HER COUNTESS
TO CHERISH

Praise for *Her Lady to Love*

"If you are looking for a sweet, cozy romance with grounded leads, this is for you. The author's dedication to the little cultural details do help flesh out the setting so much more. I also loved how buttery smooth everything tied together. Nothing seemed to be out of place, and the romance had some stakes...Highly recommended."—*Colleen Corgel, Librarian, Queens Public Library*

"Walsh debuts with a charming if flawed Regency romance... Though Honora's shift from shy curiosity to boldly stated interest feels a bit abrupt, her relationship with Jacquie is sweet, sensual, and believable. Subplots about a group of bluestockings and a society of LGBTQ Londoners add depth."—*Publishers Weekly*

"What a delightful queer Regency era romance...*Her Lady to Love* was a beautiful addition to the romance genre, and a much appreciated queer involvement. I'll definitely be looking into more of Walsh's works!"—*Dylan Miller, Librarian (Baltimore County Public Library)*

"[I]t's the perfect novel to read over the holidays if you love gorgeous writing, beautiful settings, and literal bodice ripping! I had such a brilliant time with this book. Walsh's novel has such an excellent sense of the time period she's writing in, and her specificity and interest in the historical aspects of her plot really allow the characters to shine. The inclusion of details, specifically related to women's behaviour or dress, made for a vivid and exciting setting. This novel reminded me a lot of something like *Vanity Fair* (1847) (but with lesbians!) because of its gorgeous setting and intriguing plot."—*The Lesbarary*

By the Author

Her Lady to Love

Her Countess to Cherish

Visit us at www.boldstrokesbooks.com

HER COUNTESS TO CHERISH

by

Jane Walsh

2021

HER COUNTESS TO CHERISH

ISBN 13: 978-1-63555-902-6

THIS TRADE PAPERBACK ORIGINAL IS PUBLISHED BY
BOLD STROKES BOOKS, INC.
P.O. BOX 249
VALLEY FALLS, NY 12185

FIRST EDITION: AUGUST 2021

CREDITS
EDITOR: CINDY CRESAP
PRODUCTION DESIGN: STACIA SEAMAN
COVER DESIGN: TAMMY SEIDICK

Acknowledgments

Many thanks to Radclyffe, Sandy, Cindy, and everyone on the Bold Strokes team for everything they do. I am thrilled that my Regencies have a home with BSB.

I am particularly grateful for the time and effort that my sensitivity reader, Kai, spent on my work to review the bigender representation.

My wonderful wife's thoughtfulness and support carried me through writing this book. Thank you, Mag, for your advice and encouragement, and for all the bouquets of flowers that adorned my writing room as I worked. Your love means the world to me.

This book is first and foremost about family, and community. I am forever grateful for the friends and family that I am lucky enough to have in my life.

For Mag, my endlessly curious bluestocking

Chapter One

England, 1813

The party to celebrate the upcoming nuptials of Miss Beatrice Everson and the Earl of Sinclair was sadly below average. At least, that was Beatrice's opinion. For all she knew of the earl, maybe he considered it to be a smashing success. She took a deep breath, smiled at the guests who didn't wish to be wishing her well, and wondered how gauche it would be if she were the first to leave the party thrown in her own honor.

It wasn't as if she didn't like parties. In fact, she should be in her element tonight as the center of attention. Long ago, she had perfected her arts: a throaty laugh for the fun-loving gentlemen with little means, a doe-eyed simper for the older men with their vast estates and bank accounts, and witty banter with a droll roll of the eye for the fashionable set. For the women of the ballrooms, however, she employed but one sort of look: a snide judgmental sneer. An all-encompassing expression that spoke volumes. *They're all mine. Come no closer. I daresay, isn't your hemline* terribly *last season?*

Bea hesitated to use any of these practiced efforts on the company tonight. None of them were friends, but as it was her own engagement party, none of them were rivals either. In fact, most were strangers to her. The Duchess of Hawthorne had arranged the event—and had made it clear to her that it was for the earl's benefit. Presumably because she considered Beatrice to be no more than a vulgar upstart.

Her parents were present, but she had no desire to endure their conversation.

Her dearest friends in the whole world were absent, barred from the guest list.

And her fiancé, who had ignored her during the entirety of their two-week engagement, continued to do so tonight in the company of his former men-at-arms. Sinclair had been a captain in the army for the past half dozen years before inheriting the earldom from his late brother. No doubt he was having jolly good fun with his friends, with the promise of billiards and brandy later.

Beatrice's jaw clenched. But a tight jaw would lead to a pinched lip and a furrowed brow, and she was too young to court wrinkles, so she smiled instead. Blinking to brighten her eyes with false merriment, she glided over to a stranger and cried, "Is this not the most glorious party?"

The woman looked at her with reproach. "Indeed," she said and turned away.

As she scanned the room for someone—*anyone*—who would talk to her despite the scandalous nature of her engagement, she failed to notice her father approaching until it was too late.

"The Eversons always come out on top," he said in her ear. "You've done us proud at last."

Her father was a small man, dapper and sharp and showy. Silver glinted at his temples, and rubies shone from the pin stuck in his cravat. Fake rubies, Bea knew. More than a few interested matrons were eyeing him, and she hoped her mama couldn't see them. They weren't faithful to each other but would seize any opportunity to have a screaming match. Bea wasn't convinced that being guests tonight at the ducal residence would prevent their theatrics.

He clinked his glass against hers. "Haven't you one of your little witticisms to add?" He smirked, then frowned at his wine. "There's a speck in this." He thrust it at a passing footman, who stumbled with his tray of glassware.

Beatrice gave the footman an apologetic look, then glared at her father. "There is not much to be proud of, is there?"

"A girl has to get married at some point. Even one well on her way to spinsterhood. But it was a good thing in the end that you frittered all those years away, because you had a fine use. We don't breed weaklings, after all. Strong hardy stock, we are."

"And yet so much of *our* stock has been lost to the banks of the gaming hells," she snapped.

"We're out of the thick of it now, my girl. Thanks to the deep pockets of your betrothed."

He grinned at her, and she had a flash of memory of living for those smiles when she had been a child. His confidence had always been infectious. Financial ruin had done nothing to affect his buoyancy.

There had been years in her youth when they had survived on the generosity of distant relatives, interspersed with years where her father gambled coins he didn't have at a shocking rate. But this had been one of the lavish years. She had been delighted when her dressmakers' bills had been paid promptly and in full, a first in her six London Seasons.

Three months ago, the luck turned south. Again. Letters were followed by creditors who knocked on their door day and night, this time with the threat of debtor's prison. Her father decided to use one final ace up his sleeve—Beatrice. Her mission from that instant had been to find the wealthiest man on the market to wed.

Despite his impressive military career, the Earl of Sinclair hadn't stood a chance against the onslaught of Beatrice's desperation.

Beatrice looked her father in the eye. "Whatever Sinclair gave you, keep it in your pocket and away from the tables."

He smirked. "My luck will run better than ever, girl. Just you wait and see. You think you're so fancy with your titled husband now, *my lady*? I will have my own house to rival this one when this year is through."

"You will take what was given and you will ask for no more," she said. Sinclair had already saved them once. Bea refused to see him bankrupted for her father's pleasure.

"Your husband is a good man. Now he's family. Family looks out for each other, don't they?"

Tension crackled between them.

"I say, this is a splendid party, is it not?"

Beatrice started. Mr. George Smith popped up beside her, beaming. He had a face full of freckles and sported a copper red pompadour. "Miss Everson, I must offer you my congratulations on your engagement."

She had the pleasure of meeting him once or twice during the Season and had always appreciated his style and boyish charm. Now she could add excellent timing to the list. Oh, why could she not have had the choice of a man like Mr. Smith to marry?

She knew the answer, of course. The Mr. Smiths of this world might have real rubies in their cravat pins, but they would never wield the power of a title.

Mr. Everson eyed the bright colors of Mr. Smith's waistcoat, which stood out from the crowd of fashionable black and navy, and dismissed him from notice.

"I will leave you to your guests, my dear," he said to Beatrice, and he strode into the gaggle of matrons who had been flirting with him with their fans.

"Did I appear to be a damsel in distress?" she asked Mr. Smith. He must have overheard the argument with her father. She waved her fan to cool the flush of embarrassment from her face, glad that it was an expensive one with ostrich feathers. "I assure you, I can take care of myself."

"I have no doubt," he replied, and his blue eyes twinkled at her. "But your father seemed to have an aggravating effect on you."

"I've been told I'm very like him," she drawled. "We both take what we want and live only for pleasure."

"Forgive me, I thought you might need some cheering up. You looked miserable at your own party."

"When it is one's own party, doesn't one have the right to misery?"

"Ah, but why court misery when one could court pleasure instead?"

Beatrice raised a brow. "I'm a woman to be wed, Mr. Smith. Some might say I ought never to court pleasure again."

He frowned. "And others may say that's enough of a strike against the institution to abolish it. I know many such ladies who would agree."

"I'm sure you do," she said. She touched her fan to her cheek, thinking of the women he would have brought to bed. Probably a merry widow or two. Nothing like herself.

He looked at her, and the pulse in Beatrice's throat picked up speed. It was a pity that she had no room in her life for sincere men. There was something about him that felt comfortable, like a cozy pair of wool socks in winter. She shook her head clear. She was strictly a silk stocking type of woman.

He bowed and gave her a little wink as he straightened. "I have monopolized you enough, Miss Everson. I hope to see you out and about in London as Lady Sinclair soon."

Beatrice sighed as she realized that she was standing alone again. She flicked her curls over her shoulder and sauntered over to her future husband. The Earl of Sinclair was easy enough to locate in the crowd. After all, the guests who had ignored her all evening almost fell over themselves to congratulate him.

He was a big blond man with an imposing presence and a face that belonged on a classical painting. He could not have been more blessed in society's eyes—young and handsome, wealthy and titled, war hero and gentleman.

Beatrice had to call upon a decade of practice to keep a bright smile on her face as she slipped into his circle, taking up space as if she could ever belong among them.

Sinclair's military friends looked at her with appreciation, and their easy flirtation heartened her. One leapt to her side, asking if she would like another glass of wine. Another kissed the tips of her gloved fingers and declared that Sinclair was the luckiest of devils to have landed her. A third swept into a bow and told her with a sly grin that he would be happy to be of service if Sinclair was ever not up to the task.

Sinclair growled and moved to her side. "Gentlemen, you forget yourselves," he said. "Is this any way to greet my soon-to-be *wife?*"

"I know how I'd like to greet such a wife," one of them muttered with a laugh.

"Enough," Sinclair snapped, and his fingers dug into Beatrice's upper arm. "I need a moment to speak with Miss Everson."

Sinclair only released his grip after he marched her up the stairs and down a long hallway, stopping just outside her bedroom.

"Are you looking to anticipate our wedding vows, my lord?" she cooed with false enthusiasm. She was seething inside. "It would be no more than anyone would expect, as we are supposed to have done so already."

He glowered. "This behavior is abhorrent," he said. "You cheated me of a demure, innocent wife. A woman who would be respected, who my sisters could look up to. But instead of respect, *you* invite passion, Miss Everson. Everyone downstairs could see it. They couldn't help but to lust over you."

She glared at him. It was always so, wasn't it? Men like him celebrated their sexual adventure. Women like her were expected to be desirable—but untouchable. Her behavior downstairs had been nothing more than the usual flirtation that she had enjoyed with any number of men over the years. In fact, she had flirted like that with *Sinclair* before the engagement. He hadn't chastised her for it then.

"If you are speaking of your military friends, you are being ridiculous," she snapped. "They were gibing you and welcoming me, as the bride-to-be of their friend."

Beatrice was surprised that he didn't see it. When she and her best friends, Phin and Jacquie, teased each other, it was out of love. She felt a pang that neither of them could be here tonight to support her.

"That isn't the type of *friendship* that I would hope to see you enjoying as Lady Sinclair," he sneered.

"They would never even dare to dream of seducing your wife, if that's what you are worried about," she said. "At the very least, you outranked them. Were you not Mr. Fitzhugh's commanding officer for half a decade? Did you not save Mr. Atkinson from certain death on the battlefield?"

Sinclair paused. "You did your research."

"In the game of courtship, one studies the players," Beatrice said. "You weren't the only gentleman whose past I looked into."

But after she heard Sinclair was on the market, she stopped considering anyone else. All accounts of the earl tallied up together, like a gift. Endless tales of chivalry, where he appeared like a hero in a Banbury tale.

She had decided that he must be a man who would treat a wife with kindness. Even one who had trapped him into marriage. It had been a gamble that she was no longer sure would pay off.

"This isn't the union that either of us would have chosen. We don't have to pretend otherwise, at least with each other," Beatrice said.

"That much is true. This is no love match."

She hated that sarcastic smirk on his face. "No, but perhaps we could learn to be friends."

He laughed. "I'm afraid that is unlikely, Miss Everson. All I require from you is an heir. After that I wish never to see you again."

That gave her pause. "I beg your pardon? What on earth are you expecting—for me to disappear?" The endings to a dozen gothic romances ran through her mind.

"Of course not. I have several estates. You may live at any one of them after the birth of my son, but you will leave me to my main holding in Yorkshire and the London townhouse. I never wish to see your scheming, albeit very charming, face again."

This wasn't what she had expected at all. "You would forbid me from staying in London?"

He glowered. "I was coerced into paying your family's considerable debts. You owe me this, Miss Everson. Give me a son, then give me a lifetime away from your wiles."

"And if I disagree?" Her nails bit into her palms as she clenched her fists.

"Do not forget that we are not yet married. It would be scandalous in the extreme, but I can call off this wedding. I have yet to pay your father's biggest debts."

Beatrice wavered, but it was clear that this was no choice.

He stuck out his hand. "Agree to the bargain, Miss Everson. Let us forget this sorry state of affairs after the birth of my son."

She shook the hand of the man whom she had been desperate to ensnare and whom now she felt desperate to escape, and hoped she wasn't making a mistake. "I agree."

A husband like the earl was going to prove more difficult than she had bargained for, Beatrice thought as she watched him walk away to rejoin the celebration. He didn't like her, he didn't trust her, and he didn't listen to her. It didn't bode well for marital happiness.

But then, happiness wasn't part of his deal. All she needed to do was provide an heir.

CHAPTER TWO

The Duke of Hawthorne sat a horse the way he did everything else, with effortless style, an air of danger, and a reckless lack of concern for self or state. He jumped fences where he really ought not, and galloped hell-bent to leather whenever the fancy struck him. He was magnificent in leather breeches that clung to his thighs like a second skin, and he moved as one with his stallion.

Georgina touched her horse with her knees and bent low, murmuring encouraging words, but knew it was a useless endeavor. Her chestnut mount had plenty of heart, but Georgina wasn't as skilled a rider as Hawthorne. She had ridden sidesaddle her whole life, only venturing to ride astride years after she had started wearing trousers.

It hadn't taken long for her muscles to adjust to the sensation of horseflesh between her thighs. Riding felt safer and more enjoyable without heavy long riding skirts pinned up at the side. The thrill of pounding out for a morning ride through the London fog never got boring to her, and riding had become one of her favorite pastimes.

The duke slowed down and Georgina caught up. God, but he was impressive. Deep hooded eyes gave none of his thoughts away, and they stared down an aquiline nose at her. His imperiousness was equal parts aggravating and charming. Jewels that would beggar a lesser nobleman's estate winked from his fingers and on the buttons of his coat.

"It was decent of you to have that party for Miss Everson and Sinclair," she said, though she couldn't shake the notion that this engagement was nothing to celebrate. Miss Everson had looked so upset last night.

He glanced at her. "Decent of my wife, you mean. The earl is her cousin, and she wanted to fête him properly. My role was to bless the idea of the union with my presence, and then be gone. So here we are, on the road back to London."

"You are so concerned now for her wishes that you would go to Hawthorne Towers and back to London within the span of a few days, after being away from her for ten years?"

His horse whinnied from the tight hand on its reins. "I've been known to make mistakes, young George," he said, his tone sharp. "Perhaps that was the biggest one of my life."

"It's Gina today, if you please," she told him, and he nodded.

Hawthorne always respected her name and her identity regardless of how she dressed, and she would have loved him for that alone.

She looked down at her breeches and boots and the brass buttons of her riding coat. It had been practical to dress in her male wardrobe today, as the four-hour journey to London was preferable on horseback than in the carriage. It had also been necessary. Mr. Smith had been invited to the engagement party, which meant that Lady Gina had no business being spotted stepping out of Hawthorne Towers the next morning.

"You were saying?" she prompted him.

"Gina, my marital woes are the least of your concerns right now." Hawthorne considered. "It should be the least of mine, too, from the glares that Anne was giving me last night. I think she preferred me on the Continent. We shall have to continue to live our lives apart." He grinned. "I have no complaints about that. For now, my life involves the man who has made me the happiest I have been in a long time."

Georgina's heels pressed too hard against her horse, and she sprung into a gallop which Hawthorne matched without difficulty. By the time they slowed to a walk, she had regained her composure. "You are continuing to keep company with Sir Phineas?"

"I would have returned to England much sooner had I known what awaited me here," he said. "Phin is the one worth waiting for."

It ached like a bad tooth to remember the years she had pined for Hawthorne. She had been his constant companion for most of his time in France. But it hadn't mattered. He had always seen her like a little brother. Or sister.

She was thirty now. Old enough to be past the youthful infatuation that had burned through her, driving her into the arms of men and women alike to forget about the duke's magnetic appeal.

When Georgina had come back to London, there had been no great love of her life waiting. She had managed to shake off her attraction to Hawthorne with the breadth of the English Channel between them, but now the damned duke had returned to British shores to haunt her dreams like a specter. She had no time for love anyway, she told herself. She was far too busy for such things.

It was after ten o'clock by the time they arrived in the city and parted ways. After she finished her letter writing late that morning, Georgina's fingers ached from scribbling so fast, and she had a new ink stain on her sleeve cuff. It never seemed possible to keep up with correspondence anymore.

Every day brought a fresh stack of newspapers to be annoyed with, compelling her to draft letters to their editors to debate all the topics that she disagreed with. Most mornings brought a pile of notes from friends across Europe and America, as well as letters from poets and lecturers and scientists.

At luncheon, she stepped out to visit one of the coffee shops that was friendly to men like her and Hawthorne so she could catch up on the news from the past few days when she had been at Hawthorne Towers. She loved the culture centered around the camaraderie of other men here. The aroma of tobacco and coffee mixed with the scent of fashionable pomade, and it felt like home.

Still tired from the morning's journey, she downed two cups of strong black coffee and flirted with a pair of barristers who were on break from the courts. One of them turned her head enough to consider slipping upstairs with him for a few minutes of pleasure in one of the rooms that the establishment kept for such things, but she caught sight of the clock. There wasn't enough time.

She left the barrister with nothing more than a knowing nudge of her knee against his under the table. It felt good to acknowledge one of her own, and by his wink in reply, she knew he felt the same. It was a relief sometimes simply to be *seen*.

But it was Tuesday, after all, and she needed to be home.

Every Tuesday afternoon at two o'clock for the past five years, without fail, Georgina had opened her Mayfair townhouse to host a literary, educational, and social salon where she held court among bluestockings who thrived on talk of politics and empowerment.

She changed into a white muslin day dress, looking down at the pin tucks on the bodice and the lace frill at the sleeve and the white floral embroidery that covered it all. She loved the freedom of breeches and was particular about the fall of her cravats, but she also loved all the embellishments of her lady's wardrobe. She was lucky that she had found a way to carve out a life for herself that suited all sides of her. Finally, she slipped her long red wig onto her head and went down the stairs.

She had only been at Hawthorne Towers for three days, but it was longer than she had been away from London in half a decade. She would be gone again soon enough, and for longer. But for now, she was glad to be home.

The salon was held in a large drawing room on the main floor. Years ago, she had arranged renovations to open the space and make it wider, allowing for groups of people to congregate and discuss different topics without feeling constrained. When she held readings or lectures, the salon could hold fifty people.

Georgina stripped off her gloves and gave the velvet armchair near the window a squeeze, the texture silky smooth under her hands. She had picked out every textile in this room. Chosen every piece of furniture. Curated every knickknack and ornament and fixture, agonizing over the perfect placement of each individual part of the whole. She had even thrown her back out dragging this chair from the fireplace to the window and had been bedridden for two days, she remembered, pressing a hand to the base of her spine.

The best part of making her dreams come true was that this space inspired others in pursuit of their dreams. One of the letters she had received this morning was from a scientist who had decided to study botany after attending a lecture in this room, and now she held lectures of her own as she traveled across America. Georgina wished sometimes she had the luxury of traveling, but her work attached her to London.

Madhavi Roy entered the room, tossing a stack of pamphlets on the table beside the door. She wore a practical dress as always, sturdy fustian dyed a bright blue that complemented her brown skin. Her dark hair was braided and coiled in a tight bun at her nape.

"Fresh from the press," she announced, taking a seat and picking up one of the pamphlets to thumb through it. "It looks good, Gina. This treatise on trade unions for women's labor are ready just in time to pass around at today's meeting. It's fortunate as we have the lace makers visiting us from Nottingham. Remember, they wrote to you last week to talk about tensions in their neighborhood?"

"They are visiting today?" Georgina asked, blinking. How had she lost track of this?

The Luddites had rioted and broke a lace making machine a few years ago in one of the workers' homes, creating anxiety in an already troubled industry that was fighting to survive after the post-revolution collapse of French demand for lace.

It was one of the reasons she purchased as much of it as her purse allowed. Her affection for hand-worked trims and embellishments and her choice of intricate patterns for her dresses weren't for aesthetics alone. It was a decision to support industries that she knew were rooted in female labor.

"Mrs. Lewis is worried that more riots are going to erupt now that the militia has moved in. They're starting to deport people." Madhavi scowled down at the paper in her hand, crumpling a corner.

Madhavi had been by her side working with the salon for almost as long as the doors had been opened. She was efficient and brilliant in her critiques, which had endeared her to Georgina at their first meeting when she had marched up to her after a speech she gave once on education and listed everything wrong with her opinions. She had been entirely correct, and they had been fast friends ever since.

"She's right to worry," Georgina said. "The militia isn't helping by assaulting innocent people."

Madhavi pushed the pamphlet aside and peered at her. "You have bags under your eyes," she announced. "Have you been sleeping poorly again?"

Georgina bristled. She had thought she had put enough face paint on to cover her exhaustion, but apparently not. "I was up early on the trip back to London."

"You should have taken more time in the country air. You're working yourself to the bone, Gina. It's not good for you. If you are over-exhausted, you risk making mistakes. And with some of the issues we handle here—mistakes mean that you might risk your life. And the lives of others." Her voice was stern. "You've been forgetting events. You need to rest."

She hid a yawn behind her hand. "You may be pleased to know that I will be spending more time in the country by the end of the week."

"Already? Where?"

"Miss Lockhart and Lady Honora have invited me to stay with them at Rosedale Manor in Wiltshire. They flattered me by telling me that they wish to open a salon in the same style as mine. I will help them to set it up, and then they will run it themselves after it's established."

"You're stretching yourself too thin," Madhavi warned her. "I didn't mean that you should take time away from your work in order to do more work somewhere else."

"But think of the legacy we would have," she said. "No one has set up this kind of endeavor in multiple places. If we could have the salon in London, with an offshoot in the country, think of how many more people we could reach."

Madhavi looked skeptical. "No one person is here to save the world. We stand together. As a community. It's bigger than any of us, and bigger than any venue we could establish. No, Gina, I think this sounds like a recipe for exhaustion."

"I will take time for myself as well," she said, only half-convinced that she would. "It won't be all work."

She sighed. "Well, I can run the salon here for as long as you're gone."

"Thank you, Madhavi."

More women trickled in, filling the room with laughter and debate and commentary. The lace makers from Nottingham arrived, and a long discussion ensued about the textile industry in general, and more specifically about the hardships encountered by specialized sectors like lace making and embroidery application. Mrs. Lewis clearly was not happy with the situation in her neighborhood and was looking to create change.

Georgina suggested the names of a few other people they could connect with while they were in London, and although nothing could be resolved in an afternoon, the women seemed relieved to have been able to talk about their burdens and to have a group of people rally behind them in support.

Her day didn't end when the ladies departed. Georgina and Madhavi had dinner together to plan for the weeks that Georgina would be away in Wiltshire before they attended a lecture on geography. Afterward, Georgina went her own way and made an appearance at a ball where she flirted mildly with a few other ladies before deciding that none of them seemed to understand what she might be asking for.

She contented herself with encouraging a group of debutantes not to consider matrimony as their sole goal in life and slipped them a crisp trade card with the standing meeting time for the salon.

After two in the morning, she sank into the bay seat of her bedroom window and pressed her forehead against the glass. "Legrand, I am well and truly spent," she announced to her valet.

She didn't have a lady's maid, preferring the services of Legrand whether she dressed as George or as Gina. He had been one of a handful of people she had met on the Continent who felt much the same way as she did, frustrated with the narrow options in which society expected them to express themselves. Unlike Georgina, Legrand didn't relate at all to his birth gender, and he had struggled to find employment because he didn't always look to the *haut ton*'s eyes like the man that he was.

Georgina had hired him after learning that he had been let go from three jobs in a row as a tailor, even though he was the finest craftsman she knew. Now he was both her valet and her personal tailor, which suited them both.

He lifted the wig from her head, placing it on a wooden holder on the dresser before he brushed out the waves that he had curled earlier that night. "At this hour, of course you are done. You work too hard," he chided her. He was ten years her elder, but sometimes had a strong paternal side to him.

"We will be in the country again soon enough," Georgina said. She rolled her neck, loving that moment of freedom that came with removing the wig. The breeze teased at her nape. "Would you be agreeable to travel with me?"

"I will always go with you," he said, patting her shoulder. "I am not afraid."

His answer was always the same, but she felt compelled to ask because she worried about his safety among an unfamiliar set of servants.

"You are in need of another haircut before we go," Legrand said, frowning at her untidy red curls.

"You always think that," she said. "You are aware that it is the fashion for a man's hair to be unkempt, aren't you? I am quite enjoying the pompadours that you have been styling for me."

He snorted. "If you prefer such a windswept Byronic mane, far be it for me to dissuade you." Legrand's own hair was a meticulous Brutus cut, which favored his sharp features and large eyes. He settled her hairbrush beside the silver comb and the pot of pomade.

"By the by, I heard at the coffee shop today that the raids are becoming more frequent at the molly houses," she said. "I think the police might be planning something soon at one of the taverns— possibly Mother Mary's. You may want to warn your friends before we depart from London. I'll pay a few visits tomorrow to anyone I can think of who frequents there."

"I'll do the same," he said with a sigh before he left her for the night, and Georgina wished with all her heart that this was a less common conversation between them.

It was a relief to sink into the thick mattress and pull the covers up to her chin, even though her mind raced with thoughts of everything she hadn't accomplished. There were always more letters to write. More soirees to attend. More things to do, events to plan, people to see. Unbidden, Hawthorne's dark eyes and chiseled lips wandered into her mind. Her last thought before she relaxed into sleep was that maybe it would indeed do her good to be away from the frenetic pace of London life, and away from thoughts of the duke.

CHAPTER THREE

The newly minted Countess of Sinclair looked around the room while her husband moved one last time over her and flopped onto the bed. She had always been told that one's wedding night should be something to remember, but God only knew it wouldn't be because of the act itself. Sinclair had done his duty with expediency, as if he couldn't bear to touch her for longer than necessary.

He was quiet for a moment, then sat up. "It is a fine thing for a man to discover in his marriage bed that his wife is no virgin," he said, glaring at her as he yanked a shirt over his head.

She hadn't thought he would notice. Bea widened her eyes. "Why, my lord, I don't know what you could be talking about."

"Your lack of—of a hymen," he muttered, unable to meet her eyes as he spoke the word. "There's no blood on these sheets. I didn't expect you to have embraced a nun's chasteness in the years you lived in London, but I did think you would come to this marriage with your most prized possession intact!"

Male outrage. How very tedious. Beatrice frowned and studied her nails. Tomorrow she would ask her maid to apply a new polish to them. Just the other day she had learned that there was a lotion made with crushed pearls to enhance the nail's natural luminescence. She sank back into the bed, the thick mattress supporting her in a way her new husband seemed incapable of doing.

"Well?" he barked at her.

"I didn't realize you had asked a question?" she said.

Sinclair raked a hand through his hair. "*Why* are you not a virgin?"

"I think you mistake the situation," she said, rolling her eyes. "It must be a result of my girlhood habit of riding horses astride. I have heard that such exercise can have *such* an unfortunate result."

"You lied to me," he said, sounding more surprised than angry.

"I never lied," Beatrice said sharply. "I was never even asked."

"Well, I am asking now. Were you a virgin before tonight?"

"No."

A sound of disbelief wheezed out from him. "The entire earldom will now be in question."

Bea scowled at him from her den of soft pillows. "There is nothing to question. Nothing affects you in any way unless you count the bruise to your ego. The earldom is quite safe from my wiles, I do assure you. I finished my courses this very week. You have my permission to interrogate my maid for how often I changed my rags, if you do not believe my word."

Sinclair opened his mouth to speak, then closed it with a snap.

Satisfied that she had taken the wind out of his sails, Bea turned on her side away from him. "I plan on fulfilling our bargain, my lord. You will have your heir. Now if you don't mind, I would like to rest now."

The mattress shifted as he got to his feet. "Of course, my lady," he said sardonically. "Whatever you wish, you shall have."

Finally, she thought to herself with satisfaction. It had taken her whole lifetime, but it was about damn time she got what she deserved. As the bedroom door closed behind her husband, Beatrice closed her eyes and embraced the sleep of the righteous.

❖

Breakfast the next morning was a strained affair. Beatrice took one look at Sinclair, glowering from the head of the table and gripping his fork until his knuckles whitened, and decided it was wise to limit the conversation to the barest niceties.

She turned her attention to breakfast instead. There were four different jams on the credenza, she marveled. Each one had a tiny silver serving spoon with a fruit carved into the end. How unnecessary and completely charming.

"How long shall we stay in London, my lord?" she asked,

tapping her index finger against the handle of her teacup. It was the thinnest of china, and she was delighted to see that the rim was gold leaf.

He scowled into his cup. "A month or two. I have business to arrange here first. Then we will go to Yorkshire so I can introduce you to my sisters. I had a letter from Cecilia, the eldest. She was most upset at having missed our wedding."

"It was such a short ceremony that I rather feel like I missed it myself," Bea murmured.

"It could have been the event of the year if you hadn't proclaimed in such ridiculous fashion that I had ruined you," he bit off. "As such, I thought a special license and marriage within the month was the most appropriate action to take. Was a wedding breakfast thrown by a duchess perhaps not enough for your ambition, my lady?"

"The duchess was most kind," she lied. In fact, the duchess hadn't spared her a second glance during her stay at Hawthorne Towers, and her time there had been miserable.

"At least one of us was spared lectures," he said. "I suppose you would have been richly congratulated by the other guests at the house party. I am given to understand that my suit was much looked for this season."

"It was a tough field, but I did end up the champion in the hunt. What a wonderful reward to have won your heart, my lord." Her tone was insipid, though in truth it was a reward. She couldn't forget that her family had been saved through their marriage. She frowned as she thought of her father. "By the way, if I may request it, I would ask you to refuse to give my father any more money."

"How very mercenary you are," he said. "Interested in hoarding up the Sinclair fortune for yourself? I didn't think it even of you."

The words stung. "He is unwise with money—"

"The way he spun the tale, he fell in with a group who took gross advantage of him."

"It may be true this time, but it doesn't matter. He is addicted to cards and will stop at nothing to sustain his habit."

"You don't have to worry your pretty little head about my business, my lady," he said, stepping back. "I shall not be ungenerous, if that's your concern."

It hadn't been. But it sounded like paradise not to worry about finances ever again.

He waved the servants away. "We will need to try again," Sinclair announced as soon as they were in private.

"I beg your pardon?"

"In the bedroom."

"Of course, we will try again," Beatrice said, and took a bite of her toast. She wondered if there was anything in life more scrumptious than lemon curd. The amount of sugar Cook would have used to make the lemons so sweet must have been exorbitant. Her mouth sang with its riches.

"I did not expect you to be so compliant."

"This is the marriage contract, my lord. I told you, I understand my end of the bargain."

She had every intention of fulfilling their deal. The sooner she could bear an heir, the better, even if he *was* planning to banish her to one of his estates afterward. At least then she could live a life of her own, free from obligation and responsibility.

"But we shall not meet in the bedchamber until after you have had your courses again," he said stiffly. "I cannot trust that your wicked ways have not ruined everything."

She dropped her toast, and lemon curd slid onto the pristine white tablecloth. Beatrice gripped the arms of her chair to prevent her hands from shaking in rage. How dare he decide that she must be a liar? How dare he make such a decision, without even talking to her about her experience?

She had not had a male lover in years, though she had entertained more than a few women in her bedchamber in recent memories. However, nowhere in the wedding vows had she promised to entrust her husband with her innermost thoughts, so she kept the facts to herself.

"As you wish, my lord."

"Good."

"I am most regular in my functions, so you may expect to visit my chambers again in…oh, I suppose twenty-one days hence." She was too furious to feel embarrassment.

The chair legs scraped against the wooden floor as Sinclair

rose. "I shall leave you to your breakfast, madam. I find I have lost my appetite."

Beatrice found it in herself to beam at the footman who eased into the room after Sinclair stormed out. The servants shouldn't have to bear the brunt of the family's ill humors, after all. "Thomas, do tell Cook how much I have enjoyed the lemon curd," she said. "I am *so* appreciating my new life here at Sinclair House."

❖

The next day, Beatrice strolled along the most popular avenue in Hyde Park in the middle of the most fashionable hour, on the arm of one of her dearest friends. She enjoyed the fresh air on her face, and the way the sunshine dappled through her hat just so. What she didn't enjoy was the suspicion that she was being snubbed.

No one was being rude about it. This was Hyde Park, after all, and the ladies and gentlemen who walked here behaved with the height of civility. But she knew the *ton*, inside and out. She could understand the message in a languid wave or the flutter of a fan from across the grassy expanse.

"Here I thought you wanted to walk in the park so we could talk, dear Bea," Phin said. "But alas, all you want is to look your best for the other ladies."

"I wish to look my best for *myself*," she said, drawing closer to him and threading her arm into the crook of his elbow. "Looking good for others is a bonus."

It had taken well over an hour for her maid to pin up her hair and to help her get ready in her new sprigged muslin. Despite what she had said, she was disappointed that no one came close enough to appreciate the effort.

Sir Phineas Snow was one of her dearest friends. As he was the Duke of Hawthorne's lover, the Duchess of Hawthorne had refused to invite him to the engagement party that she had hosted. The Earl of Sinclair was the duchess's cousin, so he hadn't approved Phin's name for the guest list at the wedding either. This was the first Beatrice had seen of him in weeks.

"I seem to be rather less than popular today," she said. "I

daresay you will tell me that it is my just desserts for stealing another woman's fiancé." The truth of it was a lead ball in her stomach, though she preferred to pretend that it didn't bother her one bit.

He gave her arm a squeeze. "I admit it wasn't well done of you to keep aiming for Sinclair when his sights were set on Lady Honora. He would have married her if you hadn't lied to everyone by saying that he slept with *you* instead. But all's well that ends well, isn't it? Lady Honora didn't want the earl, despite the fact that he wanted her. You saved her from a miserable marriage, and now she's happy with Jacquie."

Bea waved at another young miss, still unmarried at the end of the Season, and watched her scurry away with her mama. Poor dear. That had been her own fate for so many years. She and her very best friend and sometimes lover, Miss Jacqueline Lockhart, had been out in society for six long Seasons, determined not to settle down before they had their fill of London's pleasures.

Now she was married to an earl, and Jacquie had followed her heart and ruined herself by declaring herself in love with another woman. Beatrice could admit that Lady Honora Banfield was beautiful, though not to her own taste. She was too reserved. One never could tell what she was thinking.

"I am in alt to have saved her from an unhappy marriage, thereby making me the happiest of women as the new Countess of Sinclair."

"Are you happy indeed?" His eyes bored into hers.

"Thrilled," she said. "Married life is nothing but a constant delight."

Phin sighed. "Beatrice—"

"That is Lady Sinclair to you, dear sir."

"Too many years have I called you Bea, darling. I am not about to stop now." He gave her arm another squeeze.

"I should be happy, shouldn't I?" she asked. "There are real diamonds in my ears, after all, instead of paste. I am a married woman, so I have no chaperone at my heels. My family's troubles are over. It's a dream come true."

Beatrice had thought she would feel wild and carefree on the signing of the marriage papers, guaranteeing her the security of a noble title and a fortune. But instead she felt as trapped as she had ever been in her father's house. Now she had become another man's problem, and that man was determined to pack her away like an old suit of clothes after he determined that she had outlasted her usefulness. Her blood boiled anew at Sinclair's bargain.

"Maybe happiness takes time," Phin said, placing his hand on hers. "It might feel unfamiliar now, but you have time to find the joy in your new situation. I know you don't like people to see it, but you're a good sort, Bea. You deserve to be happy."

Her marriage to Sinclair was unlikely to bring either of them joy. However, Phin was right in one regard. She hated anyone seeing much of herself. Her father had always told her to play her cards close to her chest, and that life was nothing but a gamble. She had perfected a layer of bored sighs and sarcastic laughs that didn't allow people to get too near.

"Are you and Sinclair staying in London for the rest of the Season?"

Beatrice pulled a face. "He wants to trot me up to his estate in the wilds of Yorkshire to meet his family. I shouldn't be surprised if Vikings still abounded up there."

"A Viking may give you some excitement." He wiggled his brows.

"I may well be in need of a lover. Sinclair noticed that I came to him as no virgin and he is behaving with medieval outrage."

"He didn't cause you any harm, did he?" he asked, a thunderous frown on his face.

"No. But he shouldn't have spoken the way he did!"

"Think of it from his perspective, darling. He does have the title to consider."

"Whyever should he care?" she asked, exasperated. "If he is choosing to marry *me* then he would still be the father in any way that mattered. In any case, it *doesn't* matter! I haven't had a lover in ages."

"Simply say the word and you can have one again," Phin said, jostling her elbow.

She laughed. It was an old joke between them. "You cannot be pried away from your current lover, so I know how insincere your offer is. The Duke of Hawthorne must be a special man indeed if he can make you forget about all others."

His smile was wide and shy and proud. The dear man was so very much in love, she thought, and the pang of jealousy that she felt surprised her. For all that she had sought the security of marriage, she'd never wanted love. It came with too many expectations.

"We are passing time together, but I don't know how long it will last. He's a duke, after all."

"Even if he loves you for a season, it's worth it. To be loved by a *duke*!" Beatrice was impressed that Phin had pulled off such a coup. Hawthorne had returned to England a few months ago after being in France for who knew how long, and immediately embarked on an affair with Phin. "I should have taken a crack at him myself if he had made eyes my way."

"A duke's mistress is not as good a position as an earl's wife," he reminded her.

"Oh, *are* you a mistress?" Beatrice asked with interest. "Is he paying you? Is the money good?"

Phin laughed. "Of course he's not."

"You should propose it," she said. "In all seriousness! Why shouldn't you be compensated? Then you could reduce the amount of time you spend gambling to support yourself. Less time at the gaming tables means more time in His Grace's bed. Is that not a worthy trade?"

Phin was a prudent gambler and never risked more than he could afford. She knew he was nothing like her father, but a lump of dread grew in her throat when she thought of him at the mercy of the tables.

"Bea, not everything can be measured and bargained and compensated. Some things don't have a price."

"Well, one ought to be able to turn a situation to one's advantage, if at all possible."

"One day, you shall fall in love, and instead of admiring a bank account you will admire the person. I shall be very happy when that time comes."

The lump in her throat was joined with the hot sting of unexpected tears behind her eyes.

"Such a thing shall not come to pass." Beatrice took his arm and refused to hear another word.

"If you aren't going to Yorkshire right away, I shall be pleased to have your company in London."

Beatrice was outraged all over again by her husband's edict. Did he truly think that he could dictate how and where she lived? "If Sinclair thinks he can have me under his thumb, I will have to prove him wrong."

"Somehow I don't think you would ever be subject to another's whims," he said with a smile.

"I have time enough to take a little trip," she announced, inspiration striking. "Jacquie has gone to Wiltshire with Lady Honora, hasn't she?"

"Yes, they left for the country last month," he said. "Bea, you can't mean to start anything up again with Jacquie. She loves Lady Honora."

She blinked. "Of course I am not after a romance with Jacquie," she said. "I cannot believe you think I would stoop so low when she is so in love!"

"I *know* that you would stoop so low," he said, sighing.

"I do not mean to make waves! But until Sinclair comes to his senses, I am not going to lie about, pining for his touch. I can well entertain myself."

The more Beatrice thought about it, the more she liked the plan. Sinclair was a stuffy bore. A married woman had the freedom to travel by herself to visit friends. She deserved some entertainment of her own if Sinclair refused to provide it for the next few weeks.

CHAPTER FOUR

B eatrice peeked out the carriage window. She had announced yesterday morning to Sinclair that she would be visiting friends in the country, as he had no urgent need of her. She had been his wife for such a short period that she doubted her presence would even be missed from the household. Choosing to interpret his speechlessness as assent, she had made arrangements for the carriages to be brought round posthaste.

With her maid and a mountain of luggage that belied the fact that she meant to stay a fortnight at most, she had set out for Wiltshire to rusticate. She and Jacqueline had known each other since girlhood in London—during the years of plenty that her parents had spent there, anyway. A note wasn't necessary to be sent ahead to announce her, she had decided. Jacquie would never expect her to stand upon ceremony.

She tucked away the worry that she would not, in fact, be welcomed. After all, she had never behaved well to Lady Honora, who owned the estate. Would either of them be pleased to see her? She breathed deep and told herself to focus on the facts and not on the problems. She was here, not in London. She would be with a friend, and not her husband. These were things to celebrate.

Rosedale Manor was a snug little estate. Three stories of warm yellow stone with plenty of mullioned windows, it squatted on a low hill overlooking the rose gardens. Turrets flanked either side of the house, which gave it a fanciful charm if one was partial to such things. She looked at the delicate wrought iron embellishments beneath the windows and along the stairs. It wasn't imposing enough for her tastes, but she could admit that it had a dignified air about it.

The only time she had spent in the country had been shuffling around with her family in her youth to beg largesse from relatives. Those had been years of misery, and she had sworn never to spend much time in the country again. Yet here she was. Beatrice shook her head, exasperated with herself. After all, there was a world of difference between a week or two in a country estate, and a year or two in a run-down cottage with a leaky roof. There was no need to remember such times.

Birds chirped as she put her nose in the air and stepped up to the front door with as much magnificence as she could muster.

The butler opened the door and blinked at her. "Madam?" Confusion was apparent on his face as he took in the sight of her servants and baggage pouring out of the carriages and onto the cobblestone drive.

"I am the Countess of Sinclair," she told him, and sashayed into the house. "I am great friends with your mistress."

"Lady Honora? I shall inquire—"

"No, your *other* mistress. Miss Jacqueline Lockhart," she clarified. She wasn't sure what the servants knew about Jacquie and Lady Honora's relationship, but hoped they were treated as equals in their own home.

"Ah. Yes, my lady. Friends with the—*other* mistress." He gave a shallow bow and left the entranceway.

Jacquie came bouncing down the stairs, black curls streaming behind her, a light pink flush on her white cheeks from the exertion of running through the manor.

"Beatrice!" she gasped. She threw herself into a tight embrace. "Bea, you didn't tell me you were coming for a visit! I was ever so astonished when I saw the carriages pull up."

"It wouldn't have been a surprise if I had told you," she said. She pressed her face for a moment into Jacquie's hair and then kissed her cheek. "You don't wish for a visit from your dearest friend?"

Jacqueline laughed. "I am hardly settled in here, you know."

"I shall need some pointers myself about country living. In a few weeks, I will be off to Yorkshire."

"Yorkshire!" Jacquie exclaimed. "Well, let us get you settled, and you can tell me all about marriage." She linked arms with Beatrice and they ascended the staircase together.

"You could tell me about it yourself," Bea said. "What you have here with Lady Honora is like a marriage, isn't it?"

Jacquie's smile was brilliant. "It is," she sighed. "Oh, Bea, I didn't realize how wonderful love could be."

They reached the second floor, and several doorways were open off a long hallway. "I don't know all the proper names of our guest rooms," Jacqueline said, pursing her lips. She threw open the first door on the left, then peeked into another on the right. "I'm afraid everything will need a good airing, as we weren't expecting more guests. This room here is nice. You would have a good view of the woods surrounding the lake. Did you know we have our very own lake here? We should arrange a picnic at our earliest convenience."

Beatrice stepped into the airy suite. White sheets were draped over chairs and tables to prevent dust from accumulating. But even with the furnishings covered, it was charming. The walls were papered in pale yellow with tiny white flowers scattered across it, and the windows were enormous with billowing white curtains. It felt cozy. Clean. Inviting. A sense of peace stole over her.

Such fancy was most unlike her. After all, the room was far from luxurious. There were faded spots on the wallpaper, and dust motes dancing in the air. "This is adequate," she said, stifling the joy she had felt when she walked in. "I suppose it's the best that the country could offer."

Jacquie rolled her eyes and gave her a push. "Blink your eyes, Bea, and rid them of that London fog so you can see your surroundings properly."

"Is Rosedale Manor not to your taste, Lady Sinclair?"

"Lady Honora." Beatrice flinched and wondered if it was too late to tell the servants to stop unpacking the carriages. She turned around to face the woman whose fiancé she had stolen. "I am so very pleased to see you again." She curtsied, more polite than she had ever been in her presence. After all, she owed Lady Honora for Sinclair, even though he may not have been the prize that everyone claimed him to be.

"I had not realized that you would find yourself in this part of the country so soon after your marriage to the Earl of Sinclair," Lady Honora said. She moved closer to Jacquie and took her hand, lacing their fingers together.

"I am not here to steal your lover," Bea announced without preamble. "You may assume by my rapid engagement that I am opportunistic, but I assure you that I am not *gauche*. You have nothing to worry about, Lady Honora."

She gave her a long look, and Bea gritted her teeth at the scrutiny. At least she was wearing her best traveling dress. She always felt better in finery.

"You are welcome to stay as long as you like," Lady Honora said. "Any friend of Miss Lockhart is welcome in our home." The frosty expression on her face belied her words.

"Thank you," she muttered, shame sinking like a stone into her stomach. A moment passed as she struggled with the unwelcome emotion. "Oh, damn it all. I—well, I am sorry for my actions during the Season, Lady Honora. I behaved terribly toward you."

She couldn't remember the last time she had apologized for anything. Her muscles tensed, and her feet itched to run away.

But Lady Honora smiled, and it felt like a cool glass of water that washed away the acidity of her embarrassment. "I accept your apology, Lady Sinclair. You did treat me poorly at society events and of course I did not enjoy it. The behavior was beneath you, and I didn't deserve any of it."

Beatrice swallowed past the lump in her throat. "You did not deserve it," she agreed, her voice thin. She thought of the barbs that she had tossed at Lady Honora over the weeks where they were both vying for the earl. She had been desperate to win Sinclair's hand, and she would have done anything to succeed. But she should have drawn a line somewhere. "I was dreadful to you. You have been nothing but kind, and I truly am glad to see you that you have found happiness with Jacqueline. I am sorry for my words and actions. I know they must have hurt you."

"Thank you." She cleared her throat. "The fact of the matter is that I didn't know what was going to happen when Sinclair announced to everyone that he and I were engaged, against my will.

You decided to bear the brunt of that scandal when you announced your own engagement to him, freeing me of any part of it. Perhaps the score between us is even now."

"How wonderful that my best friend and my lover are on cordial terms now." Jacqueline beamed at them and seemed determined to overlook their tepid smiles in return. "I shall ring for the servants to bring up your luggage, Bea."

Lady Honora nodded. "I will inform Cook that we will be four to dine tonight."

Beatrice blinked. "Four?"

"I suppose when you decided to visit us that you did not consider that we might already have a houseguest? Lady Gina has been with us these past two days and has plans to stay for several weeks."

Beatrice restrained herself from wrinkling her nose. Could they not have invited *anyone* else for a visit?

"Her cousin, Mr. Smith, is also a guest here, but I think he is more interested in the village than the estate," Jacqueline added. "I doubt he will appear for dinner."

Bea perked up. She hadn't forgotten Mr. Smith's kind eyes at her engagement party—or those adorable freckles. Time spent with him would be the perfect way to forget all about her husband for the month.

"I would not miss dinner for the world," Bea said throatily.

"We dine at country hours," Lady Honora said, eyeing her.

Bea sniffed but otherwise kept her opinion to herself. After a long day of travel, an early dinner would be most welcome, but she refused to admit it.

❖

Georgina toweled off her body and rubbed the thick terrycloth through her short hair, making sure that it was as dry as it could be before she donned her wig for the evening. She had lost track of the hours reviewing the newsletters that Madhavi had enclosed in this morning's post, and then had to rush her washing up. She should have planned her time better, she thought, annoyed with herself. It would not do if the maid returned before she had a chance to look like what the servants expected of her.

She had just enough time to slip on her wig before the door to her room opened to let in the woman that Nora had assigned to be her lady's maid. "Hello, Amy," she greeted her, and the maid gave her a shy smile in return.

Nora hadn't been pleased when she had arrived yesterday with only Legrand to accompany her. She had tried to explain that Legrand always did for her, but Nora insisted that she must have a lady's maid while at Rosedale. "The servants are at sixes and sevens with Jacquie's arrival," she had confided. "I think it will take some time for everything to settle. Everything will be easier this way."

Amy helped Georgina into a white muslin frock and slid each of the dozen pearl buttons through their tiny loops at the back. Her white gloves had another row of buttons that pressed the silk snugly against her arms. Strands of pearls and opals were hung around her neck.

"My lady, how would you like your hair arranged tonight?"

"My hair is fine the way it is," she said, resisting the urge to give her wig a reassuring pat.

Amy's face didn't show any surprise. This had been Georgina's answer last night, too. Georgina dismissed her, grateful for a moment alone.

She leaned forward to peer at herself in the mirror. Her brown freckles stood out starkly against her white skin and she considered powdering her face but decided against it. A hint of color would do for her eyebrows, though, so she swept on a powder to darken them. Sometimes she liked a full face of cosmetics, and sometimes just a touch of it helped her feel more like herself. Other times she didn't wear any.

Thoughts about her body had confused her growing up, and it had taken her a long time to accept how she felt about it. Sometimes it had felt right to her, and other times it didn't feel like her own body at all. Georgina could remember every detail of the day that she had found a suit of worn servants' clothes in a pile that the housekeeper was bringing to the charity shop. Her heart hammering, she had sneaked them into her room.

After years of yearning and worrying and emotions she could not name, she had donned the patched shirt and faded breeches and pulled her hair away from her face as she looked in the mirror. Staring back at her was the boy she often wished she could be.

It was easier after that to cobble together outfits with garments nicked from her father and the grooms, or purchased with fumbling fingers from shops where she explained that they were for her nonexistent "brother." Waistcoats became her favorite item of clothing, and she had a collection of neatly polished watch fobs to tuck into their pockets.

She spent as much time as she could manage during her youth dressed in shirts and coattails and trousers, perfecting her swagger in taverns and coffee shops, tipping back glasses of gin and cheap wine with the lads. The heady rush of acceptance and *rightness* almost overwhelmed her. For once, her opinions on politics and society were listened to, instead of dismissed. At last, she could flirt with the girls that she had always watched from afar.

But over time, Georgina realized that she might often feel like a man—but she also still felt like a woman. She loved lace and parasols and fans and kissing the boys behind the stables. She also liked attending the few lady's salons that she came across when she was young, long before she ran one of her own, and challenging the idea that only men could have a rational thought in their heads. It just didn't feel right being a woman all the time.

As she approached her twentieth birthday, Georgina had realized the simple truth. She was *herself* and also *himself*. She was *both*. She might not fit into society's understanding of a man or a woman, but it no longer confused her after she decided that she would simply live her life how she chose, instead of how others tried to dictate. She loved her body, however she chose to adorn it.

Legrand slipped into the room with his usual discretion, entering the room from the adjoining door instead of from the hallway. "Amy did a good job tonight."

"Yes, she did. I need your help again with my hair, though. I can't have her touching it and discovering it's a wig. To be honest, I wish I didn't have to wear it at all tonight. It's so much warmer here than it was in London." She considered discarding it. Nora and

Jacquie wouldn't blink, but then there were the servants to consider. Best to keep it on.

Legrand picked up a wide-toothed silver comb and ran it through the long curls. He pinned it up into a loose chignon and nestled a silver tiara in the locks. "That should do," he said. "But you know this cannot last forever. We cut your hair years ago, and it's a miracle this wig with your natural hair has lasted as long as it had. You are tempting fate, Gina."

"I won't look like Gina without the wig."

"You know you can have short hair and still be Gina. Half the time when you're in breeches you're *still* Gina."

Irritated, she picked up a glass vial of cologne from the table and spritzed on a blend of cedarwood and bergamot. "Short hair in a men's fashion is not quite the thing for a lady these days."

Legrand gestured at her outfit, pin-tucked and embroidered, all in gleaming, glistening white. "Neither is this. But it's *your* fashion, your custom, and you look elegant. You can do the same with the hair."

He left her as the clock on the mantel struck four. Too early to gather for dinner. Georgina thought about writing a letter or two. Madhavi's treatise was interesting, and she wanted to ask a question about it. But she remembered her promise that she would take time to relax during her visit to the country. Although her fingers itched to put pen to paper, she stepped into a pair of backless evening shoes and opened the door in search of strong spirits.

The drawing room had a credenza stocked with sherry, where Georgina had shared a drink with Jacquie before dinner yesterday. However, she wanted solitude. She strode past the drawing room to the library at the back of the house.

The library wasn't large, and it was past its glory days. An oakwood desk was pushed against the windows, its surface scratched and nicked. Well-worn sofas and chairs were placed at haphazard angles, none of them covered in the same fabric or even belonging to the same period. The bookshelves sported tomes with mismatched spines and missing covers, and portfolios were rolled up and shoved in whatever cubby would hold them.

She wasn't sure if there had always been brandy and whisky

decanters hidden beside the ledgers on the side table, behind the globe. But last night, one of the footmen had given George a knowing wink and showed him where he could enjoy a snifter in the evenings away from the ladies.

She knew that the footman would never have dreamt of revealing the liquor's location if she had been dressed in women's clothes. The servants would be shocked to see her now in her gown and jewels, riffling through bottles of spirits.

Settling into a dark brown leather chair by the empty fireplace, she sighed as the liquor hit her tongue and warmed her throat. Closing her eyes, she leaned back and took another sip. There must be at least a half hour to spend as she pleased by herself before she would be expected to be in the drawing room. She welcomed the peace.

The heavy door opened without a creak, but Georgina's eyes flew open and she shot to her feet.

The manor, it seemed, had another houseguest.

CHAPTER FIVE

M iss Beatrice Everson swanned into the library, and the air felt thick with heat and tension and the rich scent of jasmine. She filled Georgina's eyes with quick flashes of imprints—a cloud of brown curls, a smear of cherry red lip stain, the froth of petticoat near a slim ankle.

"Miss Everson," she said, then caught herself. "Lady Sinclair now, isn't it?"

"Lady Georgina, what a surprise," Lady Sinclair said. Her eyes wandered from the pearls nestled in her hair down to the cut glass beads on her shoes.

She hated hearing her full name on other people's lips. It felt much more intimate to her than hearing either of the halves of it. "Please, call me Gina."

"Of course. *Gina.* How could I forget the lack of formality that you insist upon?" Lady Sinclair tittered.

Georgina had heard far worse from people far more dangerous than a bored social climber, so it was easy to disregard her sneer. "How are you and Lord Sinclair these days?" she asked, infusing her voice with warmth.

Lady Sinclair sniffed. "We are quite fine, I assure you."

Yet here she was in Wiltshire, not one week after her rushed wedding to the catch of the Season. There was a story there. Something told her, however, that the lady would be loath to share it with her.

Maybe she would have shared it with George, though. When Georgina had spoken to her at the engagement party, she had seen a hint of vulnerability in those beautiful eyes. There had been the spark of something interesting between them. But of course, then the lady had married, and now those eyes were looking at her with disdain.

"Is that *brandy?*" Lady Sinclair asked. "Why, Gina, I didn't expect such a thing from you. You seem more of a weak tea sort of person. Do forgive me, I don't mean to offend."

Her lashes fluttered, and Georgina noticed that they had been darkened and curled. A dramatic line of kohl lined her eyes, which needed no embellishment. But she knew well enough that makeup wasn't always applied for beauty.

"No offense taken," she said. "Tea can be very sustaining. I have also been known to enjoy a nightcap of warm milk in the evenings. Very good for digestive health."

"Then you won't mind if I finish your brandy? You can't mean to imbibe the whole thing yourself? It's almost two fingers deep."

It had been closer to four when she had poured it. Georgina had caroused with men twice her size and drank them under the table when she so pleased. She started to say that the brandy was behind the globe and that Lady Sinclair could pour herself her own damn glass, then stopped. It wasn't worth revealing how she knew where the liquor was kept, and Lady Sinclair had a hint of strain around her eyes that indicated she could use the drink.

Georgina remembered the heated exchange between Lady Sinclair and her father at the engagement party, and her sympathy rose. She passed over the glass.

Lady Sinclair took a long sip and hummed with approval. "This is lovely," she said. "You know, I had come to the library in search of your cousin. My dear Jacquie told me that Mr. Smith is here, but I can't seem to find him. Has he told you where he went?"

Georgina studied the deep decolletage of Lady Sinclair's dress. Pale blue fabric marched in tiny pleats across her bodice, with delicate lace lying as light as breath on her breasts. A ribbon was tied tight below her bosom, which was hoisted nearly to her chin. Gathered muslin flowed down her body in a skirt so gauzy that Georgina could see the petticoat underneath, and more than a hint of leg beyond that.

This was a gown that declared seduction. Although judging

from the look on Lady Sinclair's face, she didn't need a dress to do the work for her. Her determination was enough to see her through.

"I think George is at the village tavern," Georgina said brightly. "He makes friends wherever he goes. I doubt you will see much of him while you are here."

"Oh, but he shall tire soon of the country bumpkins. I would expect to see him rushing back to what little society awaits him here." Lady Sinclair took another sip of brandy.

Georgina meant to defend the countryside and its pleasures, but all she could think of was that those lips were touching the glass where hers had once rested.

"How long are you planning to stay in the country?" she asked. It shouldn't be much of a stretch to fib about her "cousin's" presence for a few days.

To her surprise, Lady Sinclair seemed discomfited. "As long as I wish," she said, and drank again.

Georgina nodded. Just as she had suspected, things were unsettled between the newlyweds. She might not be able to avoid Lady Sinclair after all, if it was meant to be a long stay.

"I do as I please," Lady Sinclair continued, drumming her fingers on the arm of her chair. "Perhaps I shall stay for a week. Maybe two. Sinclair has another thing coming to him if he expects *me* to be biddable."

Georgina nodded again. She might not quite like Lady Sinclair, but this was a notion she could wholeheartedly endorse. "There is no reason why marriage should limit your choices," she replied. "I know a great many people who eschew the entire institution."

"Yes, your bluestocking friends at your salon." Lady Sinclair rolled her eyes. "I am sure they are ever so happy with their choice. However, some of us must wed to survive."

"And some of my friends must work for their living," Georgina said. "Yet you do have it very hard, don't you?"

Lady Sinclair's eyes flashed and she set the brandy snifter on the side table. "You wouldn't know the first thing about it, would you? Aren't you wealthy in your right, living alone with your house in Mayfair? Where are the hard choices *you* have had to make to survive?"

Georgina thought of the long years in Paris. Nights spent

shivering and walking to the Duke of Hawthorne's residence across town, clad in borrowed breeches and fighting off men who wanted to rob her. And worse.

"Yes, I have lived a charmed existence," she lied, her face placid.

Lady Sinclair was scrapping for a fight, her body taut as a bowstring. Georgina waited for those poisoned barbs to sing their way to her. Instead, she surprised her by doing nothing of the sort.

"Do tell your cousin that I was looking for him," she said, and rose to her feet in one graceful move. "Or perhaps I shall have the pleasure of telling him in person."

She whisked herself out of the room. Georgina sighed, then picked up the glass and drained the leftover brandy. Dinner would be interesting.

❖

Beatrice scowled as she listened to the clock ticking away its seconds and minutes on the mantel. It wasn't even midnight, but here she was, tucked away in bed. In London, she would have been whirling around a ballroom at this hour.

Dinner had been a severe disappointment. As Jacquie had predicted, Mr. Smith had not appeared. Beatrice had been surprised to find Gina enjoying a secret brandy before dinner, but she supposed that could be considered wild rebellion to the bluestocking. Overall, it had been an awkward meal. Jacqueline had been chatty, Nora had been reserved, and Gina had been earnest. Bea had stopped listening about halfway through and entertained herself by making eyes at the footmen.

Maybe coming to Rosedale Manor had been a mistake. Sparring over dinner with Gina was hardly the stuff of London entertainment. She marveled that Jacqueline found Rosedale to be a satisfactory replacement for the delights of the capital. She couldn't wait to return.

But in London, her husband awaited her. Beatrice didn't belong with him in his unfamiliar townhouse any more than she did in this quiet country manor. She wasn't sure when she had last felt like she belonged anywhere. None of the places she had ever lived with her parents had felt like a home. Her mother was too wrapped up in her own affairs and crises of epic proportions. Her father was charming but callous, except when he was drunk and effusive. She had been all too glad to leave them and their uncertain livelihood behind at last.

Bea pushed thoughts of her father's gambling problems away. Sinclair had settled all the debts, after all. It was one more cross for him to bear, along with her own recalcitrant nature, the scandal of their marriage, and her family's lack of noble breeding. But this was the way society marriages worked, wasn't it? She would give him that all-important son that he wanted, in exchange for saving her family from penury. She had enough honor to stand by the terms of the contract, even if it meant leaving her beloved London for good after the birth of their son.

Nothing much was left for her there anyway, now that Jacquie had moved to the country and Phin was so preoccupied with his duke.

She heard a distant footfall downstairs. It must be Mr. Smith, coming home from whatever carousing was available to a young man in these parts. She couldn't imagine the village was much more interesting than the entertainment offered at the manor. At this very moment, he was likely enjoying a snifter of brandy and thinking of what good fun he was missing in London.

The clock kept track of another minute, then another. Bea remembered how Mr. Smith was the only person who talked to her of his own volition at her engagement party. He had rescued her from the argument with her father. He had been generous to Jacquie when she needed a friend the most, offering his carriage and bringing her to Lady Honora when Jacqueline had decided that love was more important than scandal.

It would be a kindness for her to seek out Mr. Smith and greet him. He might not even be aware that the manor had another houseguest. Wouldn't finding him and telling him be the polite thing to do?

She smiled. Society marriages didn't preclude flirtations with other people. All Sinclair insisted on was that she not be pregnant with another man's child when she lay with him next, not that she remain *unkissed* during all this time. Given that her husband's romantic nature had withered upon their marriage, most unlike his dashing courtship style that sank a thousand hearts in its wake, she could use a kiss to raise her spirits.

She threw off the thin blanket and lit a candle so she could peek into the wardrobe that her maid had unpacked that afternoon. She selected a dress that was easy enough to put on by herself. It would be inappropriate to greet Mr. Smith in her nightclothes, much as a certain part of her fairly sang with joy at the thought of appearing in the library with nothing but her shift and a smile.

Beatrice pinked her cheeks with a pinch, blew out the candle, and sailed out the door. She was a *married woman*, she reminded herself with a shiver of delight. Though it could cause tongues to wag, enjoying a nightcap with Mr. Smith wouldn't ruin her. There weren't any tongues to wag out here anyway. Snorting, she thought of Gina's proclamation that she enjoyed nightcaps of warm milk. Her cousin would be no such milksop.

She slipped down the stairs and through the great hallway. Light glimmered from the crack beneath the library door, and anticipation thrilled through her. Taking a deep breath, she flung the door open.

CHAPTER SIX

Blinking, Mr. Smith looked up from the book in his hands. In one fluid motion, he uncrossed his legs, threw the book onto the desk, and went into a deep bow. "Lady Sinclair. I didn't think to see you here."

He didn't seem happy to see her. She could understand. As a married woman, he must presume her to be forbidden fruit. She graced him with a smile that she had practiced in the mirror many times for potential lovers.

"Mr. Smith, I appear in all sorts of unusual places. Wherever takes my fancy, mostly. Today, I fancied a country air."

"And tomorrow?"

"Heaven only knows what tomorrow shall bring," she said, lifting a shoulder.

He laughed. "Living for the moment. I say, I do admire that. I wish I could learn how to do it."

She entered the room and crossed to the window, hoping he was taking advantage of the opportunity to look at her derriere. But when she swung around, he was leaning against the desk with his eyes fixed on his brandy.

"Aren't you going to offer me a nightcap?"

"Is it wise?" His eyes were yearning, but his voice was serious. "Or would I be at risk of a dawn appointment with pistols? Your husband was in the military—my odds aren't good at ten paces."

"Let us not be *wise*, sir. I have found that wisdom interferes with a good time." Her laugh was a practiced trill, a most effective tool for seduction. To her surprise, George moved away with a frown.

"I cannot claim always to be wise, but I do value common sense."

"We are alone here, and my husband is far away. It would be the height of prudence to take advantage of the moment." She pitched her voice low and fluttered her lashes.

He shook his head and pushed away from the edge of the desk. "Maybe I should leave."

She dropped her flirtatious act. "Please. It's been a trying month."

His eyes softened as he looked at her, and he drew in a deep breath. She saw the moment that he gave in to temptation.

"I will help you settle your nerves tonight, but no more."

"If all you have to offer me is one drink, then I shall accept with open arms."

He unstoppered a crystal decanter of brandy, swished a scant finger of amber liquid into a glass, and handed it to her with a flourish. "Your heart's desire," he announced, his treble voice earnest and sweet.

Bea took a sip and allowed the brandy to warm her all the way down to her belly. His dark blue eyes warmed her the rest of the way down to her toes. He was a slender man, half the size of her husband and only a few inches taller than her. She liked that about him. His freckled cheekbones were high, his chin was pointed, and a dimple appeared in one cheek when he smiled. Her true heart's desire was to slide her hands through those fiery red curls and let herself get burned.

"Thank you, Mr. Smith," she said, her voice husky.

He waved his hand. "Please, call me George."

She sighed. "You and your cousin, so quick to dispense with honorifics."

"Old habit. We are cut from the same cloth, after all."

"You are nothing alike," she exclaimed. "You are ever so much easier to talk with."

He smiled at her. "I am here to listen, if you need a friendly ear."

"I wouldn't mind a friendly pair of lips, if you were willing," she said, throwing caution to the wind with another deep sip of liquor.

George raised a brow. "You have moved on from Sinclair already?"

"Isn't a husband always a less exciting lover than a bachelor?" She hid her scowl in the glass that she raised to her lips again before noticing that her brandy had somehow already disappeared.

But there was dear sweet George, at her elbow already with the decanter. With dreamy pleasure, she watched as another finger or two splashed into her glass. Splendid stuff, brandy.

"No one has ever taken care of me before," she said suddenly. She never allowed anyone close enough to try. "Are you in truth a knight in shining armor, rescuing forlorn ladies everywhere you go?"

"Didn't you tell me once that you were no damsel?"

"I could pretend."

"Then I'm sure brandy is hardly the rescue you're dreaming of."

It wasn't. "I wouldn't mind that kiss now," she whispered.

"Are you sure, Lady Sinclair?" Her name fell from his lips like a caress, and she sighed. Here was the courtship that she had yearned for from Sinclair, but he had never gone so far in flirtation as to kiss her before their marriage.

She frowned. He hadn't even kissed her on their wedding night. "No?" he asked.

"Yes," she sighed, closing her eyes and leaning forward, but no answering lips met hers.

"Have you enjoyed too much brandy for such a decision?" George asked, his brow furrowed. "I had forgotten that you already had as much to drink earlier at dinner—or so I would assume, that is to say. Come, let us sit for a moment while you regain your head."

Beatrice sank onto the sofa beside him, surprised to feel so relaxed. It must be that she was so far from London, far from any demands and expectations. These days at Rosedale were like a little pocket of time carved out just for her. Days, perhaps weeks, of leisure. And pleasure.

She leaned against his wonderfully steady shoulder, kicked off her shoes, and tucked her legs beneath her. Her eyes drifted closed and she inhaled, wanting to remember this moment in the woodsy citrus scent of his cologne and the lingering aroma of brandy from his lips. The mustiness of the books and maps stacked on the shelves. He must have opened a window, for she could also smell the roses from the gardens, and the warm night air.

"Lady Sinclair?" His breath was warm and sweet against her cheek as he whispered her name.

"If I am to call you George, then you must call me Beatrice," she murmured. She opened her eyes and angled her head on his shoulder until she could see his face, so close to hers that she could have counted the freckles that danced across his cheeks if only they weren't so blasted innumerable.

"I think perhaps that you are a damsel in disguise," he said, brushing her hair from her face. "You flirt with me like you want a knight in shining armor, but when I lift my helm, I discover that you're as strong as I am."

She sighed and closed her eyes again. She rather liked that idea.

"Beatrice?" he said, giving her a little nudge.

"George?" she questioned him right back.

"We should get you to bed," he said, and then laughed as she grinned at him. "Alone," he clarified.

"For now," she said with one brow raised, and was thrilled to hear his quiet laugh again.

George helped her to her feet. "I wish I could sweep you up into my arms and carry you to your door, sweet damsel, but alas I am not as broad in the shoulders as your husband."

She smiled. "I am capable of finding my own way, my dear chevalier. This is far from the first time that I have enjoyed a trifle too many spirits."

He escorted her to her bedchamber door anyway. As he was so solicitous, Bea felt it only polite to wrap her arm around his for extra security to make sure he felt useful, pressing herself close as they ascended the staircase.

George bowed to her, and she dipped into an unsteady curtsy. "My thanks for your gallantry, dear sir," she cooed, and then surprised herself by giving him a rare but real grin. "Worry not, I shall merely blow you a kiss good night."

She touched the tips of her fingers to her lips and waved them at him, pleased to see his ears go scarlet in the dim candlelight.

Dinner had been a disappointment. But the after-dinner entertainment had been the best she had enjoyed in a very long time.

❖

The local inn was a whitewashed building with a thick thatched roof in the center of Rosedale Village. A tavern occupied the ground floor, and rooms available for rent made up the second floor. It looked to be the picture of a good old British establishment that had served its patrons faithfully for centuries of celebrations. A weathered sign proclaimed it to be the Rose & Thorn. Pushing open the door, Georgina blinked as he entered a bright room redolent with ale and meat pasties, with a good-sized crowd making an even greater sized din.

It was a relief to be among the throng. Last night's flirtation with Beatrice had been unexpected, and he had felt the irresistible and familiar lure of a beautiful person who needed him. It was easier when he was in a dress because then Beatrice paid him no mind except to snap at him. But as soon as he put on a striped waistcoat and his cravat was tied in a neat mathematical, she was all smiles and fluttering eyelashes.

When she had leaned against his shoulder, so close that he could smell her jasmine perfume, he had known he was in trouble. Part of him relished the feeling of desire that rushed over him at the thought of Beatrice. Since the Duke of Hawthorne's return to England, he had been struck with full force by all his old feelings, unable to think of anyone else but the one man who had never loved him back.

Until he was faced with Beatrice's tinkling laugh and her cherry red lips.

Georgina sank onto a stool at the bar and smiled at the woman who bustled all over the room as quick as a wink. Her black hair was piled on her head in a haphazard bun, and she had laugh lines around her eyes and mouth. She dipped low with a ready smile over the older men in the corner at the dartboard and gave a quick pat on the shoulder of a young man at the window, before coming to the bar and greeting him.

"I've not seen you here before," she said.

"No, I've not had the pleasure."

"I know who you are, of course," she said. "Mr. George Smith. Of *London*, you are." She laughed in delight when Georgina blinked. "Have you never been to a small town? We don't keep our own secrets for long here, much less anyone else's. I hope you're enjoying your stay with Lady Honora and her companion Miss Lockhart at the manor."

He smiled. "If you already know my name and my business, then I must be well met among friends. And yet I know nothing of you. How very one-sided friendship is in this part of England."

She bobbed a curtsy then pressed her lips together. "Oh dear, this sort of welcome won't do at all for a gent. You London folk with your dandified airs expect such fine manners, don't you? We've had your like here before."

She set a pitcher of ale on the bar, grabbed her skirts by the fistful, and gave the most ludicrous curtsy Georgina had ever seen in his life except on the stage. To the hoots and hollers of the men, she slowly hoisted her bottom into the air and slid onto one heel with a fair amount of grace, the other one quite scandalously extended before her. No stockings covering the whiteness of her exposed legs as she lowered herself to a rousing cheer from the crowd.

The barmaid's curtsy was half performance and half insult, and wholly intended to have a laugh at Georgina's expense.

He joined in the laughter and put up his hands in protest. "You do me too much honor! I am no king," he proclaimed, then added with a grin, "Merely a prince of a fellow. Drinks all around, on me."

The crowd roared with laughter and Georgina received a genial thump or two on the back for being a good sport.

He grasped the barmaid's hand in a firm handshake. "I say, that was a good spot of fun."

She squeezed his hand. "Good show, Mr. Smith. I'm Sally."

"George will do just fine for me, Sally. It is a pleasure to meet you."

The bartender leaned over with a tall cold tankard. He was a brawny Black man with short-cropped hair and an easy grin on his face. "You might be paying a pretty penny tonight to cover all the drinks, but yours is on the house for keeping our Sally entertained," he said. "I'm Keith. I own the Rose & Thorn."

Sally beamed at him before picking up a tray and making the rounds of the tavern.

The local brew was excellent, and so was the local cheese. A farmer wandered over to praise the braised beef pasty that Georgina had ordered for dinner. Raised on his own farm, he said, and reckoned to be the very best in the area. This was said with a sidelong glance at some of his friends, who booed him down and started touting their own beef as best.

Georgina relaxed in the camaraderie of the men around him. His lace-edged cravat and engraved buttons were outlandishly fashionable compared to the farmer's garb and the local solicitor's coat, so of course he was scrutinized for being an outsider. That was what Sally's curtsy had been meant to remind him. But no one had batted an eye at *him*.

He had enjoyed his fair share of smoky evenings in London taverns, enjoying the combined bliss from an alcohol-induced fog and the pleasure of being at home where he was in his skin, without anyone giving a second thought to whether they thought he belonged there or not.

Sally came over and tucked herself between Georgina and another customer, her hip pressed against his chair and her elbow on the bar. "Enjoying all that Wiltshire has to offer?" she asked.

Georgina gestured down to his plate, empty save for a few crumbs and the barest sliver of the best cheddar he'd ever eaten, and patted his stomach. "Too much enjoyment and my tailor would despair of me," he said, thinking of Legrand's displeasure if he had to adjust his wardrobe. "Then it's all over for a gent like me, isn't it?"

"Your tailor might despair, but the lasses round here would rejoice," Sally said with a laugh. "A young man like you needs feeding up, you know. Words from my mother."

"There's more that a lass could do than just feeding and serving," he said.

Sally shoved away from the bar. "I am not that kind of woman, sir," she said. "Before was just a show."

Georgina was alarmed at having been misunderstood. "Of course it was. I would never proposition you that way. No, I meant that my friends at the manor have a lot of ideas of what women can accomplish beyond just hearth and home."

"This hearth earns my keep, Mr. Smith." Her voice held a warning.

He shook his head. This wasn't coming across at all the way he meant it. "George, please, if you will. Sally, I'm not trying to draw you into anything here. All I wanted to say is that the ladies are thinking of holding a poetry reading sometime soon, and they thought maybe people from the village might like to come."

She snorted. "A poetry reading? You think that will interest us?"

"Yes. I do. I've brought my copy of Shelley's latest poem— *Queen Mab*. It's all the rage in London these days."

She raised her brow. "'The broad and yellow moon shone dimly through her form—that form of faultless symmetry,'" she quoted.

The farmer next to her nodded sanguinely. "Aye, who doesn't know a bit of Shelley?"

Georgina was taken aback. This wasn't what he had expected at all. "So you are a literary neighborhood?"

"The vicar holds a club every third Friday of the month. It's quite popular." She grinned at him. "Perhaps you thought us country folk couldn't read?"

Georgina flushed with embarrassment. "I apologize for under-estimating the community here," he said. "But this is wonderful. Wouldn't you wish to continue your discussions together at different sorts of events?" He thought for a moment. "Perhaps a scientific demonstration?"

Sally shrugged. "Once a month is plenty for me, with people I already know. I don't know if I need to be hobnobbing with ladies and London folk."

He hadn't expected this outcome. He had thought it would be easy to get people interested in attending the functions he had planned at the manor. Maybe it had been naive, but he had assumed that the townspeople would be excited at the opportunity to enjoy events that typically were held in the largest cities.

He hated being wrong. He would have to reconfigure all his ideas for the salon now, and his stay in Rosedale would be extended for far longer than the two weeks that he had planned.

Georgina tried again. "Do say you'll attend. Trust me, the ladies at the manor aren't stuffy do-gooders full of vinegar."

Sally refilled his tankard with ale. "That's not what I remember of the dowager countess from her visits to the manor," she said. "A good woman, the sort you can rely on to give out bolts of cloth to the poor and soup to the sick. But starchy as a potato, as my mum would say."

"Well, the aunt is one thing," he conceded. "But she isn't here. Trust me, the niece and her companion are a different sort altogether."

Sally pursed her lips and gave a sidelong look at Keith, who jerked his head toward a table of rowdy farmers who looked due for a refill. "I'll think about it," she promised and sidled away.

Keith gave Georgina a hard stare. "You thinking to fix her head with nonsense?" he said gruffly. "She's a good one, Sally is, and she knows where she belongs. Not mincing about a lady's parlor with her nose in the air."

He leaned back. "Sally can go where she chooses, can't she? Nothing wrong with a change of air. The friendship of the ladies at the manor could have its advantages."

"Pah. That's nothing like friendship, I'd say. We all have our place in the world, and God doesn't smile on them any more than on the rest of us. That's just how it should be, if you ask me. The young Banfield lady has no airs about her, I'll give her that, and it's sad how her parents passed a few years ago. Now, they were good folk. People round here liked them just fine."

"Then why not give the daughter a chance?" Georgina asked, shifting in his chair and moving closer. He was curious about what the general feeling was in the town about Jacqueline's arrival at the manor.

But Keith only shrugged and went back to pulling ale. "Just don't know much about her. Lady Honora is a quiet thing and doesn't come to town much, does she? I guess you met her in London at one of those fancy parties. Too bad nothing came of that. We thought she would come home with a husband."

"That isn't the life for everyone," he said, and sipped his beer.

"Maybe London folk don't like the quiet type too much. Then again, she could make a good match of it with our vicar if she were of a mind, but I can't blame her for not wanting him. He's a good man, but a bit...*fussy*, if you know what I mean. Might not be a marrying type of man."

"Fussy, eh?" Georgina tucked that away, always on the lookout for hints and codes about people who shared the same inclinations as himself. A visit to the vicar would be in order soon.

He tried to figure out the best way to organize the visit into his week. He wanted to be sure that he utilized every moment to the fullest. Madhavi had things well under control in London, but he itched to get back to his own salon.

"Anyway, the point is—don't fill Sally's head with nonsense," Keith said stoutly. "She's just fine the way she is."

CHAPTER SEVEN

Beatrice woke up early, the sun shining brightly through the curtains that fluttered in the windows. The room was somehow even more charming than she remembered it being when she first arrived, though it was a far cry from the finery that she enjoyed.

There was a pitcher of water and a basin for washing on a side table, both of which were solid crockery and sporting more than a few chips and hairline cracks. Thin towels were stacked beside the basin, clean but mended. The mirror propped up behind it showed spots in places and had a wavering corner that distorted her reflection.

And yet, the pretty yellow paper on the walls was soothing. The wood floors weren't covered with expensive carpets, but they shone and gleamed with pressed wax. The quilt on the bed was beautiful. The room was simple but nourished her like broth after an illness.

She was the Countess of Sinclair now, she chastised herself. A woman of power and fortune. No house of hers would ever show its age like this one. Chipped crockery in the Sinclair estate would sooner find itself in the dustbin than in a guestroom. She had married into wealth and leisure, and she was going to squeeze every last drop of pleasure from it that she could. It was nonsense to yearn for a simple country living.

A feeling of unease trickled through her. If Lady Honora had married Sinclair, she would have had the funds to renovate Rosedale Manor in the height of fashion. Lady Honora had told her that she hadn't wanted to marry the earl. But had she taken something important away from Lady Honora after all?

Beatrice rang for her maid, who soon appeared with tea and toast.

"You are a blessing, Reina," she said, taking the tea in bed. She scanned her face, looking for any sign of strain or worry after her first few nights in the new household, and finding none. "The staff is treating you well?"

"Everyone has been polite, my lady." She drew the curtains open and peeked outside before opening the wardrobe to withdraw one of her morning dresses. "But they are awfully reserved here. I always thought country folk were the chattery sort."

This piqued her interest. "Their mistress is reserved," Beatrice said. "Lady Honora didn't have more than two words to offer at a time when I knew her in London. Maybe they follow her example."

She finished her tea and sat before the mirror so Reina could arrange her hair.

Reina slid a yellow rosebud into Beatrice's curls. "I am just saying it might be a bit lonely, is all."

Bea scowled at her reflection. "I don't want you to be unhappy," she muttered, wondering if she should return to London. Reina was dear to her.

"Oh, it's no hardship, my lady."

She chose a shift in the finest weave she owned to combat the summer heat and dressed in a mint green frock, the light cotton cool and airy around her body. A thin kerchief covered her bosom for modesty in name only, as it was so translucent that one could almost see right through it. As Reina was finishing up, Jacqueline knocked on the door.

"Imagine seeing us both awake at this hour!" Jacquie said. "How times have changed."

"For you, perhaps," Bea said. "I intend to go back to city hours as soon as I may."

Yet it was nice to be awake early enough to see the morning sun slanting through the room. She felt refreshed. It unnerved her.

Jacqueline leaned against the windowsill. "Have you had new dresses made up already with the earl's money?" she asked, looking at her gown in appreciation.

"I had a few ordered before the ink was dry on the betrothal contract," Bea admitted.

"Well, you look wonderful. And Lucy has never done a better job with your hair! Lucy, it's marvelous. You have always had a knack with the latest styles, but these curls are divine."

"Oh, miss, I go by Reina now," she said cheerfully, bundling up Beatrice's discarded nightclothes as she readied to leave the bedchamber.

"Reina?" Jacquie's brows shot up and she frowned at Bea. "*Reina?* You've been a countess for a scant week and it's gone to your head enough to assign your maid a new *name?*"

"Don't I deserve to be waited on by queens?" Beatrice demanded. "I think it's fitting for my new station. Reina is a *regal* name."

"Now, you know I am that happy to be a Reina, miss. I always liked Lucy. It was my mum's name after all. But now, I am treated ever so much more nicely by the earl's staff. The butler stopped giving me those awful looks and I think the housekeeper started to take a real shine to me. *Reina* is a name to be treated with respect!"

She bobbed a curtsy and left the room.

Jacqueline leaned over and gave Bea a tight hug.

"What was that for?" she asked, allowing herself one sweet moment where she leaned her head on her shoulder before pushing away.

Jacquie gave one of her curls an affectionate tug. "You aren't nearly the spoiled upstart that you want people to think you are. That was a kind thing you did for Reina to help her fit into her new life."

"I am every inch that upstart, thank you." Bea put her nose in the air and pursed her lips, and they both collapsed into laughter.

It felt good to be here, laughing with her best friend. Everything had changed since the Season had started, but for one moment she could pretend as if nothing was different at all. There was a rightness to it that made Bea's heart feel as featherlight as her muslin frock. Maybe she could gain some sense of peace here in Wiltshire that she could take with her to face her marriage.

"How shall we spend the day?" Beatrice asked. "Getting up to mischief gallivanting about the village, or settling in for a gossipy coze in the drawing room?"

"There is not much mischief to be had, I'm afraid."

"Come on, Jacquie," she complained. "There must be some

entertainment in this town, quaint as it may be? I don't wish to waste all the effort that Reina has put into my hair today."

Jacqueline squeezed her hand. "Dearest, you know that's not the life for me any longer," she said. "Besides, today I'm off to visit Mrs. Wilkins with Nora. She's our closest neighbor, and she is in her last few weeks of her confinement. We thought we would bring her some of our roses to cheer her up."

Beatrice stared. "You? Miss Jacqueline Lockhart of London, shameless flirt of a hundred dinner parties, now visiting a sickbed? I would never have guessed such a happenstance to occur."

She laughed and poked her shoulder. "You jest, Bea. I would have guessed more like two hundred dinner parties, at the very least! But those days are behind me." She sighed. "I hadn't realized how wonderful it would be here. I think I was looking for constant diversion in London because I was unhappy, and I didn't even realize it. My life here with Nora, in the country—well, we might not have much, but we have each other. We have *love*, Beatrice."

"I love nothing more than to see you happy," Bea said, and was surprised at the sincerity of it. She hadn't thought that Jacquie could be satisfied here, but the proof was before her eyes, was it not? She studied her face. Yes, Jacqueline's green eyes were dancing, her skin was glowing, and she radiated domestic bliss.

"Can you not entertain your guest, just for today?" she asked one last time, batting her eyelashes. "Out of long love for me?"

"You could have stayed in London and been well entertained there," Jacqueline said. "You could have stayed by the husband you fought so hard to win."

Beatrice bristled. "The winning was in the wedding," she said. "Now what need do I have of him?"

Jacqueline bit her lip. "Are you so unhappy?"

She hated to show such vulnerability. Even to a friend who had known her for most of her life. She didn't want to admit that Sinclair had been so cold to her, or that he had vowed to banish her out of his sight forever after the birth of their child. It was humiliating, and unfair, and she preferred to pretend that it hadn't happened at all.

"Who cares for happiness in a *haut ton* marriage?" Beatrice said with a wave of her hand and a practiced little laugh. "Now you must be away on your errand of mercy to Mrs. Wilkins. The poor dear must be dreadfully uncomfortable and ruing the night of her wedding much more than I rue mine."

Without Jacquie's company, the morning seemed endless. The problem with being an uninvited guest was that there was nothing in particular to do. This wasn't a house party, and thus there were no planned entertainments. Lady Honora's estate existed on straightened means, so there were no horses to ride in the stables. There wasn't any sewing in her reticule, as she had decided upon her marriage that she needn't ever pick up a needle again. Her valise held no novels. The only person to whom she would have penned a letter would have been Jacqueline.

Then Beatrice remembered there were two other houseguests. Gina was the sort who would have suggested the mission to cheer up the pregnant ladies of the county, so she must be with Lady Honora and Jacqueline. George, however, might be around. Kicking up his heels. Looking for adventure.

Pleasure blossomed deep inside as she thought of his warm smiles. He could pass the time with *her*. Rosedale was no big estate. It shouldn't take her long at all to find what she desired.

To her surprise, she found Gina instead, buried up to her elbows in papers and books in the library. Beatrice was disappointed. She had looked forward to seeing George's tousled coppery hair and sincere blue eyes, but she cheered herself by remembering that there was time enough for that in the moonlight.

Gina didn't look thrilled to see her either. She sighed and closed the book in front of her, some dusty tome that looked the same as all the other ones on the shelves, and set her pen aside. "Good morning, Beatrice."

Her hair was pulled back in a simple tail, though a few bright red strands had straggled out of it. Her freckled face was drawn and tired, her lips pulling down at the corners. Her dress was a fine weave that looked as lightweight as Bea's but was made heavier with the elaborate embroidery that she favored. Varying textures made the thread thistles and leaves stand out from the thin fabric in vivid relief, even though it was white stitchwork on white fabric. It was beautiful, but Beatrice wondered if Gina regretted the choice of attire. The windows were wide open, but there wasn't any breeze.

"Already hard at work?" Beatrice asked, peering down at the

desk. She picked up a piece of paper, but it was written in Latin. *Of course* Gina could read Latin. Was there anything she couldn't do? She shook her head and let the paper slip back to the desk, and with the tip of a finger pushed a book around so she could see its title. *A Study of British Geography*. How tedious.

Gina shot a hand out and pulled the book back toward her. "Please don't," she said. "There's a lot to be done, and it is much easier for me to know exactly where everything is." She leaned back in the chair and folded her arms across her chest.

Beatrice stepped away from the desk. "What is it that you're working on, anyway?"

"Why would you want to know? So you can deride it?"

"No," she said in defense. "I'm just curious."

"You're *bored*," Gina corrected her.

There was no use to deny it. She shrugged. "I might be."

"Why don't you visit with Jacqueline instead of wandering around here?" She picked up her pen again. "I should get back to what I'm doing."

"Jacquie and Lady Honora have gone visiting. My options are limited to walking around the gardens in the heat, or to converse here with you."

"You've chosen me? I say, I am surprised."

Gina was scrutinizing her with those dark blue eyes that looked like they saw into one's soul. That steady focus made Beatrice's stomach flutter.

"Maybe I could help with what you're doing," she said, though she only partly meant it. She just wanted those fathomless eyes directed elsewhere. "Explain it to me?"

"Jacquie and Nora asked me to visit so I can help them set up a salon, like the weekly one I hold in Mayfair." She began stacking the books on the desk, running her finger along the spines to align them, staring down at them as if it were the most important task in the world. "But it turns out that the people of Rosedale Village might not actually be interested in attending one. I wanted so much for this to be a success, to build an extension of what I had created in London. I don't know anymore if I can make it happen."

The words sounded forced, as if it had been difficult to get them out. Her shoulders hunched upward, the puffed sleeves of her dress almost reaching her ears.

It was the first time she had ever seen Gina seem less than sure of herself. Beatrice wanted to reach out and tuck that strand of hair behind her ear. She wanted to smooth a finger across the creases in that freckled brow.

Beatrice frowned. Where were these thoughts coming from? It must be that Gina looked so much like her cousin George. She could not possibly be attracted to Gina, the intellectual bluestocking who thought that Beatrice was nothing but a shallow flirt.

"Country folk might not be as interested as Londoners in your particular agenda," Bea offered, thinking back to her years spent in a little village like this one. "Perhaps you argue all night in Mayfair about progress and fair wages and the best stratagem to fight off Napoleon. But can you rely on that kind of engagement here about the same topics?"

Gina drummed her fingers on the desk. "Show me one person in all of England who has no opinion of the war, whether it's the impact on the price of beef, or the sad lack of gentlemen to dance with in the evenings, or the excitement of the militia passing through town."

"But they gather in their own drawing rooms to share these thoughts. Or they have a lively chat in the tavern. Or they talk about it on washing day with their neighbors when they hang their clothes on the line. Why should they come *here*?"

Gina sighed. "I prepared pamphlets to pass around for discussion and paid for subscriptions to some of the most popular newspapers in London. I chose a series of piano quartets, all written by women, so we can have a musical evening. I wrote four lectures about local archeology, and I think just about everyone should have an interest in that!"

Beatrice threw up her hands. "What if no one in this neighborhood even likes archeology? Then who would come to your *four-part series*?"

"You think that *you* would know what it is that people want? Aren't you more occupied with your latest hairstyle or cut of your gown than in your fellow man?"

"I am not so preoccupied to notice that people don't like condescension. Which is what this must seem like to them. Londoners waltzing into a town that they know nothing about, taking one look around, and wanting to change everything."

"Nora has grown up here. These are her countrymen—how can you say she knows nothing about it?" she contested.

"I'm not talking about Lady Honora," Bea shot back. "I'm talking about you."

Her mouth gaped open, then snapped shut. Bea felt a tiny rush of satisfaction. So maybe Gina didn't know everything after all.

"I didn't think about it that way," she said slowly. "All I want is to help people. Nora thought that we had a chance, but maybe you're right. I haven't taken into consideration that the interests here might not be the same as in the capital. Perhaps I should pack up for London and focus on my own salon again."

Bea picked at the worn fabric of the armchair. She hadn't intended for Gina to leave. She didn't want to examine that disappointment too closely. It was just that there would be so few to dinner, should Gina depart.

"Why is the salon so important to you, anyway? Isn't it just sipping tea and gossiping, but about philosophy instead of hemlines?"

Gina's eyes flashed. "It is my life's work. Nothing will ever be more important to me."

She was beautiful when she was animated. Her passion shone from her face and illuminated every inch of her. The sun streamed in from the window behind her and turned her hair into a fiery crown. She looked more like a warrior than an academic.

Gina pushed away from the desk and paced in front of the bookshelves. "This is the only space most of us have where we can talk about politics, women's rights, and scientific and technological advances. There are no men to tell us to be quiet, that we don't understand, that it isn't our place. Can you imagine being in a room full of encouragement, with every soul cheering you on as you talk about your passions? Anything is permitted. Nothing is denied."

She whirled around to face Beatrice. "Is none of this important to you? Because all of it is sacred to me."

Beatrice suddenly remembered her first Season. She had been

eager for any opportunity to escape from her family, and to find friendship instead. But competition between women was fierce on the Marriage Mart. When the other debutantes had sized her up as a threat and treated her with scorn, it hadn't taken her long before she shut the door on that search for friendship. It was a shock to realize that Gina might have come across the same door, but instead of shutting it, she had turned around and created a whole new room for herself and anyone who might care to join her.

Bea swallowed hard. "I never thought about it. About any of this."

Gina sighed. "It's been so hard to try to explain to people that this is important. Women deserve to have their voices heard, and I am determined to hear as many as I can in this lifetime. But if even you can't understand it, when you have friends like Jacqueline who champion such things, then what chance do I have here?"

Beatrice leaned closer. "You shouldn't give up. Maybe there is another approach we could take here in Wiltshire."

She saw the swift tangle of emotions cross Gina's face before she leaned back against the edge of the desk, her eyes darkening as she stared up at her. "Whatever are you suggesting we do instead?"

"If I knew, I would be the queen of the bluestockings, not you," Beatrice said with a grin. "But when you figure it out, let me know and I will be happy to help. God only knows there's not much else to do here in the country. This would be a fun distraction."

She left the library before she could regret the offer, but not before she enjoyed the look of astonishment on Gina's face.

CHAPTER EIGHT

Georgina swung her parasol by her side. She considered herself a patient person, but this was testing her limits. She had been standing with Jacqueline and Nora in the front hall for almost half an hour when they could have been to the village by now. Lady Sinclair was nowhere to be seen.

It was annoying enough to have rushed through her own toilette, but she was eager to talk more with the people in the village to gauge their interest in the idea for the salon. Wasting time when she could be doing something useful was the very worst of sins in her book.

"Beatrice has an affection for making an entrance," Jacqueline said. "I am sorry, Nora. I know she's an uninvited guest, and now she's throwing everything off schedule. We shall have to reschedule luncheon, won't we? You're a darling for not tossing her out on her rear."

"Why haven't you done so yet?" Georgina asked, trying not to imagine Lady Sinclair's lovely rear in her mind's eye.

Despite her words, she didn't want her to leave Rosedale. Lady Sinclair's careless words about her work had stung. On the other hand, she had been oddly encouraging. She wouldn't want to admit it to anyone, least of all to the lady herself, but she had inspired her yesterday to continue to pursue the idea of the salon at Rosedale.

"I do not like her," Nora admitted. "She wasn't kind in her pursuit of the Earl of Sinclair when she noticed that he favored me. But, Jacquie, you do consider her to be as close as family. And family is important."

The look that they exchanged was charged with grief. Nora's parents had passed away a few years ago in a carriage accident, and Jacquie's parents had disowned her when they discovered her liaisons with other women.

Georgina understood that the bonds of friendship could be complicated. Not everyone that she had surrounded herself with over the years were people she liked. But the unspoken loyalty between herself and others who had the same desires and feelings was what bound them together into a community. She would do anything in her power to help them, regardless if they were friends or not.

"Bea was there for me at every turn in my life when it was hard," Jacquie said quietly. "She will always be the dearest of friends. But she is not an easy person, and she hasn't had an easy life. I had hoped that marriage would bring her peace."

Georgina snapped open her parasol. Lady Sinclair had guessed correctly the other night in the library. Damsels in distress were her weakness, and she loved nothing more than trying to rescue them. How many women had she invited to her salon because the vulnerability in their eyes brought out her protective side?

Lady Sinclair didn't fall into that category, Georgina reminded herself. Despite her troubles, she was about as vulnerable as a hawk, with the sharp beak and talons to match.

The click of a heeled shoe brought their attention to the top of the staircase where Lady Sinclair stood in striped muslin splendor. Her bonnet sported a ribbon tied into an impressive bow beneath her chin. Lace gloves covered her hands to the wrist, leaving plenty of arm bared up to the tiniest of sleeves at her shoulder. Georgina had an urge to reach out and touch that flawless creamy skin.

"You're late," Georgina announced.

"I was attending my toilette," Lady Sinclair replied with a toss of her ringlets as she descended the stairs. "As a countess, I have a certain station to uphold."

She was now close enough that Georgina could see the fine line of kohl on her eyelids, and the lip color that made it appear as if she had been eating cherries all morning. Those honeyed brown eyes swept over her own outfit and lingered on her parasol, made with delicate linen lace in a pattern of Celtic knots.

"How very charming," Lady Sinclair said.

"Bea, do let us go now," Jacquie broke in. "Gina is right. It's getting on and I want to have enough time to peek in at the milliner's as well as the mantua maker's today."

She and Nora headed out the front door together, and they began their trip to Rosedale Village. Georgina was soon left to walk by herself as Lady Sinclair lagged behind them. No doubt mincing her steps and preening at the few passersby that they chanced to see on the road.

It wasn't a long walk to the village. The gravel path was well-worn, marked with a few neat hedgerows here and there to delineate the many farms in the area. A flock of sheep ambled in the distance.

"To see sheep is to know that we are in a dismal location indeed," Lady Sinclair muttered from behind her.

Georgina couldn't resist slowing her pace to walk beside her. "I daresay you care for a wool pelisse in the winter though, don't you? British fashion starts with the lowly sheep. I would have thought you would be more appreciative of its origin here in the country."

"*Country* and *fashion* are two words that do not go together," she huffed.

"Wiltshire is a fascinating part of the country, isn't it?" Georgina asked. She twirled her parasol against her shoulder and tipped her head back so she could better view the farmland from under its lacework panels.

"Fascinating if one cares for either sheep or cheese," Lady Sinclair said. "Both of which are odorous and unremarkable."

Georgina frowned. "Rosedale was once the site of a Roman settlement. Nora tells me that there are still traces of one of their roads near town. They had an impressive fabric trade in the area until recently."

"There is nothing so boring as people who wallow in past history and refuse to move on." A shadow crossed her face, and she adjusted her hat to cover more of her eyes.

"There is nothing so tedious as watching people refuse to learn from the examples of what has already happened," Georgina retorted.

"Dusty old facts that happened to people a long time ago have no relevance to current affairs."

Georgina blew out a breath. "Are you always so close-minded?"

"I prefer to think of myself as *specifically interested*," she said. "Close to things that happen within my sphere. Nowadays, thanks to the great good fortune of marrying the earl, I plan that sphere to encompass nothing more than clothes, entertainments, and lovers."

"There is more to life than frivolity."

Lady Sinclair made a show of ruffling her skirts and admiring the scalloped hem with a little hum of pleasure. "Why shouldn't I enjoy myself? I had precious little enough times in my life to be grateful now for plenty."

Georgina tried not to peek at the ankle that Lady Sinclair had exposed. "You could be helping so many people with your new title and riches, you know. You could be a patron of the arts, or a champion of the downtrodden. How are you planning to pass your days as Lady Sinclair?"

"My days are my own to spend, as is my coin," she said sharply. "You have your own fortune to throw at the masses, don't you? Yet isn't there still poverty? Don't you still see children sweeping the streets? One woman can only do so much."

Georgina slapped her parasol into her hand. "Don't you see? This is why we need to come together. One person can start an avalanche, but it takes the lot of us together to *be* the avalanche and effect change."

"I should prefer to be a single elegant flake of snow than a great big churning disaster," she said.

"Some of us like disasters," Georgina said with a sidelong look at her.

Lady Sinclair gasped in outrage. "I am *not* a disaster."

"Of course not. Do forgive me, Lady Sinclair. I spoke out of turn."

After all, Lady Sinclair had hardly held the title for a week. Perhaps it wasn't fair to expect her to make all these decisions straightaway. There would be time enough for that when they returned to London, if Georgina could interest her to visit on Tuesdays.

"Are we close to the village yet?" Lady Sinclair asked. "I have endured a lecture when all I was promised on this excursion was fashion and shoes and perhaps a quaint rustic view."

"I say, do be fair. I tried to speak of fashion, but you were disinterested in discussing the sheep," she teased her, trying to lighten the mood.

She was relieved when Lady Sinclair laughed. "Lady Gina, we shall never see eye to eye. On anything."

"I would be pleased if you called me Gina," she said. She never liked to bother with honorifics if she could help it. But at least Lady Sinclair hadn't called her Georgina. In fact, she hadn't called her by her full name since Georgina had first requested her not to, which was a mark in her favor.

"Fine. Gina." She heaved an exasperated sigh. "If you must insist on a shocking lack of formality, then you might as well call me Beatrice. Though it's a fine thing to eschew one's title when one has just received it."

"Have you been enjoying the toadying?" Georgina asked. "It gets dull after a while."

Beatrice touched a finger to the brim of her bonnet and spent some time adjusting it on her curls. "No one has done so yet," she replied. "I have paid no calls since my marriage, except once to walk in the park with Sir Phineas. No one cares much to socialize with an upstart countess."

She seemed uncomfortable with the admission, and Georgina frowned. "Well, we must tell the villagers that they have a brand-new peer of the realm come to visit," she announced. "The mantua maker will be in alt."

She sniffed. "It should be below my notice to shop in such pedestrian areas now."

Georgina grinned and leaned close. "I bet you cannot resist the siren song of a faux fruit arrangement for your bonnet no matter where it may be found, can you?"

"However did you guess my secret?" Beatrice asked, some of the hauteur easing from her face. Georgina was charmed to see the curve of her natural smile. It wasn't anything like the arch curl of her lip that she so often displayed, and was different again from the seductive smile that she directed at George. Georgina wanted to see more of it.

"We are almost to the shops now," Georgina said. "You may indulge to your heart's content."

Beatrice's lashes lowered, and there was a chasm between

them again. "You needn't remind *me*—I only ever indulge myself," she said.

By the end of their shopping trip, Georgina was impressed by the extent to which Beatrice was capable of indulging. She cast a bored eye over the merchandise in the general store, but it didn't stop her from purchasing a dozen bolts of cloth and twice as many lengths of trim. Her largesse continued when she insisted on visiting the candlemaker ("You aren't using the finest beeswax at your table, Lady Honora—*do* let us dine in style tonight."), and the butcher ("Shall we not eat beef? I tire of mutton, whether it's on the plate or on the hoof as we saw it today."). Her spending was extravagant at the milliner's, where she bought every hat she chanced to pick up, adding enough silk ribbon to the final tally that could put a bow on all the hats in the village combined.

"I shall spread my custom where I may," she snapped when Georgina questioned her, and sailed out the door after settling the exorbitant payments.

Georgina tried at every turn to interest the shopkeepers in the idea of the ladies salon, stressing the importance of supporting female industry and the role of education for girls in improving the future of those industries. But instead she found herself listening to them marvel at the amount of money they had made in just one day from just one customer. They were gratified by the custom of a London-bred countess, and relieved that they wouldn't have to worry about settling their quarterly bills after today's sales.

As she listened to their appreciative chatter, Georgina started to wonder if there was much more to Beatrice than met the eye.

CHAPTER NINE

Was there anything as perfect as a summer night for seduction? Beatrice curled herself in the chair by the open window of her bedroom, feeling the warm night breeze on her face as it ruffled the curtains like a lover ruffling her hair.

This had been a good week. Surprisingly good.

She had lived in a small country village like this for two years, until her father charmed enough money from a friend to whisk them back to London. She remembered not having a farthing to spend in the general store, her face pressed up against the window until her mother grasped her by the arm and hauled her home. It was a thrill to go inside such a shop now and spend a small fortune.

The items for Lady Honora's table...well, that had been an impulse. Although she had apologized already to Lady Honora when she arrived at Rosedale, she felt the need to do penance over her behavior during the Season. Every day that she spent as a guest in her home humbled her. She knew there wasn't a lot of money in her coffers, so she had decided to contribute to the household in lieu of more words that she wasn't sure if Lady Honora wished to hear from her.

It had been helpful to have Gina at her side, she admitted to herself. She had felt uncomfortable when Gina had asked what she was doing with her fortune and station in life. But if Gina hadn't asked, Beatrice didn't know if she would have thought to use them to Lady Honora's advantage. She had hidden the truth of her feelings in the only way she knew how, under the cover of self-indulgence and derision. Beatrice hated how the words had sounded as they fell from her lips, but she shrank away from the idea of showing any hint of vulnerability.

Maybe before she left Rosedale she could find it in herself to gift something to Lady Honora with honesty.

The heavy scent of roses from her dresser perfumed the room, and she shivered. Every ounce of her body felt tight, coiled, and taut. Primed and ready and *aching* for a lover's touch. Dusk had just touched the gardens, and she could see pale orange and pink staining the sky from the last moments of the sunset. It wasn't late enough, though. George wouldn't be home from the tavern.

And yet, this moment felt *unbearably* late. She was seven and twenty, a woman full grown and married, but tonight had her feeling like a debutante waiting for the opening set at her very first ball. She remembered the agony of that reception line. The interminable mingling before the music started. The impatience of waiting for a gentleman to appear, asking for a dance. The fear that it wouldn't happen at all. She and Jacquie had been lucky, grinning at each other in delight as they twirled all night long on the arms of men whose names were beyond recall now.

That long forgotten combination of hope and wonder and anticipation bloomed deep in her belly like a flame. She had felt cynical and jaded since that first Season, and never more so than during her weary husband hunt this year.

Now, deep in the wilds of Wiltshire, hours away from any ballroom whatsoever and miles apart from her husband, she felt fresh.

Bea pushed herself away from the chair and went to the mirror to smooth powder on her cheeks and salve on her lips. "I am in sore danger of countrifying if I am excited about the *night air* of all things," she murmured to herself and gave a sarcastic laugh that somehow didn't feel quite right despite how often she had rehearsed it over the years.

A familiar refrain started to echo in her heart, which she tried her best to ignore. If only, it whispered. Oh, *if only*. She sighed. Hadn't she wasted her childhood papering her life with those words? If only the maids hadn't been let go. If only she could have a new doll for Christmas.

If only her parents had loved her.

If only she had met some man in those early Seasons with a warm disposition and kind hands who could have swept her away from her family before she could be forced to sacrifice herself to save them.

Instead, Bea had sought out wild gentlemen who seduced her with shallow entertainments and laughter, with nary a thought of matrimony. She had never been in danger of losing anything of importance around them, though now she wondered if she had ever gained anything either. The women she had loved had been no different, except for the long years she had spent loving Jacquie.

If only she had met George sooner.

Well. It was no use trying to solve the past's problems when there were plenty piled up for her to tackle today. And tomorrow. And next year.

A night of lovemaking with George would be just that. One night. Perhaps a week if she wished to be hedonistic. Then Beatrice would return to Sinclair and concentrate on her wifely duties. She would have the rest of her life in front of her.

If only she could give him a son right away.

The minute hand of the clock ticked its way to eleven, and before much more time had passed, she heard the now familiar footfall downstairs that could only mean one thing.

George had returned. *Finally.*

Bea spritzed one last puff of perfume on her neck, applied another coat of salve to her lips, and slipped out the door to run to her soon-to-be lover and the temporary oblivion of an affair.

❖

Georgina downed his second tankard of ale in the back corner of the Rose & Thorn. The men in the tavern had wives and daughters and sisters and mothers, and he thought it might be easier for some of those women to attend if they had the support of their family. Although he continued to meet with polite disinterest, he persisted in talking to anyone who would listen.

Today was Tuesday. He took another long pull of his ale, his foot tapping against the rung of his chair. This was the first week he had missed attending his own salon. Had Mrs. MacArthur been there, complaining of rheumy knees and gloating about thwarting her nephew's plans to enclose his estate? Had Alice Andrews arrived to discuss the latest story that she had sold to the newspapers?

The only person he didn't wonder about was Madhavi. She was always marvelous with the ladies on Tuesdays. Her manner was firm but warm, and she was excellent at moderating debate and encouraging discussion. He was impatient to receive the letter he knew she would have written the instant the women had dispersed.

Sally bumped him with her hip as she took his tankard. "Awfully long face for a fine London gent," she remarked. "Are you staying another round?"

He shook his head. "I'm afraid I'm not good company tonight."

Sitting here in the tavern reminded him of the camaraderie he was missing in London. If he were there now, he could hie himself off to Hawthorne's for a drink and an evening of entertainment with anyone the duke chanced to invite to his estate. Guilt gnawed at him as he thought about the threat of the raids on the molly houses. Men like him had it easy enough, with the security of wealth and powerful friends.

But so many lacked those privileges. How many thousands thronged the streets at night, full of longings that they couldn't safely satiate? He felt exhausted enough doing all the work he could for women with the salon, but he worried that he should be paying equal attention to men who didn't quite fit into society's expectations.

The moon was full and bright, and the air was fresh. Georgina left the heat and the rowdiness of the tavern behind him and walked down the main street until he found a stretch of brick wall between the bakery and the haberdashery, where several shopfronts had been boarded up. During last week's shopping expedition, he had noticed that this corner was as busy as village life could be. Plenty of people walked to the bakery every day, and a fair amount of carriages bustled past to change horses at the inn.

It was the perfect place for advertisements. The brick was barely visible beneath the pell-mell of posters and handbills, and they were pasted all over the boarded-up windows too. There were announcements for lady's hand creams, apothecary's cures for gout and chilblains, and claims about various services and wares of the shops in this town and the next.

Georgina pulled out a thick wad of handbills from the pocket that Legrand had sewn into the front of his coat and set them on top of a barrel. He withdrew a pot of glue and a thick bristled brush and placed them beside the bills. He studied the wall. There was no space for new posters. Most of them were already plastered on top of older ones, giving the wall an uneven thickness.

Deciding that the vulgar caricatures of London Society would be the best thing to cover, he uncorked the bottle and spread a thin layer of adhesive on the back of the bill before pressing it to the wall. It was a treatise on suffrage, as succinctly written as he could manage it, with an illustration contributed by one of the ladies at the salon. He pasted a bill about workers' rights beside it and added one more about abolition.

He stuffed the supplies into his coat and started up the path toward Rosedale Manor. The least he could do was draw attention to those issues any way he could manage it, even if he couldn't inspire people to congregate for discussions about them.

Georgina opened the front door of the manor and thought about going straight to bed. The library now held the memory of Beatrice's intoxicating jasmine perfume. What if she appeared again, like some tempting apparition? Would he regret it if she didn't?

He threw open the library door and poured himself a drink. Beatrice was a willing woman, and she intrigued him more with every day that passed. The problem was that she didn't really *know* him. His appearance, either as a man or a woman, was no deception in itself. He was both George and Gina, male and female, and although it had taken him a long time to become comfortable with himself, he knew deep in his bones that it was his truth.

Frowning into his glass, he wondered why it felt different with Beatrice. He had slept with bored matrons of the *ton* before, without feeling the need to tell them anything. Why would he want her to know?

The real problem, he realized, was that he found himself drawn to her, and not just sexually. He liked that saucy smile and those amused eyes. There was even something about her haughty airs and manners that charmed him. At first, he had thought it was because they reminded him of Hawthorne and his ducal arrogance, but it was different entirely from his attraction to the duke. He wanted to strip away those artificial layers and discover who Beatrice was at her core. He had been watching her since her arrival at Rosedale and was starting to put the pieces together that there was a softer side to Beatrice hidden underneath her sharp exterior.

At meals, she was full of snappy retorts that she flung at himself and Lady Honora and Jacqueline, but Georgina had noticed that she only behaved that way when the servants weren't in the room. She was sweet to the footmen and flirtatious with the butler, who was eighty years old if he was a day. She never failed to compliment either the service or the meal or both. Legrand had told him that Beatrice's maid was devoted to her and spoke often of her kindness.

Georgina took a deep sip of the liquor and drew the curtains open. He lit but one candle tonight above the mantel, preferring the dusky romance of the evening to permeate the room. The moonlight gilded the rose gardens, turning everything to silver and indigo and charcoal, so many shades of darkness.

Should he tell Beatrice the truth? But for what purpose—just for the chance to lay with her tonight? Would it be worth it?

Jacquie and Nora knew about his identity, as did Phin and Hawthorne. A few others had known, over the years. He had found enough ways to seek sexual satisfaction whether he chose to talk about his anatomy or not, often aided by the nature of pleasures taken in hurried enclaves where neither party expected to undress.

Given who her friends were coupled with, Georgina thought Beatrice might be open to the idea that if not everyone shared the same sexual preferences, then perhaps not everyone shared the same gender identity that society expected.

However, although Beatrice might be attracted to George, the ne'er–do–well charmer, she would never want to have an affair with Gina, the bluestocking. He thought they were becoming friends, of a sort, though it was tentative at best.

The library door was well-oiled, but nevertheless he heard it swing open. The hairs on his neck rose. His blood heated. Georgina turned to see Beatrice slink into the room still clad in the diaphanous silvery evening dress that he remembered from dinner. Where he had sat across from her in his own dress, covered in the white lace and little frills and sparkling beads that he loved and that Beatrice had scorned.

He couldn't tell her. Not without trusting her first. The risk was too great.

But it was clear that temptation was about to be put to its test.

CHAPTER TEN

Georgina's heart beat faster when he saw a delighted smile cross Beatrice's face as she entered the library. It was a flash of sincerity that he never saw as Gina. This was the side of Beatrice that he yearned to know, and she wouldn't dream of sharing it with him in a dress.

"We meet again, George," she said, her voice sweet as an angel. Those honeyed eyes gleamed at him with the knowledge that no heavenly creature should have.

He grinned. She was becoming his idea of heaven. He turned to the sideboard and fixed her a brandy.

Georgina thought for a moment. He couldn't seduce Beatrice, for all that she was now sprawling herself on the sofa with the brazen confidence of an orange seller at the opera. A silky smooth leg was bared from the knee down beneath a froth of petticoats. A creamy expanse of bosom peeked out from the bodice which she had obviously tugged down while he had been pouring her drink. Her cherry lips curved in a mischievous smile.

Then she licked those full lips, and the sight of her tongue ignited a fire beneath his trousers. No, he wouldn't give in to her seduction. But something had to be done to satisfy this wild desire between them.

"Have you given any more thought to granting my wish of a kiss?" she asked, taking the glass from his hand. "You see, I have asked you before I even had one drop of liquor. You need have no worries about what I want from you."

It wouldn't be easy to stop after he had a taste of those lips. Yet he would be undone if there was anything more than kissing.

Inspiration struck. If he didn't want to complete the deed, he could find a way to delay. "A kiss...for a confidence," he said.

"A confidence?" Bea pouted. "I hardly think you would be interested in learning my secrets, George." She looked down at herself and inched her skirts higher. "Although I do have one secret that you would be most interested in seeing."

He sat beside her, pulled her legs onto his lap, and smoothed her skirts down. He stroked the fragile skin on the inside of her ankles with his thumb and heard her quick gasp. "I am interested in more than your body, luscious though it is."

She breathed deeply. He wondered if she was affected by his statement, or his hands on her legs, or if she just wanted him to watch her breasts rise and fall beneath the thin silk with every inhale. Whichever it was, he was captivated by the quick play of emotion that he saw in her eyes. Against his better judgment, he slid a hand up one warm calf under her petticoats.

"Tell me secrets and no lies," he whispered as he brushed the hollow at the back of her knee with his fingers.

Beatrice sipped her brandy. "Perhaps I shall choose neither, sir."

He removed his hands. "By all means. You are always free to walk away, Beatrice. This library is no prison. You are under no obligations to play."

"Only if I wish to be kissed," she said slowly.

"Precisely."

She eyed him. "Is this library meant to be a popish confessional? Nothing said within these four walls will be revealed outside of them?"

"Well, I'm Church of England and hardly drawn to the vicarage, but I suppose the metaphor stands."

"I agree to your terms, George. A kiss for a confidence." She straightened her shoulders. "But I think the kissing ought to come first."

"Oh?"

"How can I judge how intimate my secret should be, if not for the intensity of the kiss?"

He gave her a peck on the cheek and grinned at her expression of mock outrage.

"That wasn't worth the barest remark on the weather," she said.

"It still counts," he defended.

Beatrice nestled against the arm of the sofa. "Let me see," she said, tapping one finger against her chin. "I think you are rather handsome." She closed her eyes and puckered her lips. "Anything more requires further motivation."

Georgina gently pressed his mouth to hers, sensitive to every nerve that fired in response. He tasted brandy and heat and he craved more, sliding his fingers through the hair at the nape of her neck and drawing her closer to him. She grasped his shoulders and held on tight, moving against him so her breasts lay snug against his own. He was small-breasted and was wearing a shirt and waistcoat beneath his coat, so he wasn't concerned that she would notice.

His body shifted so one trousered knee was pressed against her thigh, and he craved nothing more than full body contact. It would be easy enough to topple her over onto the sofa, or the floor if she wasn't opposed to it. God knew he wanted it enough.

But by his own rules, there was to be kissing only. He had to remember that it was for the best. Reluctantly, he drew away and she opened her eyes.

"That was a very nice kiss, George," she drawled, her eyes shadowy and half-lidded. Georgina frowned. Her guard seemed up again, and he kept his touch light and soothing on her knee to comfort her. "I suppose you wish me to unearth very detailed secrets tonight. All you may have is that Sinclair is an utter ass, and I may have made a terrible mistake by marrying him, except for the fact that his money saved my family from penury."

"Marital bliss doesn't happen for everyone," Georgina said. "There is far more to the reality of love and family than words written on a paper."

She huffed, but she seemed to relax. "Now you sound like your cousin. Gina seems to think that no woman needs marriage or some such nonsense. Not all of us can make the choices she has made."

"Gina is very dear to me," he said and leaned in for another long kiss.

"Another secret is that I slept with other people before my marriage," she told him.

"Many people do, damsel," he said, stroking her cheek.

"Sinclair was beastly about it." Beatrice shifted, folding her arms across her chest. "It's why I ran here. I was so furious with him for making such a fuss, when I am sure *he* was no saint before our marriage."

"Your experience is yours, and yours alone, no matter what anyone thinks of it. You deserve to have had pleasure in your life. We all do."

Georgina felt a flash of rage at the people who decried certain acts of human pleasure, and who passed judgment on when and how those acts were experienced. There was such hatred toward women who loved women, men who loved men. People like him who loved both, who *were* both. People who were neither, and people who loved neither. It escaped him how some had such narrow views on the vast and endless experience of humanity.

"I am glad you don't subscribe to such nonsensical ideas," Beatrice said, and the smile on her face was open and warm and all the more dazzling in its sincerity.

"I have many thoughts on manhood, and womanhood, and everything in between," he told her, his anger dissipating.

"Now you remind me of your cousin again. Enough serious talk, please. My turn," she said decisively, and leaned forward to kiss him.

Her lips were warm and insistent, her tongue pressing against the corner of his mouth and slipping inside, quick and delicate. It was a sweeter kiss than their first. He had thought tonight would be all fire and spice, an explosion of passion, an expression of physical urges that would be easy to handle. But this was different. He felt the danger of it tug at him. He wanted to nestle into its comfort and never emerge.

"Now you must tell *me* a secret," Beatrice said, her eyes bright. She leaned toward him but didn't bother to tug her bodice down again, and he knew that this wasn't just about sexual impulse anymore for her either.

Georgina paused. Somehow, he hadn't thought this through.

He had wanted to know if he could trust her, without thinking that he owed such honesty in return. He took a deep breath.

"I wish I still lived in Paris," he said.

"What could you do there that you can't here?" she asked.

He looked at her in reproof and she giggled, giving him a token kiss to continue the narrative.

"Paris is exciting. There is a thrill, an energy that comes just from walking its streets. The entertainments are scandalously legendary." He hesitated, then decided to be blunt. "I know you are aware of the Duke of Hawthorne's love affair with your friend Phin. I too have known love such as that. I have slept with men and women."

Bea tossed her curls. "It doesn't sound so very different from London. Not all of my lovers have been men. I enjoy both." She wrinkled her nose. "Though I did *not* enjoy Sinclair. He was all business in the bedchamber."

Georgina nudged her knee with his own. "You deserve to be cherished, always," he murmured, and was rewarded with another sweet, long kiss. "It's different in France, though. That manner of love isn't persecuted in the same way, which makes it safer for men like me."

"Did you meet the Duke of Hawthorne while you were there? He returned from France not long ago."

"Yes, I am friendly with His Grace," he said, noncommittal, but she saw through the ruse.

"Another kiss shall coax the truth from you," she said, and in one swift motion she was sitting astride his lap, her thighs on each side of his own.

Beatrice grasped his face, her palms pressing flat against his cheeks and her thumbs stroking his cheekbones, holding him still as she kissed him. His breath was uneven when they broke apart.

"I spent time with the duke at Hawthorne Towers during my engagement to my *dear* Sinclair," she said. "His Grace is so very regal, isn't he?" Her eyes danced.

Georgina stroked his hands along the outside of her thighs, ruffling the silk layers of her dress. He hadn't meant to talk about any of this tonight. Yet there was something so intimate about this moment that it compelled him to speak without varnishing his words with the half-truths that he usually told when describing a boy's childhood, instead of how he had been raised as a girl.

"My father works in the British embassy in France. My mother passed away when I was young, and I had been left behind in England for my education. But I didn't care much for school, and I ran away instead."

Beatrice's mouth fell open. "How old were you?"

"I was fourteen, and headstrong and foolish. I left a note and shimmied down the tree outside my bedroom window and was on the first ship I could purchase passage from." It had been his first time out of the house in breeches, his hair tucked up under a cap, shivering and sniveling when he arrived at the docks. "I thought my father would send me straight back to England, but he never did. He was too busy with foreign affairs to be bothered if I was there or not, truth be told."

He heard the touch of bitterness in his voice, but in the end, his father's focus on Napoleon had been a blessing. It had allowed him the precious freedom to escape the house at all hours wearing whatever he pleased without notice. He had encountered more than his fair share of dangers along the way, but it had been worth it to explore who he really was.

"That was terribly brave of you. Though this has nothing to do with the Duke of Hawthorne," she said, frowning. "I thought I was going to get a very different sort of story."

"I say, have a bit of patience." He tapped her nose playfully. "The duke arrived some years after I did. It was an open secret that he was a molly, and he held wild parties for anyone who cared to join. When I discovered that I shared those same desires, I took every opportunity to sneak out of my father's house. I spent countless nights carousing until dawn and casting up my accounts in His Grace's rather splendid outdoor fountain."

"You became friends?"

He sighed. "I fell in love, of course. He was older and experienced, and I was in awe of what he had created for us all. He was the first person that I told of my wants and my needs. Of *who* I am. Hawthorne accepted me from the very moment I walked into his house. But alas, he never looked at me with romance in his eyes."

"And then you fled back to England."

"Yes. I learned a lot while I was traveling, though." He smiled at her. "I learned the difference between running away because I was scared and running toward something that made me happy. When I returned to England, it was to create my own future instead of living in the shadow of the duke's life."

"That's all very romantic. I would love to hear more."

"Alas, the currency of your kisses has run out and you have already cheated enough by going out of turn."

"We never agreed to such a thing as equal turns!" she cried, and she grabbed a pillow and smacked him in the arm.

He laughed and tossed the pillow aside, catching her in his arms as she squealed.

"My question to you, Beatrice—what is it in London that you're really running from?"

The mood changed in an instant. She pouted her lips in reply, but her eyes were dark, all trace of laughter gone. He met her lips fiercely, passion flooding his senses. He wanted to forget all about Hawthorne, and to banish all thought of Sinclair from her mind with his touch. She burned for *him*. Fiery satisfaction rushed through his body. He moved his hands behind her back, molding her to him, and one of her legs moved up over his lap.

Beatrice undulated against him and he groaned, slipping his hands up her petticoats and connecting with her bare thighs. Her skin was so smooth, so soft, and he wanted to touch her everywhere and in between. He was lost in a jasmine-scented fog of desire, and he gripped her legs for dear life as her lips continued their onslaught over his, her hips grinding against his own.

Beatrice eased off and he caught a glimpse of sadness in her eyes before she curled against him, her head tucked up under his chin. He pressed his nose gently into her brown ringlets and kissed the crown of her head, pulling her skirts down her thighs and cradling her against him.

"I don't think I know what I'm running toward. I don't know where I belong," Beatrice said, her voice quiet against his shirt.

"You found yourself and what you wanted in Paris with Hawthorne, and then in London. Gina created something wonderful with her bluestocking friends. Jacquie is seeking to do the same here in Rosedale. I don't have anything like that."

Georgina stroked her back. "Is it something you want?"

She shifted. "It wasn't. But now, hearing Gina talk so much about community, and duty…I've been thinking about it." She paused. "My mother always accused me of grasping whatever I wanted in life, before anyone could offer it. I saw it as getting what I needed before anyone could deprive me. I took lovers, entertainments, flirtations. I snatched up the prettiest gowns I could afford, and the wittiest gentlemen to dance with."

"Many people in Society behave in exactly the same way."

"Yes, but in all those Seasons, I only made two friends. Jacquie and Phin. Now both of them have fallen in love, and I'm alone. I married, but without love. I suppose I didn't think how lonely it could be."

With alarm, he felt his shirt growing damp. He dropped another kiss on her head. "I wish I had all the answers about love and loss and happiness. But I do know one thing."

She looked up at him with watery eyes, then pressed one sweet kiss against his lips to earn the answer.

"You have made a third friend in me," Georgina promised her. "But I hope that is no secret." The smile that spread across her face warmed his heart.

Oh, his foolish heart. He was sinking fast. This was getting too serious. Thinking fast, he said, "You know, speaking of confessionals—I am actually going to call on the vicar tomorrow."

She let out a peal of laughter.

"Do you want to come with me?"

Her mouth snapped shut. "You're better off taking your cousin. Or Lady Honora. People with some claim to virtue."

"I am asking you," he said firmly. "This is how you make friends, Beatrice. This is how you join in. This is how you find out where you might want to belong."

She hesitated, and he took the opportunity to kiss her.

"Yes," she breathed, staring into his eyes. "Yes, I will go with you."

CHAPTER ELEVEN

Only the worst sort of lust would compel *me* to agree to see a vicar outside of Sunday," Beatrice muttered as she fluffed her curls and tried to dodge the wavering corner of her reflection in the mirror. "Reina, do remind me if we packed anything at all appropriate for such a visit?"

"It depends on what you seek to do in the presence of said vicar, my lady." She riffled through the dresses in the wardrobe. "If you were a single lady and you wished to entice the vicar, you would have a great many options."

"That's what I suspected." She propped her elbows on the table, scattering her tins of salves and soaps. "I've made a cake of myself by promising to accompany George today."

Her face flushed scarlet and she turned from the mirror. What had come over her last night? When he had suggested his game, she had planned on lying her way through. Instead, honesty had poured forth. She was still struggling to understand how it happened. She had never talked of such things before. Not with Phin, not even with Jacquie. How had it all spilled from her lips with George?

"Mr. Smith is a fine man. Would you know anything about his gentleman's gentleman, my lady?" Reina's voice held an air of studied disinterest as she took out a day dress and considered it.

"His valet? Legrand? I know nothing at all except that George thinks highly of him," she said.

"He's so gallant. Why, he holds the door for me at every turn— even when I'm coming from a long ways off. He remembers how I like my tea when we break our fast together at dawn. We laugh ever so much in the morning as we're getting things ready for the day." Her voice turned wistful. "None of the men in our household in London are like him."

Reina had been her maid for years, and she had never heard her speak like this about anyone. "If he's a nice man, and he respects you, then I am happy for you," she said. "I hope he returns your feelings."

With a rush of unfettered joy, she realized that as the Countess of Sinclair, she was wealthy enough to dower Reina if she so chose. She could settle enough money on her to ensure her comfort no matter what happened with Legrand. Reina would never need to be dependent on a man for her livelihood.

It occurred to her that what she had said to George last night hadn't been quite true. After all, Reina had also proven over and over to have been her friend, hadn't she? It was only their situation in life that had prevented her from seeing it. How snobbish of her, Beatrice thought with surprise. How many times had they laughed together after a ball, and chatted during long strolls through Hyde Park? How often had she urged Reina to take tea with her in secret, when the household had enough money in its coffers to provide luxury for the family but bare comforts for the staff? How many times had Reina comforted her over her love affairs?

Her heart was light as she selected a cornflower blue dress and debated with Reina for a quarter hour over which shoes best matched it, interspersed with teasing comments about their prospective beaux.

Bea found George outside, prowling around the edge of the garden. Her embarrassment over last night faded as his dear freckled face beamed at her. His pompadour was as disheveled as ever, raising a good three inches off his brow in a windswept tousle, and his impeccably white cravat gleamed in the sunlight. She had become so used to seeing him at night that it felt odd to see him in daylight.

"This is your last chance to take someone else with you," she warned him. "I will not take offense."

He took her hand and pressed it into the crook of his elbow. "There is no one else I would rather go with, Beatrice."

Pleased by his words, she tried to think of something droll to say, but her heart was too full. Or maybe it was the heat, she thought as they made their way down the cobblestone drive and onto the now-familiar path toward town. Or maybe, just maybe, not every moment of earnest honesty needed to scare her into giving it an insincere coating of sarcasm or laughter. The introspection didn't make her as uneasy as it usually did.

The vicar was in his front garden, busying himself with a trowel in front of a hydrangea bush. He was younger than Beatrice expected, with round cheeks and a snub nose and fair hair that flopped across his forehead.

George strode up the path. "Hello," he greeted him. "Pardon me, but are you Mr. Powell?"

He tossed the trowel to the side and stood. "That I am," he said. "And who may be asking for him?"

"I'm Mr. Smith, but I beg of you to please call me George. This is Lady Sinclair."

"This is a pleasure. Allow me to tidy up and offer you some refreshment." He frowned down at his hands and went to busy himself at the pump outside his yard before they followed him into the vicarage.

"Welcome to my humble abode. Do make yourself at home." He bustled about the kitchen and returned with lemonade and currant biscuits.

Beatrice accepted a glass and glanced around the room, with its old wooden chairs and whitewashed walls and a chimney with enough soot around the edge to indicate that it smoked in winter. She remembered such chimneys from her youth. The memory didn't bother her today, not in the face of Mr. Powell's obvious pleasure in his home.

Mr. Powell beamed. "The Banfields have been good enough to have given me the odd furnishing over the years. I also have a rather nice harpsichord, if I do say so myself. Brought it all the way from London when I was lucky enough to receive the living here in Rosedale."

"Is this a musical neighborhood, then?" Beatrice asked.

"It's more of a literary neighborhood, if truth be told," he said.

"I was told the same," George said. "I was sampling the local wares at the tavern and Sally told me that you've been reading Shelley."

He drew himself up. "I hope you are not such a one that considers reading poetry a less than godly affair," he said. "I'll have none of that under this roof."

"Of course not. In fact, we were hoping that there would be some local interest in a ladies group that they are organizing up at Rosedale Manor. If you already have a regular literary soiree here, then they will focus their planning on other events."

It was kind of George to be so supportive of Gina's salon, Beatrice thought. She had never met a man so passionate about women's causes before, and it made her enjoy his company even more.

"Ah, I see," Mr. Powell said. "Yes, we have quite a lively gathering here every third Friday evening. It's not only for the ladies, however. And perhaps not as devoted to poetry as some might like it to be. Some cards—no gambling, of course. A very little music from time to time, nothing boisterous. Mrs. Talbot, the butcher's wife, brings a delightful cake, and I make a punch that they say goes rather well with the evening."

Beatrice took a currant biscuit. A party once a month was better than nothing, even if one did have to read some poetry to gain entry. "That sounds like very fine entertainment indeed."

"I had to work hard to get people interested at first," he admitted.

George settled into a wooden chair and crossed his booted legs at the ankle. "Did you? My cousin Gina is having the same problem here. Do you have any suggestions for her?"

He frowned. "I don't know if this village needs another assembly. We do fine here on our Fridays."

"Be that as it may, I would think people would look forward to more opportunities for socialization and education."

"Maybe they will, but maybe they won't. Many parishioners have left in the past year, looking for factory work elsewhere. It's a sad sight to see their empty cottages. There are many here that rely on the parish for charity. More than we can comfortably manage, at times."

"It's sad indeed. Rosedale is such a nice village." She was surprised to find that she meant it. "You mentioned you're from London?"

"I lived there for a time, but as a fourth son I had to end up somewhere," Mr. Powell confided. "My eldest brother got the title, of course. My second brother ought to have gone into the church but chose the army, God rest him. I've a third brother, but he has a profession of all things—smart man, he teaches at Oxford. Nothing to be done for it, someone in the family had to choose the church or my mother would have had conniptions."

"London life has a lot to offer," George mused. "I would find it hard to give up. So many opportunities for friendship…and companionship." His gaze lingered on the vicar.

The expression on Mr. Powell's face didn't change, but the air filled with tension. "Mr. Smith, I wonder if you might be interested in exploring my back garden? You seem like a discerning man, and I have a lovely patch of lavender that you may care to cast your eye over."

He grinned. "I would indeed."

Beatrice pursed her lips as they headed out the door. They had just arrived, and yet she had been left to her own devices with naught but a half empty plate of biscuits for company. It had been nice to have a change of scenery, but she would have been better off staying at Rosedale for the day.

She scowled into her lemonade. Why would George be interested in the vicar's lavender, anyway? He didn't seem to have any particular affinity for horticulture. But if it had been a matter of general interest, wouldn't they have invited her as well, instead of disappearing together?

Before she could decide on whether or not she should look out the back window in case the lavender somehow was a sight that should not be missed, the door opened. Mr. Powell had a hand on George's shoulder, and they were laughing as they reentered the house.

The vicar looked more relaxed than he had when they first arrived, and he insisted that they stay for a luncheon of bread and cheese and bright red apples from his neighbor's orchard. Beatrice found herself laughing more with both men than she had in the past two weeks she had spent at Rosedale, enjoying the vicar's cheerful stories of his Oxford schooling and his time in London as a young man with no profession and plenty of idle time to spend as he pleased.

George didn't chime in with any tales of his own time at school, which she found odd until she remembered that somehow he had ended up in Paris and had never attended much formal schooling. She made a note to ask him about it, as it seemed so unusual for a young man.

Mr. Powell was such a darling, she thought as he poured her a small glass of wine. George had been right to push her out to meet him. She watched him hover over George, brewing him a cup of coffee and leaning in close to pour it into his proffered mug.

She had a startling flash of realization. Mr. Powell was of the same persuasion as they were. That was why George had wanted to visit. That must be why they had talked outside in the garden.

On their way back to the village, Beatrice asked George why they hadn't included her in the conversation.

"Everyone deserves to reveal their truth to the people of their choosing, without it being forced on them," he said, lacing his fingers with hers.

"Like we have," she said softly, leaning against his arm.

He dropped a kiss on her shoulder. "Yes. Exactly like we have, damsel."

❖

The days and nights at Rosedale started to fall into a pleasant pattern. Beatrice went for walks with Jacqueline in the mornings and took afternoon tea with her and Lady Honora. She looked forward to unfashionably early dinners and debating with Gina over soup and salad, surprised that she was easing into a comfortable sort of friendship with both Gina and Lady Honora. She would never have guessed such a thing possible in London.

Time lost its meaning in the haze of the hottest days of summer. They had no ice cellar to cool themselves down, but they took to sitting outside in the dusk with their fans, watching the sun set.

After the moon rose and the stars started to twinkle, time took on still another dimension. Beatrice and George found each other in the library, exchanging kisses and stories and secrets and laughter. The parameter that they had set out on that first night was strictly respected. In this room, truth prevailed, and Beatrice felt emboldened by the fact that none of this would follow her back to London. She felt free to be herself, and she knew she would cherish this time for the rest of her life.

After all, this was a holiday. Like Yuletide in summer. Or a special birthday treat. Soon enough she would return to London and continue her life like this interlude had never happened. She would resume conjugal relations with her husband, though she suspected she would need the memory of George's hands on her hips and his lips on her throat to help her.

But she needn't worry about that now. It was peaceful here. She let that settle over her as she marched with her widest bonnet and biggest fan to sit in the heat of the afternoon in the rose gardens. Peacefulness was not a familiar experience, nor one that she had bothered to seek before. She was surprised by how much she liked it.

An uncomfortable feeling settled in her chest and she rubbed at it, hoping the ache would cease. There would be no peace for her at Sinclair's estate. Being a countess in residence was a lot of work. Work that Beatrice had never wanted. She had wed the earl to save her family, and that was accomplished.

She had agreed to Sinclair's bargain to bear an heir and then flee to one of his estates, but she hadn't yet let herself think about what that life would look like. The very idea of it outraged her. She had a hazy escape plan in mind that entailed gathering up all the jewels she could find and fleeing England, rather than being beholden to him for the rest of her life. The last thing she wanted was to exist as some poor dependent relative, under the humiliating scandal of being known as the banished bride.

Beatrice had had enough of relying on relatives. They had provided a meagre subsistence when her family had needed it the most. That family then turned on her and used her for their gain, happy to wed her to the first wealthy man who would have her.

The sooner she left England, the better. It would be her one secret that she could never divulge to anyone, not even to George. If she told anyone, there would be the risk that Sinclair would find out. And he would come for her.

She probably would never see George again. Nor Jacquie, or Phin. She would even miss Gina if she never had the chance to see her again. But if her time here proved anything, it was that she could start again if she needed to. She wondered what it would be like to stay here at Rosedale, but it was hopeless. Jacqueline and Lady Honora deserved to create a life for themselves here without an unwanted interloper overstaying her welcome, or the threat of Sinclair's vengeance.

All she wanted was a life of pleasure, to let the days drift away in lazy splendor, but the idea of it made her uneasy now. George had told her happiness would be found by running toward something, but she didn't really understand. What could be more peaceful than escape?

Her eyes fluttered open and she got to her feet. The rose arbor was charming, but it had offered no respite at all. Perhaps she could dip her feet in the lake that Jacqueline had mentioned was nearby.

There was a small wooded area at the edge of the estate that she could see from her bedchamber window, and a narrow path had been cut into it that led to the small lake. She was charmed by the vista before her—a group of toadstools and a mossy log, the sun dappling through the poplar leaves, the aroma of leaves and bark and loam.

When she left the shelter of the woods, she saw that the lake already had a guest in its waters.

Gina stood before her, the water above her ankles and her white skirts bunched in one hand, enough leg visible for Beatrice to notice that her freckles didn't only cover her face. Bea felt a familiar heat that had nothing to do with the sun as she looked at those legs, and with an unwelcome start realized that it could only be one thing.

Desire.

CHAPTER TWELVE

Beatrice stepped forward. "Gina," she called out. "Are you play-acting as the Lady of the Lake? Searching for Excalibur?"

Gina turned at the sound of her voice. "I am no enchantress," she said, amusement in her voice. "I identify more with the Knights of the Round Table."

Beatrice rolled her eyes out of habit, but then she smiled. After all, it was an apt enough description for her. "Yes, of course. Defender of women's causes, champion to the masses. Do you consider the salon to be your quest?"

She shrugged. "You know I consider it to be important and necessary work, and my work is my life. I cannot imagine anything more important."

Beatrice slid her fan into her reticule and peeled off her gloves, finger by finger, before shoving them in the bag. "Lady Gina, patron saint of ladies everywhere."

Gina sighed. "I am no saint. I'm still not sure if I'm doing enough here to merit staying in Rosedale, especially if the vicar already has a standing literary engagement every month." She paused. "George told me about your visit to Mr. Powell. Thank you for helping. I appreciate it."

She shrugged. "Any opportunity to be with George is time well spent. He is the most charming gentleman of my acquaintance, and he has been most kind to me."

Gina swayed in the lake with the current, lithe and elegant, her eyes closed and her face tipped back to catch the sun.

"You'll freckle more if you don't take care."

"I like my freckles," she said peaceably.

Beatrice leaned one hand against a tree to steady herself and toed off one walking shoe, then the other. She reached up her skirts and tugged down her stockings, folding them and placing them in the reticule.

"What are you doing?" Gina asked.

"Why would one go to a lake in summer if not to splash around?" She tested the water with a toe, humming in approval before taking a careful step into the lake. "It's a small lake, Gina, but I think it's big enough for two."

The cool water was delicious against her warm skin. Oh, this was *heaven*. She hiked her skirts up higher, then walked past Gina until she was in up to her knees.

"It gets deep," Gina warned her. "It's safer here by the edge."

She laughed. "Whatever about me makes you think I am concerned with *safe*? Do tell me, so I may change it straightaway."

"I suppose if you were interested in safe, you would still be in London."

"You have no idea why I left London," she said, her back ramrod straight. No one did.

"You could tell me," she offered.

Beatrice hesitated. She hadn't even told the entire truth to George. But here in the sunlight, under the wide-open skies in the middle of the lake, with the least judgmental person she knew—in its own way, it felt as private and sacred as her nights in the library.

There was something about these Smith cousins that made it easy for her to confide in them. Maybe it was the steadiness in their blue eyes, or the earnestness that shone through on their faces, or their quiet acceptance of their fellow man around them.

Whatever it was, she felt drawn to them both.

"Sinclair wasn't happy that I was not a virgin on our wedding night," she said. That much she had told everyone. She took a deep breath. "He refused to lay with me until I had my monthly courses again, so he could be assured that the earldom wasn't tainted by my supposed harlotry. I don't even know how he thinks I achieved such a thing, Gina. I spent the entire month of our engagement in his own cousin's house, a guest of the Duchess of Hawthorne. I was so angry that I decided to leave London instead of waiting around for the next month, just to prove to him that I had been honest."

"He said that to you?" Gina dropped the skirts that she had been holding up and had to scramble to rescue her dress from the water.

"Yes." She thought back to the morning after their wedding. He had been so autocratic, so cold. So insistent on getting her with his own child as soon as possible, so dismissive of her aside from her usefulness to him as a brood mare. She clenched her jaw. "I don't want him to think I am going to be a wife that he can ride roughshod over."

To her surprise, Gina was beaming at her. "It's marvelous that you stood up to him like that. You are *amazing*, Beatrice."

"It is?" Over the weeks, she had started to wonder if it had been foolhardy, but now she began to feel a sense a pride. "I am?"

"Of course! This is *your body*. What you do with it is your choice, and yours alone."

Beatrice pondered this. She counted back the weeks since she had lain with Sinclair. Two more days to go until she expected her courses. She had intended on returning to London at that time, loath as she was to go back to Sinclair.

But she did have her own power, didn't she? Maybe she could just…stay. At least for now.

If she didn't lay with Sinclair again, if she could delay getting pregnant, then she would also delay the choice of either living on his charity in God only knew where, or leaving the country. She could buy herself more time.

"He might be your husband, but you are not property. He doesn't own you."

"Except in the eyes of the law," she said, frowning.

"You know, these are things we discuss and protest in my Tuesday salon. You are welcome to join us, anytime. There are many of us who feel the same way. Women should not be beholden to men, nor seen as less than equal."

"Maybe I should," she said slowly. "Do you really think I was brave? I thought—well, I thought that your general opinion of me is that I am rather unintelligent," she said, splashing her hand in the water.

"I have never thought that," Gina said quietly. The sun on her freckled face was glorious, and it turned her hair into a golden red halo. "Owning your power as your own person is always brave. I admire you for it, Beatrice."

Bea felt herself grow warm, and it wasn't just from the sun. She considered replying, and instead scooped a handful of water onto her face, letting it trickle down her neck, rivulets sliding between her breasts.

"I say, you'll get your dress wet."

"Water won't hurt it." She poured another handful over her forehead.

Suddenly, it wasn't quite enough to be wading to the knees. She made her way back to the bank, trying to avoid the rocks embedded in the bottom of the lake.

"There, I knew you would see reason."

Was that a hint of relief in Gina's voice? Or was it a challenge?

Beatrice paused where she had dropped her reticule. Without another thought, she tugged the ribbon at her waist free and dropped it beside her. With a few quick pulls and tugs, her day dress was discarded, her stays loosened, and there she stood.

In her shift.

Which was almost transparent, especially in the bright sunlight.

Own your power. This is your body. You can choose what to do with it. And if she chose to cavort in a lake on a hot summer day, what was the harm?

Beatrice strode into the lake up to her waist before flipping forward into a shallow dive. A few strokes later, she resurfaced, reveling in the feeling of the cold water sluicing off her face and shoulders.

"Where did you learn to swim?" Gina asked.

"Jacquie and I went on holiday to Brighton with my cousins one summer, and we all went sea bathing." Memories crowded her thoughts of Jacqueline shrieking with joy in the waves, and then shrieking in altogether another sort of way later that night in their shared bedchamber at the elegant little hotel. She missed the easy physicality of loving another woman.

"That sounds lovely." Was that a hint of yearning in her voice?

"Can you not swim?" she asked.

She shook her head. "This is as close to sea bathing as I've ever been."

Bea smiled. "Would you like a lesson, so you may be Lady of the Lake in truth?"

Gina beamed at her. "I would."

She touched bottom and went toward her in the shallower water, conscious that her thin wet shift hid nothing. Gina's eyes flicked down to her chest. "You will be more comfortable if you remove your gown, then."

Gina hastened out of the lake. She reached up and took off her bonnet, then fixed her hair to pile it high on top of her head. She fumbled behind her with the fastenings of her dress and let it fall to the ground.

The slight curve of her bosom and her hips and her sinewy thighs were noticeable under her thin shift. The comparison to Arthurian tales wasn't so far off the mark. She had said she was no enchantress, but Beatrice begged to differ. This heat of her arousal felt like witchcraft indeed.

Gina marched into the water toward Beatrice.

"Even your shift is decorated," she said in surprise as Gina moved closer. It was extravagant to carry her love of embellishment onto her underclothing. A woodland scene with fanciful trees was stitched into the fabric.

"It's Buratto needle lace," Georgina said. "Possibly my very favorite example of lacemaking."

Beatrice looked closer.

"Admiring the hedgehogs?" Gina asked.

On the left of the bodice, right over her heart, were two hedgehogs in a compromising position. "Are they *mating*?" she asked.

"In flagrante delicto, I'm afraid," Gina said, humor dancing in her eyes. There was a dimple in her left cheek that appeared when she was trying not to laugh, Beatrice noticed. She wrested her eyes back to her shift and saw there were a series of thread animals intertwined with each other among detailed ferns and oak leaves and ivy.

But studying the fabric also meant looking at the body beneath it. Gina's nipples were puckered on the slope of her small breasts, and she could see their rosy color through the delicate linen weave. Bea swallowed and moved her eyes elsewhere, but everything about Gina's body was beautiful. The elegance of her long neck, the enticing dip between her collarbone and the strong sinews of her shoulder, the play of her defined arm muscles as she plucked the shift away from her body to look at it.

"The fabric was a gift from a naturalist who visits my salon now and again," Gina said. "I couldn't think of another use for it, so I had it made into undergarments."

Those arms looked strong and firm. Like they were made to hold on tight to another woman as she brought her to ecstasy.

She had never thought of any bookish bluestocking like this before.

Beatrice hesitated. There was something about her tone when she talked about the naturalist. "Was she a lover?" she asked.

She skimmed her hand over the water, drawing a little circle with her finger. "For a time, yes. She travels a lot."

For some reason, Beatrice wanted to know all about the affair. About all of the women Gina had slept with. All of the ones she had kissed. Every last detail of every last intimacy.

She cleared her throat. "Swimming," she said. "Let's swim."

"What's the first step?"

Beatrice took a deep breath. "I don't know," she admitted. "When I went to Brighton, I just got in the water and moved my limbs and it seemed to just kind of happen. Have you tried that approach?"

Gina stared at her. "I need more information. What do I *do*?"

"Sometimes you have to just follow your instinct."

Gina blew out a breath. "I'm rather more fond of planning than leaping into something, Beatrice."

"You need to focus on the present moment instead of worrying about the next one. Try it?"

She stared at the water with a ferocious scowl, then fell forward and thrashed her limbs. Her head dipped below water and she stood up, spluttering and reaching for her hair. "I don't like this," she announced, firmly adjusting the bun on top of her head.

"A lungful of lake water isn't the best way to enjoy the activity."

Beatrice thought for a moment. "Maybe I could hold you while you move your arms and legs, so you can practice how to move?"

Gina smiled at her, and it was unlike any of the smiles she had ever given to Beatrice before. Most of them had been polite. Or patient. But this one was full of charm and warmth, and Beatrice felt the impact of it sneak up on her and pull her down like an undertow in the ocean.

"Yes, you should definitely hold me," Gina said, nodding.

Beatrice put her hands on Gina's narrow waist. The only barrier between them was damp lace filled with fornicating animals. She was close enough to notice the bergamot scent of her perfume, which lingered on her skin despite the lake water. Gina must purchase it from the same perfumier as George, she thought.

Beatrice cleared her throat. "Lean forward." She moved her forearm low against Gina's lean belly as she twisted. "Now move your arms—no, not like that. One at a time. Now your legs."

She thrashed again, but it didn't look right at all.

"You're thinking too hard, Gina. Focus on the moment. Stop thinking so hard about what comes next. Imagine each movement while it's happening and let the next one come naturally. You can do this."

Gina undulated against her arm and then suddenly her limbs were moving in fluid motion. She righted herself. "I did it!" she crowed.

Beatrice laughed, but the delight on Gina's face was infectious. "You did something," she said. "You'd have to do it on your own to say you did it."

With a loud splash, Gina managed to keep her head above water and swim a few strokes before she bounced back up. "There! I say, I did do it!"

Beatrice laughed. Her delight was so earnest, so sincere. Had she ever learned anything new with such enthusiasm? As she looked at Gina's shining face, she realized that she was learning an awful lot from Gina during this stay at Rosedale Manor.

It was strange, she thought as she trudged back to the house, her shift dripping lake water onto her shoes. She had found peace today after all, but not at all in the way that she had expected.

CHAPTER THIRTEEN

Nora clipped the rose bushes with precision under the hot afternoon sun, angling her shears to remove any blooms that were past their prime and trimming back errant leaves and twigs. The workman's gloves were too big on her hands, but she continued her task with care.

Georgina held out a basket for the cuttings. "Have you had to let go of the gardeners?" she asked. She had thought they were coming to the garden to pick bunches of roses for the dining room table and the drawing room vases and had been surprised when Nora had steered her first into the gardener's shed to pick up tools.

"Yesterday," she said, making another cut. She wiggled her glove down and wiped at the sweat on her brow with her wrist. "Once we had half a dozen men to take care of these gardens. My mother loved them, you know. Roses were her passion, and she cultivated so many varieties."

Georgina dislodged a bumblebee as she buried her nose into a striped cream and pink rose with plenty of petals. "They have a lovely aroma."

"That's one of my favorites. A newer variety from France. The Cottage Maid." She dipped her face into one with a shy smile. "I thought for a time I was destined to be nothing more than a cottage maid, all alone here in the manor. Until I met Jacqueline."

"You have looked so happy here over the past month."

Nora clipped another rose. "I'm grateful that I met you, and Jacquie, and that you both taught me what happiness could look like. I couldn't have imagined it otherwise."

Georgina sighed. "I do love a happy ending."

"My main concern is about money," she confessed.

"Does the manor not provide enough income?"

"For the last few years, I was able to manage with the rents. But many cottages are empty now. Wiltshire is flush with sheep, and we always had families weaving fabric with the wool and selling it at market. But the demand seems to have dried up, and the costs couldn't remain competitive, and people have moved away."

Georgina nodded. Mr. Powell had said much the same to them.

"I wish I could think of a way to help the people here. I worry about them." Nora sighed. "Thank you again for spending so much time here in Rosedale. It means the world to me that you are willing to help us build something here."

Georgina thought of the men at the tavern who had yawned through her conversations recently, and the tepid smiles on the women in the bakery where she had picked up bread yesterday. "It's my pleasure," she murmured, but she was afraid that she was still making little headway.

"It may be selfish, but I also worry about me. The best thing for me to do might be to sell the manor. I know the estate isn't as well-managed as it once was, but it should fetch more than what I need to live somewhere smaller." Her voice trembled. "I don't want to move. This is my last link to my parents. But if needs must, then I will do what's necessary to provide for myself and Jacqueline."

Georgina dropped the basket and hugged her. "Whatever happens, you have friends that will support you. Always."

She sighed and clung to her. "I almost hate to admit it, but I've been deeply grateful to Lady Sinclair for helping out with the household. It has been nice to have fine things on the table again. She thrust yards of fabric at the housekeeper yesterday and told her that she had bought too much, and did she think Rosedale could use new curtains or if the maids would like new frocks? She isn't who I thought she was."

They moved over to the rose arbor, where Nora examined the tall arch and gave a brisk nod before heading to a cluster of bushes sporting yellow roses.

"I have grown very fond of her," Georgina admitted. She hadn't told either Nora or Jacquie about her evenings with Beatrice. Those moments were for them alone, time that existed in its own separate universe. She had thought she had it under control, limiting their wild flirtation to the safety of nighttime, but their romp in the lake had blurred the lines. She couldn't deny any longer that she wanted Beatrice, and not just in bed.

"I'm told that the staff loves her. A basket of sweets and oranges made its way to the butler last week to distribute as he saw fit, and it met with great acclaim."

"She has a kind heart. She just doesn't like to show it," Georgina said.

Nora gave her a sidelong look. "You sound perhaps more than just fond of Lady Sinclair."

"Beatrice would be a complicated woman to love," she said.

What she didn't add was that her complexity made Georgina want to delve even deeper, burrowing her way beneath all of her layers, and finally lay siege to her heart. This was the secret that she had been unable to say in words during their evenings together, but which had been expressed through every touch and every kiss and every look.

"Does it matter to you that she's married?"

"Theirs is no love match," she said.

"Jacquie says she's loyal," Nora said. "If you earned her love, she wouldn't be the type to let it go."

"Maybe not. But I don't want some clandestine affair forever, secreting away our nights together while she lives during the day as another man's wife."

Georgina heard the wistful tone in her own voice with surprise. She didn't have time in London for a lover, whether it was during the day *or* the night. She was always too busy working. Hadn't Beatrice told her in the lake that she should learn to focus on the moment before her? Why shouldn't she grasp what she wanted for now, and worry about the future later?

"Maybe I want a clandestine affair for the summer, though," Georgina said.

Nora clipped another rose. "If you're developing real feelings for her, then you should explore them and see where it goes. You'll never know what could happen if you do nothing."

Georgina paused. "I haven't told her yet that I'm George. I

know I don't owe the truth of myself to anyone." She had learned that a long time ago in Paris. "But I want to tell her. I feel like I've been getting so close to her over these weeks, and I want her to know *all* of me. I know that I can trust her—I would never consider telling her if I didn't."

Georgina was worried she would lose her head entirely if she went any further with Beatrice. Kissing and talking during the long summer nights had deepened their relationship further than she had ever intended. Her feelings for Beatrice grew stronger by the day. How could she survive the loss if Beatrice decided, like Hawthorne, that Georgina was a fine enough companion to pass the time with— but wasn't enough to love?

But Nora was right about one thing. If she didn't try, she would never know.

❖

Georgina was unable to resist the siren song luring her to the library, tantalizing her with thoughts of Beatrice. She had tied her cravat with reluctance tonight, mussing her pompadour with pomade and wishing that she could greet Beatrice in the library in her dress.

Maybe after tonight, she would.

They had already revealed so much to each other in this room. The timing felt right. Neither of them might be at Rosedale for much longer, after all, and she couldn't bear it if she never took the opportunity to be with her. Even if it was only a temporary love affair.

She didn't want to be in love. Beatrice was another man's wife, and a prickly, self-centered new aristocrat with more fashion than sense. Except she had learned over the past few weeks that this wasn't really true. Beneath the glittering facade, the arch humor and all of her affectations, she was a passionate, interested, intelligent woman.

When the clock chimed midnight, Georgina stifled her disappointment and snuffed out the candles. Beatrice wasn't coming tonight, and she would have to plan this all over again for tomorrow night. Sighing, she opened the door and collided with a warm laughing bundle of woman.

"George!" Beatrice gasped, steadying herself in her arms. "This is the sort of welcome that makes me wish I had tried to maneuver it earlier."

Her heart lightened and she smiled down at her. "Were you out here this whole time while I waited just beyond the door, my heart beating out of rhythm for missing you?"

She lost herself in a deep slow kiss that rattled her to the bone. This didn't feel like seduction. It felt like trust. Hope.

Beatrice smiled at her as she leaned back, and it flooded her with such uncertainty that she kissed her again, wildly.

When they broke apart, Beatrice's light laugh tinkled through the library. "That felt like something major is on your mind, Mr. Smith," she said playfully. "Do tell me all about it."

This was the moment, then. There would be no turning back. Georgina's heart knocked against her ribs. Was she ready to trust Beatrice and tell her everything?

CHAPTER FOURTEEN

G eorgina lit a trio of candles on the desk, and then decided to light a wall sconce as well. "That's better," she said with false heartiness. But her heart was in her boots.

Beatrice must have seen something concerning because her face turned serious and she pulled her toward the sofa, tugging her down to sit beside her. "What is it, George?"

"Beatrice, I have something to tell you." Georgina took her hand and looked deep in her eyes. "I am telling you this because I care about you. Deeply. And I want you to know who I am."

"Are you some disenfranchised duke?" she asked, a puzzled look on her face.

That startled a laugh from her. "No. That would be a good deal easier." She hesitated again. "It's complicated. But I want you to know that this is me, Beatrice. I'm Mr. George Smith, through and through. But at the same time—I am Lady Gina."

"Gina?" Her confusion was clear as she studied her face. There was a long pause. "*Gina*? Does George know you have been wearing his wardrobe all summer?"

"Beatrice, listen to me. It's me. I'm still George. I am both a man, and a woman."

Beatrice blinked. "*George?*"

Then she was all action, leaping to her feet and grabbing Georgina's hand, which she knew was clammy despite the summer heat. Together, they sped out of the library and into the night air, down the garden path through the rose trellis and away from the house. Georgina allowed herself to be led, unsure of what to say or why they were in a rush.

At the edge of the gardens, Beatrice turned, shadowed by the night sky. "I thought you might need more privacy, far away from the manor," she explained, grasping both her hands in her own and holding them to her chest. "What if Jacquie and Lady Honora were there to overhear? Or the servants? Oh, Gina. *George*. I couldn't bear to see you thrown out of the house in the middle of the night!"

Although she was touched to the core by her thoughtfulness, her words also raised a pit the size of an apricot in her throat. She withdrew her hands from her grip. "It's safe, Beatrice. No one is going to throw me out. They know about me."

Beatrice paused. "Oh," she said. "Both of them? It's only me who didn't know?"

"Not many people know that I live both sides of my life. I am careful about who I trust to tell, and when I choose to do it," she said, gently but firmly. "This is my body. My choice. Myself."

Understanding flashed across her face as Georgina repeated those words that she had used in the lake about Beatrice's body and her power over her sexual congress.

"I know people who have misunderstood me in the past, so I want to be clear in case you are wondering. I don't *dress* like a man. I am a man. I am a woman. I am both."

Beatrice was quiet. The moon was a crescent in the sky, and it was dark in the gardens. Her eyes were hidden beneath her eyelashes. Then she placed her hand on Georgina's shoulder and pulled her into a tight embrace, burying her head into her neck. After a long moment, she looked up to meet her eyes. "Thank you so much for trusting me," she said. "What a beautiful thing to share."

The adrenaline left her body and she felt limp with relief. It was always difficult to trust someone with her truth. This was the first time she was telling a potential lover. She pressed her lips to her forehead, too emotional for speech.

"I am surprised," Beatrice admitted. "I had no idea, Gina! George? Yet…is it so surprising that the bluestocking who crusades on behalf of women is also the man who saves any damsel in distress that he comes across? Oh, I have so many questions." She looked at Georgina expectantly and laughed a little. "And so many kisses to give you in exchange for those details. But, more importantly—how do *you* feel?" she asked, holding her tighter.

"Happy," Georgina said and smiled. "I think I would even say that this is one of the best nights I've ever had."

"Me too," she said quietly.

They held each other for a long time, listening to the leaves rustling and the nightingale's song in the woods, before returning to the house.

❖

Beatrice skipped breakfast the next morning.

She paused for a moment after she pushed open the front door and saw the dark clouds overhead. She should be glad that it was threatening to rain after so many weeks of heat, but it was gloomy weather. Unwilling to go far lest she ruin her new satin shoes if it started to rain, she contented herself with a stroll around the front garden. The air was thick with humidity, even hotter than it had been last night.

Oh, *last night.*

When she thought about it, it all made so much sense. Not just the resemblance. Nor even the fact that she hadn't noticed that Gina and George were never in the same room together. No, it made sense on a deeper level. Why *shouldn't* Gina take what she could of the world and live her life to the very fullest?

She returned to the house and found Jacquie walking up the front stairs.

"Jacquie darling, where have you been?"

"Over to the neighbor's for a slice of lemon cake and to catch up on all of the Rosedale news," she said. "You might not think it, but there's as much gossip and rumormongering in a village as there is in London! They have been nothing but kind to me since my arrival here. I think I might truly belong to the neighborhood now."

Beatrice grasped her hand. "Don't you wish sometimes to go back to the way things were?" she asked.

Jacquie laughed and extricated herself before taking the last stair and entering the manor. "Bea! Whatever has brought this on? You know that I was in perfect accord to leave London for Wiltshire.

I have no regrets, if that's what you're asking." Her tone held a mild rebuke.

"Some mornings I wake up here and I hardly recognize myself anymore. I'm not sure if I like it." It was disconcerting.

"Your problem is that you always want to run," Jacqueline said. "You never trust anyone, and you hide behind your airs so you don't get hurt. But I am not cut from the same cloth. I want the steadiness and reliability that we have here. I have such wonderful *independence* now, Bea."

"Oh, Jacquie. I'm in a muddle," she said.

"Then we need to unmuddle you," she said cheerfully. "Come to my drawing room. We can enjoy a spot of tea and a comfortable coze, like we used to do."

Beatrice allowed herself to be pressed into an armchair, a steaming cup of tea soon appearing at her elbow. A well-run household always seemed like magic, Bea thought. It was the magic of hard work and precise timing and an excellent staff. She had known the lack of it for too long to be unappreciative.

She sipped her tea and made idle conversation until Jacqueline came to sit on the arm of her chair. She stroked her hair, tucking a curl behind her ear. "My dear, do tell me what's troubling you."

Beatrice sighed. "I am not quite sure what to do with my feelings about George."

"Ah. Did he talk to you?"

"Yes. And now I feel like such an utter ass." She was silent for a moment. "I have been getting close to George, you know. I have told him things that I have never told anyone. Even you. But now it's not just George, but *Gina* who knows everything about me. I understand now that I was talking to the same person all along. But it's strange for me to think about it, when I am so used to thinking of George and Gina as two different people." She looked at Jacquie, her eyes imploring. "Almost no one really *knows* me. I don't make a habit of being so…emotionally intimate." She hated feeling vulnerable.

"Well, George must be in the same position," Jacqueline pointed out. "I don't think many people know his situation. Maybe he's feeling the same way."

Bea hadn't thought about it that way. George had been much

more vulnerable than she had been, and she admired him for it. Perhaps it was no bad thing to be more open about herself. Maybe it didn't have to be so frightening. After all, the sky hadn't fallen and the earth hadn't shook at anything that either of them had said in the library all summer long. She leaned back and took a petit four from the tray. "That helps," she admitted.

"Now you both know each other better. There's no need to be so distressed. Gina is wonderful. She just has a fuller life than you thought."

"But how do I keep it all straight? George? Gina?"

"I don't think it's so complicated. Why don't you just ask her?"

"Oh. Yes, that would be best." Beatrice gave Jacqueline a crushing hug. "Thank you," she whispered, and she tried to put all the emotion of their years of friendship into the embrace.

Then she went in search of Gina. Or George. Her heart was fair leaping from her chest at the thought of seeing the person who had become so special to her. The library was empty, and so were the other public rooms on the ground floor.

She hesitated on the second floor, where the bedchambers were. Somehow, meeting in a private room felt scandalous, even though their nocturnal behavior in the library was far wilder than this would be.

Gina's door was open, and she peeked her head in but didn't find her. George's room was next, and she found him sitting at a table by the open window writing letters. Probably trying to get what light he could, she thought, as she caught sight of the gray storm clouds looming.

He didn't notice her. His head was bent low over the page, his rumpled red hair sticking up at the back where he must have moved his hands through it. His cravat was as neat as ever, and she wanted to slip her fingers through its intricate folds and tug it away from his coat. He moved his head and she could see his face in profile, elegant with that pointed chin and high cheekbones. He was beautiful.

Could he be hers?

She swallowed and tapped on the doorframe with one fingernail to alert him to her presence. "I hope I'm not disturbing you," she said.

His head swung up to reveal a brilliant grin on his face. He rose and bowed. "You could never disturb me, Beatrice."

They stood there for a moment, and then she leapt into his arms. Never had she been around someone that she wanted to touch all the time. She felt like she had been starved of contact all her life, and she couldn't get enough. Even being held by George without the promise of sex had a magnetic draw that she couldn't resist.

"Last night meant a lot to me," she said. Standing outside with him in the night air, surrounded by nature and truth and inky black sky, had been special. "It was one of the most profound moments of my life. Thank you again so much for telling me."

He murmured in her ear, "Has anything changed for you?"

She relaxed into him. The tension and worry that she had expressed to Jacqueline fled in the security of his embrace. "Nothing, except that I would rather like to see you in the library again soon. Perhaps with rather less clothes."

He put his hands on her shoulders and drew her back. He looked down at her, his dark blue eyes searching hers. "Is it just George that you want to see?"

She smiled up at him. "You may remember that I've already seen Gina's scanty attire at the lake? I definitely want to see more. That afternoon helped to warm me up to you, by the way."

He laughed. "I'm glad."

She hesitated. "I do have a question, though. How should I address you? Or is either name appropriate? Do you always feel like both genders?"

He shook his head. "You can tell by my clothes. Today, for example, please call me George. Though it isn't always possible for me to wear the clothes that suit my identity, and sometimes it's not practical. If I feel differently than how I dress, then I would tell you."

"But it isn't just the clothing, is it?" she asked, remembering what he said about it in the middle of the night.

"I prefer my appearance to match how I feel, but my clothes are not a costume that I don simply because I like them. I am more at ease and more *myself* if I'm wearing what I consider to be the right clothing as either a woman or a man, if that makes sense."

"Men's garments must be more comfortable at times, surely?" Beatrice glanced at his trousers. So practical in so many ways, unlike her skirts which sometimes felt miles too long.

George laughed. "Yes, and nothing compares to the warmth of a greatcoat in winter. Yet if it were only a matter of comfort, I would wear pantaloons every day and would show up to the salon in tasseled Hessians instead of embroidered shoes. But that isn't how I feel." He paused. "Of course, I would fight to the death for the right of any person to wear what they wish on their own body, regardless of what Society dictates."

"It must be so freeing to be a man."

"As long as I look like this, I can show up to any of the London clubs, and say what I wish and be listened to, no matter how frivolous my opinion. But I wouldn't be running a lady's salon if I only wanted the personal freedom of speech that comes when I *look* like a man. I am a man, and I am a woman, and I want the same freedom as a woman that I enjoy as a man. I will always fight for our equal rights in my salon."

"That makes a good deal of sense." Beatrice was relieved. Somehow, she had expected things to feel more complicated. Instead, all she felt was joy in his presence.

"Now, I have a question for you," he said, and that little dimple appeared in his cheek. "I don't know how long you're planning to stay at Rosedale, but I'll be here for another few weeks yet. Should we reevaluate our 'kissing only' rule?"

"You were the one to make the rule, George," she reminded him. "I was always more than happy to break it. Let's agree to a few more weeks of holiday."

"I wish these summer days were endless," he said.

"Me too," she sighed. "But I will take every moment that we have."

"I didn't realize how much I needed this trip to the country," he said. "I feel better than I have in a long time. More relaxed. I am busy enough here, but in London, I never have a moment that isn't scheduled. I have no time for indulgences like this."

"You have no time? Or you *make* no time?" Beatrice raised a brow. "It sounds unrewarding."

"Some work never ends. I have devoted my whole life to it." George ran his hands up her arms. "Now, I ought to finish my letters so that my London friends do not forget all about me."

Beatrice trailed a finger around the edge of her bodice, dipping low between the valley of her breasts. "As long as *you* don't forget about *me*," she said with a wink, and was delighted to hear him groan as she glided out the door.

CHAPTER FIFTEEN

Georgina ran his eyes over the pages in front of him, though it was hard to concentrate with Beatrice's perfume lingering in the air. Summer days like this were meant for drinking iced punch and playing a lazy hand of cards or lying between a lover's thighs. Maybe he should have encouraged Beatrice to stay, he thought with a glance at the bed.

But the work called to him.

Troubled, he picked up the letter from Hawthorne that he had shoved under the others when Beatrice had entered. It was mostly amusing *on dits* about friends they had in common. Sprinkled among the gossip were coded warnings that Georgina could decipher but would go unnoticed to a casual observer if the letter should be seized and read for any reason. The coffee shops were rife with talk, Hawthorne had implied in the code. Many believed that more raids were coming and feared the harsh penalties if anyone was caught and accused of sodomy.

Georgina's throat tightened and he thought of Paris, of his life *before*. Once upon a time, he thought only of his own pleasures. The shriek of endless parties at the duke's estate, where Hawthorne invited anyone who he thought needed a duke's protection. Courtesans. The demimonde. Gamblers. Most frequently, his protection extended to those who loved their own kind, sapphists and sodomites. Everyone was welcome, for the duration of the entertainment. Because people from all walks of life attended, from footmen to politicians, uneasy truces existed to protect each other and themselves.

How many times had Georgina seen the duke's beautiful arrogant smile as he opened the festivities? "Judge not lest ye be judged," he would say, and with a languid wave of his hand, the musicians would tune their instruments. Tables of plenty groaned under the weight of banquets, barrels of wine, and faro chips. You could play as deep as you liked on Hawthorne's grounds, with cards or with love.

Georgina had played with love and lost. Yet the thought of Hawthorne didn't pull at him anymore during the day or bother his sleep with dreams of his hard body and large hands. How much of his unrequited longing over the years in London had been because he hadn't allowed himself time to move on to new love? He had kept himself so busy in recent years, but maybe it had kept him living in the past.

Things were trickier now. Georgina had indulged himself during those long Parisian nights, not a care in his mind beyond self-discovery and pleasure. Now he was responsible for so much more than just himself, and the threats felt constant. Would the work ever end? He knew in his heart that it wouldn't, and he would never stop trying. But he also knew his own frenetic pace had to slow.

The past month had shown him what it felt like to have a normal sleep schedule again. Regular meals. Less pressure, fewer interruptions on his work. He had never enjoyed such peace as he had here. And he would never have had the opportunity in London to get to know someone as well as he was knowing Beatrice.

Oh, Beatrice. How could he have expected when she arrived at Rosedale that she contained multitudes? She was teasing and kind, demanding and giving, understanding and arch. She was dearer to his heart than he could bring himself to express.

A light knock at the open door caught his attention, and he looked up as Jacqueline bounded into the room. "George, you can't write in the dark!" She shook her head. "We asked you to come help set up a salon, but not at the expense of your eyesight. It's only midafternoon, but I swear with this coming storm it looks almost like midnight. I would offer you a candle, but I've no idea if we have many left. I am learning that household matters are frightfully expensive."

"It's kind of you to think of the offer nevertheless," he said.

Nora wandered into the room. "There you are, George," she said. "We missed you at luncheon."

Feeling guilty that all of the ladies of the house had come searching for him in the past hour, Georgina pushed aside his letters. "Shall we sit and talk in the drawing room?" he suggested.

"Excellent idea," Jacquie said. "I shall ring for tea and some sandwiches. You must be starving. We have biscuits today, too. Beatrice decided to go to the village yesterday and came home with a cart full of pantry items for the manor. I didn't even know she knew what some of these things were!" Her nose wrinkled. "In fact, I don't think *I* know what some of these things are."

Georgina followed them to a sitting room near the front of the house, papered in pale pink. He knew Nora favored it because it housed the only painting of her parents.

Tea and sandwiches and biscuits arrived, and his stomach growled. He took a bite of a cheddar and chutney sandwich and peered out the window.

"I hope we get that storm soon," he said, studying the thick gray clouds. "We could use some relief from the heat."

"It has been unusually hot this summer," Nora agreed. "The servants have all been out of sorts, and maybe a respite from the weather will make everyone feel much better."

Georgina looked down at his sandwich and wondered if he should tell Nora that he had noticed the servants' behavior too, but he wasn't convinced that it was due to the weather. It wasn't his place to meddle in another household's affairs. Yet were they not friends?

"Have you considered that they aren't happy with your current living situation?" he asked, setting his teacup down.

To his surprise, Jacqueline went into peals of laughter. "Of course we have, George," she said. "I am a total nobody to these people. I come with no land, no money, no connections to speak of—oh, and I'm a *woman*."

"Women live with companions all the time," said Nora firmly, taking a sip of tea. "Our union may look more intimate, but that's because it *is* more intimate. Most people seem to be accepting of the pretense, however. If I had never gone to your salons in London, George, I might never have considered such a thing. I had no notion that I would come home without a husband, but how miserable I would have been to have gone to Sinclair's estate instead of my dear Rosedale with its gardens!"

Jacqueline went to sit in her lap, giving her a sweet kiss. "The roses have nothing on your lips, darling. I am ever grateful that you have brought me home with you."

Georgina raised a brow. "Am I to be treated to sandwiches and a show?" he asked with a wink, and all three of them laughed.

"Whatever is so droll?" Beatrice entered the room and brightened when she saw the tea tray.

Jacqueline snorted. "Bea, do you listen at doorways to choose your best moment to enter?"

"On occasion," Beatrice said. She picked up a small pillow as she glided past their chair and whacked Jacqueline on the arm with it.

Jacquie laughed and grabbed the pillow, throwing it back at her once Bea had fluffed her skirts and taken a seat on the sofa next to Georgina. This was another side of Beatrice that he hadn't seen before. Playful, easy, and unfettered.

She reviewed the tea service. "There is no cup for me?" she asked.

"We can ring for one," Nora said and started to rise.

"No need," she said and picked up Georgina's teacup. "This shall do rather well." She took a sip and grimaced. "Ugh, have you no lemon? Never mind, I shall need my own cup after all."

"By all means, indulge yourself. Add the lemon," he told her.

She chose a thin slice and added it to his cup, humming as she took another sip. "Much improved, thank you."

Jacqueline and Nora exchanged looks.

Beatrice sipped her pilfered tea. "Do you find something interesting, my dear?" she asked Jacqueline, fluttering her lashes.

"Of course I do," she said. "Bea, what is the meaning of this?"

"Lady Sinclair does have a habit of cozying up with the most handsome of gentlemen in a room," Nora said, but it was said with a shy smile directed at Beatrice.

"Can I help being so charming and so beautiful that men are drawn to me?" she drawled.

"I hope not," Georgina said with a smile, and they all laughed.

"Lady Honora, of all of us here, I realize that you and I are the only ones still maintaining any proper sense of decorum. Shall we follow suit? I would be honored if you called me Beatrice."

Her tone was airy, but Georgina could see her tight grip on the china. He knew how important this step toward friendship was to her.

Nora smiled. "I would like nothing more. Please do call me Nora."

Beatrice let out a breath and reached for a triangle of Georgina's sandwich. "Now that this is settled, do fill me in on the news of the day?"

Georgina reached out and took her other hand in his, rubbing his thumb over her knuckles, and she gave him a quick smile.

Nora cleared her throat. "We should make a decision on the first event for our salon. George, you've been marvelous at coming up with any number of programs and series that we can use throughout the year. Why, I think you've used the library more than any Banfield has in the past half century!"

Georgina's lips twitched and he squeezed Beatrice's hand. He would always have fond memories of the library.

Jacquie bounced in her seat. "We shall soon be renowned for interesting gatherings of people and ideas, and we shall encourage people to do what they want instead of just what is expected of them. After all, when one knows how much there is out there for them, it's easy to dream and to find your heart's desire." She locked eyes with Nora, and Georgina felt a bloom of happiness in her heart.

Beatrice set aside her tea. "I don't mean to criticize," she said, shooting a glare at Georgina when he snorted in disbelief. "Truly, I don't! But do you think this might sound dull to the townspeople? Jacquie, before you met Nora, would you have any interest if someone had asked you to come to a gathering to talk about the classics, or the impact of war, or to sign a petition?"

Jacquie hesitated and bit her lip. "No."

"Neither would I," Nora sighed.

All three of them looked at Georgina.

"Maybe Beatrice is being contrary," he said.

She threw up her hands. "I think you should organize something fun. Something with broad appeal."

Georgina thought of the vicar's gatherings, more card playing than poetry reading. "That does make sense. Shall we host a ball?"

"Do say yes, Nora!" Beatrice exclaimed. "Is no one else yearning for a quadrille?"

Nora considered it for a moment. "Who will we invite? There are several families in the neighborhood who would be pleased to have an invitation from Rosedale Manor. They would be very ready to come to an educational or musical engagement, but I cannot help but feel that this wouldn't be the same as your salon."

Jacqueline nodded. "If we wished to just seek out the gentry, it will become a social group where we all agree with the same old things we feel that we ought to agree on, and sip our tea and not do very much at all. But there would be nothing to challenge anyone's mind, or allow other people to see how they could live. What's available to them."

"We could invite everyone from the village to come," he said. "Anyone from the lady down the road to the barmaid in the tavern will be welcomed. A public ball, if you're willing to host it."

"How perfect," Beatrice said cheerfully. "This is what the village needs. Just you wait and see how many people will be excited for dancing. Once they arrive, then you can talk to them to your heart's content."

Noise rumbled from the front of the manor, growing louder and louder. At first, Georgina thought with hope in his heart that the rain had come at last. But the sound wasn't thunder from the gathering storm clouds.

Those were a man's boots in the foyer.

A man's voice issuing commands to the servants.

Beatrice's husband had come to claim his bride.

CHAPTER SIXTEEN

Sinclair stood in the great hall with the mien of an avenging angel, which was how he had looked from the minute their engagement had been announced. The unexpected arrival of her husband didn't interest Bea nearly as much as the sullen-faced girl who trailed behind him into Rosedale Manor, a mutinous glare on her face.

George elbowed his way ahead of the ladies, stopping just short of Sinclair. He was almost a full head shorter and far less broad in the shoulder compared to the earl, and Beatrice's heart fluttered. Sinclair was Society's idea of a champion, having just returned from war. But to her, George was the real hero.

"Sinclair," he greeted him, and they exchanged bows.

Beatrice joined George, and he gently nudged himself in front of her. He looked a heartbeat away from challenging the earl to a duel, every line of his body rigid with fury. Without a shadow of a doubt, she knew that he would fight for her to stay at Rosedale instead of returning to Sinclair if she didn't wish to go.

Sinclair looked down at her. "Lady Sinclair. How very good to see you again."

Beatrice tossed her curls and dropped a curtsy as if they were meeting at a ball. "Greetings, husband."

A pulse throbbed at her temple, but she smiled, refusing to show any sign of weakness that could be used against her.

Nora's face went white when Sinclair bowed to her, and Beatrice wondered if she might faint. Her stomach churned. She was responsible for Sinclair's arrival, and Nora didn't deserve this kind of distress. Jacqueline put a hand on her shoulder, which seemed to calm her.

"I apologize for intruding, Lady Honora. I have merely come to collect my baggage." Sinclair shot an annoyed look at Beatrice.

"Baggage, husband dearest? What a strange endearment," she drawled. If he thought she would come willingly, then he didn't know her at all.

"You have never been here before, and thus left nothing to collect," Nora said. "But if you are referring to Lady Sinclair, you should be aware that she is an honored guest of this house."

Nora was standing up for *her*? Beatrice felt a peculiar warmth in her heart.

"Is she a guest of this house? Or of your *paramour*?" he spat.

"Have a care of how you address any of the women here, Sinclair," George snapped.

Nora's eyes narrowed. "You are not as welcome here as your wife is, my lord. Please do see yourself out."

"I like it here," the sullen-faced girl announced.

"And who might you be?" Nora asked.

She jerked her head toward Sinclair. "I'm his sister. Cecilia. I came all the way from Yorkshire to London to meet my new sister-in-law, but I had no idea that my brother would then take me here to meet her. I only arrived in London yesterday morning, and I have seen *nothing* of it!" Her voice was high and petulant.

Cecilia stared at Beatrice, who stared at her right back. Her dress was rather fine quality, she was relieved to note. It boded well for the sartorial opportunities that she could expect of Yorkshire. She was tall with a long thin face, and brown hair that didn't hold a curl very well. There were too many ribbons pinned to her hat brim, and her reticule was embroidered poorly enough that she presumed it to be the wearer's own work.

"I am pleased to meet any member of the Sinclair family," she said. "Please call me Beatrice."

Cecilia scowled. "Why did you run from London? Did you not want to meet me?"

"Some people do a little traveling after their marriage," Beatrice said.

"Often those people travel *together*," Sinclair ground out.

"Details, details," she said with a little shrug.

"The devil is in the details," Cecilia pronounced with a dark look and all the ill grace and poor timing of a young person unused to society. Beatrice bit her tongue to keep from smiling. She remembered those awkward years all too well.

"Quiet, Ceci," Sinclair said. "Go back to the carriage."

Beatrice raised a brow. "I do hope you don't expect either of us to be bundled up into a carriage at the snap of your fingers, my lord." She turned to Nora. "Would the girl be welcome here? Her brother is boorish, but we can't be judged according to our relations."

Nora nodded, a smile on her lips. Except for her pallor, she looked for all the world as if nothing out of the ordinary was happening. For the first time, Beatrice understood why Jaqueline had fallen in love with her. "I have no objection to the youths of Yorkshire. Miss Sinclair, you may stay as long as Lady Sinclair is here."

Sinclair looked outraged. "Ceci, you don't know these people."

"Are they *disreputable?*" she asked. "Then I shall enjoy my stay here very much. Thank you for the invitation, Lady—Honora, is it?"

"Yes," she said. "We run an unusual household, but it is perfectly safe for you to stay with us."

"I shall take my leave," Sinclair said in clipped tones. "But I will stay at the inn until my sister and my wife come to their senses and realize that their place is beside me."

He strode out the door. A carriage door slammed shut, and the clip-clop of horseshoes striking the cobblestones thundered down the path.

"What a wonderful turn of events!" Cecilia cried, clasping her hands in front of her chest. "Is there anything very shocking that you can tell me about yourselves, or the manor? Are there any *ghosts?* I am delighted beyond measure to be here."

Clearly, her new sister-in-law had read her fair share of gothic romance.

"Well, imagine that. Sinclair arrived and departed in a mere quarter hour," Bea sniffed.

"Persona non grata!" Cecilia announced wildly, and everyone looked at her. She beamed at them. "This is my first house party, you know. My governess told me that a country house party is quite unexceptional for a young lady to attend before her first Season. How lovely to be invited to one!"

Beatrice eyed her. "Unexceptional in every way," she murmured.

She looked at Nora and Jacqueline standing so close that the folds of their skirts nestled together, no doubt hiding their clasped hands. She glanced at George and thought of her evenings in his scandalous embrace. Perhaps she should have insisted on Cecilia joining her brother in the inn after all.

"Come, let us see which room is available for you," Jacquie said with a grin, grasping Cecilia's hand and tugging her upstairs. "Nora, perhaps we should put her in the striped room at the back?"

"We will soon run out of space," she said, but she seemed pleased as she followed them up the stairs.

Bea remained in the great hall alone with George. The pulse still beat fast in her temple, her ears filled with the thrumming of her heart, amplified by the roar of thunder outside that heralded the storm.

"How do you feel?" George asked, his brows knitted low. He reached out to touch her arm, but she shrugged it away.

She laughed without humor. "Relieved, I suppose. I might have guessed that he would follow me. I should be glad that he didn't drag me out of here."

"No one could do that," George said, his voice stern. "We would have protected you, you know."

That peculiar warmth was there again, and it was spreading through her heart to her whole body. "I do know," she said quietly. Tears threatened to spill from her eyes, and she bit her lip. "Thank you." They weren't words she often used, except to the servants.

Yet here she was, safe and secure in this snug country manor. She owed a debt of gratitude to all of them. How could she ever repay Jacqueline for welcoming her as warmly as ever when she had arrived unannounced? How dared she bring such trouble to Nora, when she was trying to mend their fences? How could she even look at George, so kind and so *good*?

Did they know how much she appreciated the grace that they

had extended to her? Her knees trembled as the weight of her debts overloaded her, piling up with every new friendship she had made.

She had to get out of here.

She wasn't ready to return to London, let alone go all the way to Yorkshire. She wasn't ready to be Sinclair's wife. But would she ever feel prepared for her new life?

Beatrice forced her face into an expression of amused scorn, the muscles feeling strange from disuse. She poked her nose in the air. It was an art that she had practiced as if it were a science. Nothing could touch her as long as she remained apart from everyone.

"Everything is fine," she said to George.

She sailed out of the house and into the gardens as the heavens opened up and the rain poured down on her, mixing with the salt of the tears on her face.

George ran outside after her. "Wait!"

CHAPTER SEVENTEEN

I wish to be alone, sir." Beatrice was sobbing, her hitched breath blending into the snap of the rain hitting the cobblestones. Thunder rumbled again.

"Beatrice, I beg of you. Stop running away!" George shouted.

Was she running? Her feet were moving fast, the gardens were a blur of color beside her.

George jogged beside her, catching up. "What do you need?"

"I am not one of your charity projects," she cried.

"Of course you're not. But you're hurting, and I would do anything to spare you pain."

All the fight left her. Soaked to the skin, she plopped onto the bench beneath the rose trellis, elbows on her knees and head in her hands. "You must think I'm weak," she whispered.

George sank to his knees in the wet grass and looked up at her face. "I would never think that."

He pressed his cheek against her cold damp skirt, and she slid her fingers into his tangled curls. He reached up and grasped her hands in his own, stroking the skin of her wrists where she could feel her pulse slowing as the adrenaline left her.

"Stop touching me this way," she said, her voice shaking. "Like I'm something delicate. I am not fragile."

"It's no bad thing to come undone every so often."

George got up and sat beside her on the bench, pressing his thigh against hers and moving an arm around her shoulders to gather her close to him. His body heat warmed her in the chill of the rain, and she broke down again in tears.

"I can't remember the last time I cried like this," she said when the tears slowed at last. She leaned her head on his shoulder. This was a secret she hadn't told him yet. "I don't think I let myself care about anything enough to shed tears over them."

"It's terrifying to care," he said. "But isn't it nice to know that others care for *you* in return?"

"How can I ever repay what you have done for me?" she whispered, looking at the muddy grass.

He shifted and tipped her chin up to look into her eyes. "Why are you so concerned about owing anything? I'm here with you because I want to be. So is Jacqueline, and Nora. We're your friends, Beatrice. We stand up for each other."

She wanted so much to believe it. Maybe she could, just for the summer.

Shivering and soaked, they walked to the manor together, hand in hand.

❖

Breakfast with an energetic sixteen-year-old, Beatrice discovered the next morning, was something of a trial. The addition of one person to the table managed to increase the volume of conversation tenfold. Questions poured out of Cecilia, who wanted to talk about everything from the history of Rosedale to her insistence that she had, in fact, heard a ghost in the attic last night.

It was no surprise that Jacquie and Nora made quick work of their morning toast and tea and murmured their excuses, leaving Beatrice staring down at a slice of honey cake while Cecilia attacked a plate of eggs and ham.

After a few minutes of one-sided conversation, Cecilia scowled at her. "I am here to get to know you," she said, putting down her fork with a clatter. "Do recall that I traveled all the way from Yorkshire to meet you."

"You weren't invited," Beatrice pointed out, but she made sure her tone was mild. "You simply arrived. Had you but waited a month or two, we should have made our way north."

"Can we go shopping?" Cecilia asked. "I would very much like to see if there are any different colors of ribbon to be had here."

She thought of the fortune she had spent in the village shops already and wondered if Sinclair had received the bills yet. Her conscience twinged as she thought of his angry face yesterday, but then again, she was his countess and deserving of her husband's funds. As was his sister. And the townspeople. And the people of Rosedale Manor.

"Yes, let's go to the village," Beatrice said.

It was a strange feeling, she thought, listening to Cecilia's whoops of joy as she scrambled up the stairs to grab her bonnet. She was accustomed to considering her own pleasure when contemplating how to spend her time, but she knew she would get no real enjoyment from perusing the small shops where she had spent more than enough time this summer. She couldn't explain why she hadn't been able to say no.

It must be that Cecilia was amusing, she thought. She had met almost everyone in the town at this point, after all. Cecilia had been here for a scant twelve hours and had spent her time leaping into assumptions, bounding into conversations that she oughtn't be privy to, and squeezing her way into Beatrice's life without so much as a by-your-leave.

She grimaced as she thought of her own life at that age. Coldness from her parents, the solitude of school when they could afford to send her. Something about this bright-eyed girl was bringing out feelings of protectiveness that were as unfamiliar as snow in June.

Reina made quick work of Beatrice's toilette, arranging her hair in a bun instead of fussing with ringlets. Usually Beatrice would have demanded more fussing, more primping, more accessories. She would decide upon a bonnet and then insist on seeing the three others tucked away on the highest shelf of her closet, only to decide that the first had been the best choice all along.

But today she nodded at herself in the mirror with an amused glance at the wavering corner. "How bucolic," she said. "All I need is a wicker basket to tuck in the crook of my arm and I could be any farmer's daughter on her way to a fair."

Reina brushed at a speck on the shoulder of her spencer. "You are as elegant as ever, my lady. Are you sure you don't wish to look at any of your other walking shoes?"

"Quite sure. Now, do enjoy your free afternoon, Reina. Imagine, me a married lady, chaperoning her sister! I am accustomed to you following me everywhere in London as a chaperone, and it's altogether too odd to think of me performing the duty for anyone."

"How ever will you make the best choices for your shopping without my excellent judgment?" she asked, fluttering her lashes and making Beatrice smile.

"Oh, so you wish to take all the credit for my finery?"

"Of course," she said with a laugh. "But I will be pleased to have the time to myself today. Legrand has the afternoon off as well, and we have planned a stroll around the gardens." Her smile was bright enough to warm Beatrice's heart.

"Finally!" Cecilia cried when Beatrice came down the stairs. "Let us be off." She bounded out the front door and down the stairs.

Beatrice sauntered behind her. Had she ever had that coltish energy when she was young? "My dear sister, you must learn some decorum. At least in London," she hastened to add after seeing the indignant look on Cecilia's face.

She peeked at Beatrice from beneath the brim of her bonnet. "Lady Honora and Miss Lockhart seem nice," she announced.

Beatrice's senses were on high alert for any hint of censure. "Miss Lockhart is an old friend of mine."

"Are they related in some way?" Cecilia's voice had a studied air, and she twisted her hat ribbon around her finger.

"No, but they live at Rosedale Manor together," she said with a look that quelled most of the women of the *ton* when she chose to employ it.

Cecilia wasn't cowed. "I think they seem rather close. Not exactly friends."

Bea thought about the situation as they walked. For the first time, she wondered what it would be like to be more open about such behaviors. She only ever talked about them with people she was certain shared them. But if she had known that such liaisons could be permanent when she had been Cecilia's age, would things have been different for her?

"I do not know what you know of such things," Beatrice said. At that age, she had known her own inclinations. When she talked about it with George, he had told her that he had met many people who all came to it differently. "But your assumption is correct. Miss Lockhart and Lady Honora are very close. They love each other and they have chosen to live their lives here. Together."

Cecilia's mouth dropped open. "One can do such a thing?" she asked, a quarter of a mile down the road.

Beatrice hid a smile. Her new sister didn't sound in the least scandalized. She sounded intrigued.

"Yes, one can," she said, determined that she would give this girl any chance at happiness that she could and steer her away from the same poor decisions she had made along the way. A rush of emotion threatened to choke her. "Moreover, you don't need to ever settle down with anyone if you don't choose to, Cecilia."

"Adam calls me Ceci," she blurted out, looking at the ground.

Beatrice blinked. *Adam*? Oh, yes. It was Sinclair's given name. It was strange to feel so unfamiliar with it, given that she had taken his name in marriage.

"He has the privilege of brotherhood," she said. The reminder of Sinclair caused a wave of discomfort to wash over her and crashed her back to reality. "Cecilia will do quite well, I think."

Her cheeks went red and her back was as straight as a board. "Of course," she muttered.

Beatrice tried not to feel guilty. It would do no good to encourage any closeness. She had forgotten that she wasn't in a position to make good on any vow to watch out over Cecilia, and that forlorn look on her face was reason enough to remind her why.

Beatrice could break her own heart at the end of the summer when it was time to say good-bye to the friends she had made at Rosedale. Jacquie and Nora and Georgina all had full lives and other friendships. The loss of hers wouldn't hurt them—only herself, because she would have no one else to turn to.

But family was different, and Cecilia was so young. She deserved better than to grow close to a sister who would be forced to leave her at the first opportunity.

Her agreement with her husband was to bear an heir and then divest herself from the Sinclair family entirely. It would be much harder for everyone if there were feelings involved.

❖

Georgina wasn't sure how governesses in Yorkshire went about things, but surely they didn't teach their charges to talk over others and reach across the rolls and the gravy boat at dinner? Jacqueline had cheerfully declared that they didn't need to stand on ceremony and followed suit. Although Nora looked taken aback, that sweet shy smile on her face gave away her true feelings as she gazed at her houseguests. Beatrice entered a spirited debate with her new sister about the attractions of the countryside, laughing over their shopping expedition.

After dinner, Georgina and Beatrice sat together on the sofa as Cecilia hammered out a rendition of Mozart on the pianoforte. Nora was beside her in an instant, trying to correct the worst of her mistakes.

Beatrice sipped her ratafia and made a face. "Too sweet."

Georgina grinned. "It's to balance out your natural tartness." She laughed at Beatrice's mock indignation but handed over her own glass of white wine.

"Much better," Beatrice said with a smile.

Georgina drank Beatrice's ratafia and looked around the room. They were among friends here. She grasped Beatrice's hand on the cushion between them.

"Scandal in the drawing room," Beatrice murmured.

"The people in this room seem to specialize in it," she said dryly. "Let's hope Cecilia doesn't follow any of our examples."

"She would do well to follow yours," she said. "You're the best person I've ever met."

Georgina blinked.

"I mean it. You have given me so much to think about, about so many things. You're so strong to live the way you do, in the way that makes you the happiest."

"Don't underestimate your own strength," she said. "It took courage to stand up to your husband."

"Perhaps. But where you inspire other people to do good as you have done, I've left nothing but bitterness in my wake." The sadness in her voice pressed on Georgina's heart.

"You are a strong and vibrant person, Lady Sinclair," she said sternly. "You don't give yourself enough credit, and you hide your own goodness under your attitude. I see right through it."

Beatrice leaned close. "Come to me tonight," she breathed, meeting her eyes. "Please."

Georgina felt a burst of happiness. "I would love to."

CHAPTER EIGHTEEN

An hour later, Georgina made her way down the hallway and slipped into the first bedchamber by the stairs to find Beatrice standing in a blaze of light.

Beatrice shrugged at Georgina's raised brow. "I know it's extravagant, but I paid for plenty of fine beeswax candles for this house," she said. "I want to put my money to good use. I want to see you."

Georgina had known her share of pleasure in the past. There were parks in Paris notorious for such things, and there had been no shortage of nocturnal visits to bedchambers and boarding rooms alike over the years. She had sampled what she wanted when it was available. But it felt different tonight in the country air, in this cheerful yellow bedroom, standing in the golden pools of light cast by the candles. More intimate. Loving.

Bea's hands were soft on her hips, barely touching her, and she wanted more. Much more. Georgina clutched the fabric of her shift in one hand and tugged, pulling Beatrice snug against her. In reflex, Beatrice grabbed her shoulders to steady herself.

"Why, hello," she said, fluttering lashes that were now a mere inch away from Georgina's own.

She still wasn't close enough. Georgina wrapped her arms around her waist and kissed her, catching her gasp. She moved her lips down her slender neck and paused to inhale the jasmine scent on the hollow of her throat.

Bea sighed. "Just for you, Gina."

Georgina licked the spot on her clavicle, tasting salt and the tang of perfume oil. "Here?" she murmured. Beatrice hummed in approval.

"What else did you wear for me?" Georgina asked between kisses, squeezing her rounded bottom. She could feel another layer under the shift.

Bea stepped away and posed with her hand on her hip. "Oh, is this too demure for your debauched Parisian tastes?" she asked. She stretched her arms up, back arched, the muslin pulling tight over her breasts. "I suppose I could divest myself of my shift, though the polite thing would be for someone to offer assistance."

"I'm always happy to help a lady," Georgina said.

The garment closed with a drawstring at the neckline. Georgina thumbed open the knot and pulled the string loose, letting the fabric gape and pool around her breasts before sliding it off her body.

Beneath her shift, Beatrice wore nothing but a pair of white cotton drawers, covered in rows of lace and gathered at the waist and the knee. They opened down the front, and when she shifted, Georgina could catch a glimpse of everything she desired.

Georgina smiled. "Drawers? You do always love to be the height of scandalous fashion, don't you?"

"If they are good enough for Princess Charlotte, then I daresay they are good enough for me," she said. "I told you from the beginning that I was no honest lady."

She scowled. "If you mean that you are not inexperienced, then yes. You told me all about your lovers. But never think that any of it was less than honest, Beatrice." She cupped a hand at the base of her skull and kissed her. "There is nothing more honest than the language of your body. I think I have kissed you long enough to learn it well."

Georgina sucked her full bottom lip into her mouth and released it with a pop, hearing Bea's unsteady breathing. Her ears were filled with the sounds of love, from the scrape of her nails against Bea's back to her teeth nipping at her earlobe, to the rustle of Bea's hair, freed from its ringlets to fall in loose waves around her shoulders.

"These sounds are the very truth of you, and I want to know you to your core."

Beatrice drew in a breath. "For so long, that has been a private conversation."

"Oh, it's still private," she said with a wink. "But I am listening for you. Always. You need never say a word, and I would hear you clear to London."

Georgina pulled her closer, running her hands over her lace-covered bottom, sinking her fingers in to pull her tight against her. Beatrice moved to untie her drawers. "Keep them on for me, damsel," she murmured against her lips and felt Beatrice's hands fall away.

She dipped her head to her breasts, tonguing her pink nipples until they puckered. Keeping her mouth on one breast, she moved her hand to the opening at the front of her drawers and slipped her fingers between her thighs, delighting in the warmth that awaited her there.

Bea gasped and moved against her fingers, her center slick with desire. Georgina wrapped one arm around her back to steady her as she felt her knees buckle and pushed her fingers deeper to enter her. She stroked her gently, then swept her fingers against her nub. Beatrice's full weight pressed against her as she moaned in pleasure.

"Let's get you down on the bed," she whispered and drew her down on top of the quilt.

Bea laid bare, in the flickering candlelight that danced across her skin, was glorious. Her complexion was rosy, her skin was damp from the summer heat and from Georgina's touch, and her cherry red lip color had been kissed off until just a trace remained. She was sprawled on the quilt, her legs slightly parted so Georgina could just see her brown curls peeking out through the front slit of her undergarments.

Beatrice propped herself up on her elbows. "If you like what you see, my darling chevalier, then why has the attention stopped?" she drawled.

Georgina grinned, loving every inch of her haughty attitude. "We're just getting started."

She tossed aside her own shift and lay on top of Beatrice like she was made to be there, moving her hips as Bea's legs wrapped around her. Her kisses became more urgent, her thoughts less coherent, as she moved her fingers between them, down Beatrice's stomach, and then again between her legs with a firm steady rhythm that had her hips bucking beneath hers and her lips crying out against her own.

Encouraged, she went deep and hard to test out what Bea was looking for, which seemed to meet with approval when Beatrice gripped her shoulders as if hanging on for dear life and the rest of her body rocked against her.

Beatrice gave one last shudder and went limp under her hand. Panting, she opened her eyes to meet Georgina's and smiled. "Those years in Paris paid off," she said.

She laughed. "I'm so glad they came in handy."

Beatrice arched up beneath her for another slow kiss, and then nudged her so that Georgina was sitting up astride her hips while she lay underneath. Bea ran her fingers up her hips and over her waist to her breasts, teasing her nipples. "You have freckles all over," she murmured with a smile. "I love them."

Georgina's head fell back, and she luxuriated in the sensation of Bea's hands on her breasts. "You can touch anywhere you see them," she promised.

Beatrice sat up so that they were face to face, Georgina sitting on her lap with her legs wrapped around Beatrice's waist. Bea continued her slow exploration of her body, smoothing her hands over arms, shoulders, back, and then reached behind to clasp her bottom in both hands. "And anywhere I don't?" she breathed.

Georgina jerked her head in assent, sighing as Bea delicately stroked her bottom cheeks before she moved her hands across her hipbone and down between her legs. She gasped as her fingers found her center, knowing she was more than ready for release. Burying her head in Bea's neck, she found her jasmine scent again as her fingers worked their sweet slow magic and then found their way inside, filling her again and again as she thrust against her. Her body tensed and then quivered as a wave of pure pleasure rocked her from deep within, and she cried out against Bea's shoulder as the waves rolled over her and dragged her under until she collapsed.

She managed to roll off Beatrice and lie on her back, her arms flung over her head. Her heart thudded back into place. Beatrice curled up beside her, pillowing her cheek on Georgina's shoulder and drawing one leg up over her thigh.

Bea gave her shoulder a lazy kiss. "Not bad for a first attempt."

Georgina pinched her hip. "I think we merit a better review than that."

Bea grinned, dropping her arch manner. "You're right. It was perfect, Gina."

Georgina worried her lip with her teeth. This felt like a tipping point. All of these weeks, there had been a slow reveal of layers and secrets between them. Now she wanted to give her last truth to Beatrice. Her name.

"Please," she said finally, deciding to trust her with her most honest self. "Please, when we are alone, or when we are intimate like this—please feel free to call me Georgina."

Bea blinked up at her, confusion plain on her face. "Oh. Yes, of course, Georgina. I thought you didn't like your full name."

Georgina pulled away, wishing she could cover herself, but her shift was beyond the bed and no help to her now. She pulled her legs up to her chest and wrapped her arms around them. Bea sat up as well and started rubbing her back. Startled by the comfort at first, she relaxed into Beatrice's hands.

"The real reason I don't like anyone to call me by my real name is because it *is* my real name. No matter how I might dress, and how I might feel, Georgina is how I think of myself. I cannot bear for other people to say it because they don't understand it. They don't understand *me*." She sighed. "It's hard to explain."

She rested her cheek on her knee and looked at Beatrice. It was difficult to feel so vulnerable in front of her, but the look on Bea's face was thoughtful. It was genuine. "No one ever calls me Georgina," she said quietly. "But I feel so close to you. I want you to call me by my *name*."

"I am honored, Georgina," Beatrice said, and her eyes shone.

Hearing her name on her lover's lips made her head feel light and her heart feel free.

❖

Beatrice had just returned from a visit with the vicar when the butler informed her that she had a visitor in the morning room. She frowned. In all of Wiltshire, there could only be one person who she could imagine waiting for her, and she was in no mood to see him. It would do her no good to delay, and with a sigh she stepped into the morning room to face her husband.

"Welcome back to Rosedale Manor, my lord," she said. "How have your evenings been at the tavern? It's nothing like London, of course, but I hear its entertainments are adequate for the country. Do you not agree?"

"This is ridiculous," Sinclair growled. "Here I am, paying a social call. To my wife. In someone else's home."

Beatrice smiled. "May I pour you a cup of tea, husband? Do forgive me, I don't believe I ever learned how you take it. Our union has been so brief, after all. Lemon? Milk?"

"How does this look to Lady Honora, as my former fiancée?" Sinclair demanded. "How does it look to my sister? It's outrageous. It's bloody embarrassing." He reddened. "Pardon my language," he added.

She tipped a teaspoon of milk into his tea and stirred before placing the cup on the table beside him. "I wouldn't worry about Cecilia. You know, Gina feels that a strong female role model does wonders for a girl her age."

"Lady Gina," he repeated in incredulity. "A bluestocking! Giving advice to my sister."

"Cecilia could do much worse for models than Gina," she snapped. "She is the very best of people and an example to us all. Cecilia could have the great misfortune to be inspired by me, couldn't she?"

Sinclair shifted in his seat. "I thought you were coming back to London," he said.

"I shall," she said. "When the time is right."

"How do you need more time? It's been weeks." His voice dropped. "You said you were always punctual."

How dared he bring this up again? Georgina had been right. This was her body, and none of his business.

Except—she had promised him a child, hadn't she?

The air whooshed out of her lungs as the truth of what he said hit her. She *was* always punctual. Caught up in the whirlwind of her affair with Georgina, trying to squeeze every second of their summer nights while they lasted, she had failed to notice that time had long ago run out.

"We should stay here for another month," Beatrice blurted out.

"Cecilia has come all the way from Yorkshire. Isn't this the perfect place to get to know her?"

Sinclair stared at her. "Why should I stay in a country inn with a lumpy bed, and my wife stay as someone's houseguest, when I have several perfectly good homes lying around with no one to live in them?"

"We married so fast," she said. "Don't you wish for more time before we have to resume our lives? Can't we accustom ourselves to the way things are?"

Sinclair leapt to his feet and paced toward the window. The conversation didn't rest easy with Beatrice either. She thought of leaving Rosedale. Saying her farewells to her friends. Giving up Georgina. She had not known what she was gambling until it was too late. But there was no room in her heart for yearning. Oh, but *if only…*Yet this was all she had promised herself. One summer to herself. Only one.

"Cecilia and I will darken your London doorstep soon enough," she said, hating the idea, but they could not stay at the manor forever. "Why don't you return to the capital and we shall join you when we are ready? You must have better things to do than rusticate."

He swung around to face her, his face dark. "Someone needs to keep an eye on you."

Anger boiled in her belly. "I do not require watching. We may have wed, but my life remains my own."

"People are talking, Lady Sinclair. We pretended ours was a love match. They think we couldn't keep our hands off each other before the wedding, remember? Wasn't that the entire alleged reason of the marriage you forced on me? How can I explain that we tired of each other so fast that you disappeared within the week to be with your friends?"

She frowned. "No one is talking. London in August is deserted of good society. Is it your army friends who have noticed our lack of passion?"

"All I want is to secure an heir as soon as I can and then to forget that any of this ever happened," he said, eyes blazing. "Can you not do that much for me?"

That had been what Beatrice had wanted too, though she ached to think of it now. But a deal was a deal. Her father's example had shown her that it was a poor idea to renege, lest what was owed multiplied into something much worse. She took a deep breath. "Once the labor pains cease, I shall make my grand departure."

He nodded. "Excellent. I had wanted a wife to help bring Cecilia out for her debut Season, but I will find another way."

She felt the heavy weight of his disappointment even as she told herself she shouldn't care what he thought of her. She couldn't blame him for not thinking she was good enough to help launch his sister into good society. Who would issue invitations to the upstart countess and her sister-in-law, when no one would even greet her in Hyde Park? What kind of example was she to Cecilia, tricking a man into marriage and then embarking on an affair?

Cecilia would be better off without Beatrice. She would forget all about her by her Season next year. Sinclair would move his family along with the life that he had planned before he had ever met her.

Sinclair took his leave, and not a moment too soon. Faced with the enormity of the situation, Beatrice felt faint. She stumbled to her feet and up the stairs to her bedchamber, seeing nothing more than a dizzying blur of yellow and white as she collapsed onto the bed.

She had meant to return to London when she had her monthly courses again.

She was never, ever late.

Not one time.

Except for now.

CHAPTER NINETEEN

B eatrice buried her head in the pillow. She had been at Rosedale for almost two months. How had she not even *noticed*?

She was pregnant. She must be.

Her one intimate encounter with Sinclair on their wedding night had proved fruitful. Elation coursed through her as she realized that she might not ever need to endure his attentions again. If she were lucky, the child she was carrying would be a son, and Sinclair's heir. Within a year, she would be done with the entire marriage, and then she would be gone.

Anywhere. Away from her family. Away from Sinclair and his disapproval.

Away from London, and Georgina. Her giddiness dissipated.

She thought of Sinclair's rage on their wedding night. He had called into question the legitimacy of the earldom due to her failure to arrive in their marital bed as a virgin. Would he even believe the baby was his? Based on his attitude today, she didn't think she could she expect a different reaction.

Beatrice couldn't tell him. Not yet. She would be tossed from his household without a penny to her name, pregnant and destitute without the earldom's protection. The idea of it was enough for her to break out into a cold sweat. Marriage was supposed to mean security, but she couldn't trust the earl.

Could she tell Georgina? He had trusted her with the truth of himself. She imagined telling him tonight, giving him details between sweet lingering kisses, feeling his hands moving over her belly.

If only the child was his.

But that was just a fantasy. Georgina was far more likely to whip out a pen and paper and start brainstorming ideas to rescue her from the situation, and Beatrice wasn't sure that she needed rescuing. After all, wasn't this what she had wanted?

If she told him the truth, if she let down all of her barriers, told him everything, and relied on his help, she would fall the rest of the way headlong into love. She was more than halfway already, she suspected. Georgina deserved better than a needy countess begging him to stay at the end of their affair. He had made it clear that his work would always come first. He wouldn't have time for her once he was back in London.

No, she couldn't tell anyone. This secret burden would be hers alone to shoulder.

She had bargained another month from Sinclair. Enough time to figure out how she would handle revealing the baby to him. Enough time to have her fill of George. Enough time to enjoy these last weeks with Jacquie and Nora before she had to leave them all.

Resolutely, Beatrice wiped away her tears and rang for Reina. She needed to look beautiful tonight, to erase any emotion from her face. All of her problems would be shelved for tomorrow, while she lived for tonight.

She wanted to sparkle and flirt and forget. Just like always.

❖

Georgina passed a fresh sheaf of paper to Cecilia. Her presence was a reminder that Sinclair had descended upon Rosedale like a conquering army, intent on squiring away his womenfolk. But she had to admit that it was handy to have his sister here. Cecilia was easily distracted and prone to fanciful discourse at the drop of a hat, but she wrote a neat hand and was agreeable to doing rote work in exchange for sweetmeats.

Beatrice, on the other hand, was poking around the books on the desk and riffling through letters at random. She was a distraction to all of them gathered in the library. Georgina would have asked her to stop, but Beatrice had a new strain around her eyes these days.

The stress of Sinclair's recent visit must be wearing her down.

Georgina ached to relieve that pressure. The best thing she could think of to do for Beatrice was to help her forget her worries tonight in a whirl of passion.

"What is it you're copying, Cecilia?" Beatrice hovered over her shoulder, frowning down at the tidy penmanship.

She grinned up at her. "I'm writing the invitations to our ball. It's ever such fun to think that someday I shall do the same for a ball of my very own."

She raised a brow, and Cecilia's smile fell. "It is fitting for a woman of your station to have others do the work for you. Sinclair would set a secretary to the task."

Cecilia's face turned mulish. "Gina says it's practical for a person to know and understand the tasks she sets to others. None of us are so much higher than the others that we can't all work together to get the job done."

Georgina frowned. Didn't Beatrice see the adoration in Cecilia's eyes when she looked at her? Why was she behaving like this?

Beatrice asked, "Has it been decided how we shall decorate?"

"We do not have the funds at present to do anything on a grand scale," Nora said, adding a stitch to her sampler. "But our ballroom shall be cleaned and polished enough on the night of the party to meet even your London standards."

"*Clean* is not the most exciting thing I have ever heard said about a ball," Beatrice mused, tapping her finger against her chin. "I believe what we should aspire to is *fun*."

Jacqueline shot her a look. The return of Beatrice's arch manner was wearing thin on all of them. "Do stop being such a stickler. This is Wiltshire, and expectations will be lower."

Nora bristled. "We can meet any expectation from anyone who chances to come to Rosedale."

"I am sure we can, dearest," Jacquie said.

Georgina sighed. All of this tension was unnecessary. "This is a simple introductory ball to announce the launch of the salon. There will be guests. There will be a supper. There will be dancing. What more do we need?"

"The ballroom to be draped in roses, of course," Beatrice said. "Nora, do you think we could hire gardeners to move a trellis or two?"

"Move the rose arbor *indoors*? You wish to *ruin my late mother's garden*?" Nora went pink, and Jacqueline patted her knee. "Think of the *dirt*!"

"Nothing so dramatic, Nora," Beatrice said with a wave of her hand. "A little soil can be cleaned right up. I thought to use cuttings of flowers on their last legs. The living bush itself needn't be moved indoors. It won't be ruined, I promise you."

"What on earth would be the point?" Georgina asked. It sounded impractical.

"To create a beautiful illusion. Just think of the white trellis with red roses, maybe rose petals strewn on the ground with some greenery. Everyone will wish to stand there and gossip. It would be a marvelous focal point for a ballroom." Nodding to herself, she added, "When Cecilia and I went shopping, I noticed the store in town has a great many bolts of gold spangled gauze. It could look quite elegant, festooned around the roses."

"That does sound charming." Nora looked thoughtful.

"I like spangles," said Cecilia.

"The ballroom doesn't need a focal point," Georgina broke in. She was annoyed that Beatrice had started to throw around ideas without so much as a by-your-leave. This was *her* salon. "I beg your pardon, but how many events have you organized?"

Beatrice glared at her. "I may not have the experience that you have, but I have been to many balls." She started counting off her fingers. "They benefit from having one or more elements: a fascinating guest list, a spectacular to talk about, or a splendid setting. No one of note shall be in attendance at ours, and we can't very well hire acrobats from Vauxhall, so we shall have to make do with whatever setting we can manage."

Georgina squared the papers on her desk. "We can manage quite well by offering intellectual substance." Even to her, it sounded stuffy.

Beatrice turned to Nora. "Do any of your neighbors boast of a greenhouse or a garden of their own? Could we barter roses for a display of other flowers? Especially a tall sort of flower that we could stick in vases, large enough to take up space if we haven't any other décor."

"Yes, I think this could be arranged," Nora said.

"Gina, perhaps you could write to your friends and see if there are any London musicians looking for a night of work?" Beatrice's eyes sparked fire. "Or is a country dance not intellectual enough for their tastes?"

"The vicar told me that the farmers here are dab hands with a fiddle," Georgina said. "We would do best to highlight the talent in the area."

"If people wish to hear fiddling farmers, they can attend the harvest festival. They will expect to see variety here at the manor. It has nothing to do with London fussiness," Beatrice said.

Nora bit her lip. "We cannot finance such an undertaking—"

Beatrice cut her off. "I will fund the endeavor. Whatever have I come into riches for if not to do what I please? After all, the ball will be my last night at Rosedale before Cecilia and I go back to London. I wish it to be memorable, so we are sent off in style."

Cecilia squealed with joy, blotting one of the invitations with ink. "Oh, I cannot wait!"

Georgina's stomach dipped like she was learning to swim all over again. When had this been decided? Why hadn't Beatrice said anything to her? She tried to catch her eye, but she seemed determined not to look at her as bright spots of color bloomed high on her cheeks.

"I have such excellent taste that whatever suits me should be able to satisfy people who haven't been ten miles outside of Rosedale in all their lives," Beatrice said, tossing her ringlets.

Over the summer, Beatrice's tone had shifted from sarcasm and arch observations into cheeky humor and flirtatious banter. But tonight seemed like a return to that first night she had come across Georgina drinking brandy in secret before dinner. Whatever had Sinclair said to her that had upset her so much? Was she being forced back to London? Her heart ached as she watched Beatrice curl her lip with some semblance of amusement. She could see plain as day that this was an act to cover her pain.

"Even if most of the townspeople have lived here all their lives, they have been kind to me since I arrived," Jacquie said. "They have interesting stories to tell, and a friendly ear to listen to my own."

"Have you been telling your story?" Bea asked, brightening. "Not that you are from London, but that you are living here as Lady Honora's lover?"

Cecilia's pen dropped with a clatter and she propped her chin on her hand.

"Bea!" Jacqueline scolded her. "Not in so many terms, obviously. Can you imagine me announcing to the grocer, quite apropos of nothing, 'I have arrived as another woman's lover'? Do not be such a goose! I simply say that I am here to live with Lady Honora and she is the very best of women and I hope our relationship lasts all our lives."

"Discreet, but clear enough so that they can understand if they so choose." Georgina nodded. "Well done."

"I've received my fair share of raised eyebrows," Nora admitted. "But I am pleased that it has come to no more than that. We are happy here together." They smiled, and Georgina felt a spark of jealousy.

Their situation was as unlike to herself and Beatrice as chalk to cheese. Georgina couldn't imagine Beatrice being willing to be at her side in London, discussing the news from the coffee houses, and entertaining the women of the salon. This was a capsule of time that would be over in just a few more weeks on the night of the ball.

It was for the best that way. She needed all of her focus on her work. Her lifestyle in London kept her busy from dawn until midnight. She couldn't afford the distraction that Beatrice would bring if she were her full-time lover.

These weeks in the country had been blissful, but it was only a holiday. She would be wise to remember that all holidays must end.

❖

Beatrice swished past Georgina and into the library at the stroke of midnight, closing the door behind them. "Although Reina was delighted to deliver to me your message, as I suspect it arrived with a love note to her from Legrand, I am tired and wish to go straight to bed."

Georgina took her hand and pressed a kiss into her palm.

"Whatever you desire, you should have," she said. "We can always talk tomorrow."

She moved to open the library door, but Beatrice caught her arm. "Wait, Georgina. I'm sorry. That sounded mean-spirited. I am tired, but not too tired to see you." She smiled. "I would have been here sooner, but my new sister-in-law insisted on hanging about my room for as long as she could get away with. I suspect she wanted us to paper our curls together before bed."

"The endless curiosity of youth."

"Her curiosity seems focused on the best way to finagle a kiss without one's chaperone noticing. The chaperone in question, of course, seems to be me. My grand romantic love story with her brother is convincing enough for the schoolroom set, at least." Her tone held a trace of bitterness.

"Beatrice, don't you see that Cecilia adores you?" she asked. "She looks to you for everything."

Her eyes gleamed in the darkness, lit only by the moonlight from the windows. "Do you truly wish to know how I feel?" she asked. "I believe that warrants a kiss."

Georgina obliged, brushing her lips across hers and dropping featherlight kisses along the corner of her mouth and down her neck, pressing one last kiss at the hollow of her throat. She was relieved that Beatrice had dropped her haughtiness, but the sadness that lingered in her eyes tore at her heart.

"I never asked to be anyone's exemplar," Beatrice said, leaning her head against Georgina's shoulder. "How I wish Cecilia had remained in Yorkshire. I remember Sinclair saying that he was in search of a wife because his sister would be ready soon for her first Season. I thought I would save that headache for next year, as God knows I was pressed enough with troubles this year."

"You are a wonderful person to look up to, Beatrice." Georgina kissed the crown of her head. "You are ambitious. Determined. Strong."

She nestled into her arms. "I don't feel like it these days."

"I wrote you the note tonight because you seemed more troubled today than usual." She hesitated. "You have decided to leave Rosedale?"

Beatrice drew away. "I can't hide in the country forever. I only meant to stay a few weeks, and it's been far longer. Nora's and Jacquie's generosity must have a limit, after all, and Sinclair expects his family to live with him. It is the least I can do, given that I trapped him into the arrangement." Her voice broke.

"You don't need to go with him."

"I can't very well survive on my own without him, can I? I came to the marriage with nothing. If I leave, I have nothing. I would rather have something." Beatrice wrapped her arms around her waist. "Being a wealthy countess is much more than some may say I deserve, given the circumstances."

"You may have engineered the marriage, but you were under a great deal of pressure from your family," Georgina said.

"Does it excuse my actions? Do the ends justify the means?" She laughed a little. "Your salon is starting to rub off on me if I am philosophizing."

"From the sounds of your planning for the ball, I wonder if you're wishing to start your own establishment," she said, but as soon as the words flew from her mouth, she knew they didn't sound as light as she had intended.

Beatrice glared. "I had *one* suggestion, Georgina. About décor. Why is it so hard for you to take a recommendation from me? I thought you would appreciate the help."

"It's not that I don't appreciate it," she said. "But I have a particular vision. I have done things my own way for a long time, and I've had great success."

"But this isn't yours," Beatrice said. "This is for Jacquie and Nora to run as they see fit. Have you asked them for their input on what they might want to do after you leave for London? Or did you start planning even before you arrived?"

That stung. She did consider it to be an extension of her own establishment. She didn't think of it as *theirs*. She thought of it as *hers*.

"Of course they told me what they wanted. It's meant to be like my own Tuesday afternoons."

"From the first week we were here, you admitted that it wasn't working out the way you planned."

Georgina felt her cheeks flame. "That may be true, but I am

doing my best and working my hardest to get something done. It's not about the presentation of the event, with a rose trellis here or spangles there. The key is creating the memory of what was discussed, the feeling of freedom and openness that people experience at these kinds of events. I hadn't thought this first gathering to be a simple ball."

Beatrice folded her arms across her chest. "A ball can have plenty of meaning, and presentation is important. Balls are flush with opportunity and create all sorts of interesting avenues for people to interact. People's lives can change at a ball."

"But Jacquie and Nora could arrange for dancing at the manor by themselves at any time. If this is all that we have managed to accomplish, then they didn't need to have me stay for all these weeks. I have been neglecting my work in London. Every day I slip further behind in my correspondence. Maybe it's time for me to return to the city too, if my efforts have been for nothing."

The words were hard to choke out. If she couldn't replicate her success here, did it mean that it had been a fluke of circumstance? An accident of timing? Did the Mayfair salon's popularity have anything to do with her at all? She remembered Madhavi telling her that the community was bigger than the venue. Maybe the venue wasn't as important as she thought. But then what value was she giving to the community? Her heart clutched.

"It's not for nothing," Beatrice said, her face softening.

"Hawthorne was always able to do it so naturally." Georgina thought of Paris. Would she always play second fiddle to what she had been inspired by? "People are drawn to him, and he has made it so easy for a community to spring up around him."

"Why are you denigrating our ball when you held Hawthorne's parties in such esteem? From what you have told me, none of you were talking about Socrates while you drank your way from one end of his estate to the other."

Georgina sighed. "The entire point of his gatherings was to give people like us the opportunity to be who they really were, and to celebrate it. We didn't have the luxury to behave like that everywhere. The party itself was important. Not what we talked about—but just the fact that we could safely be together, with joy." She shook her head. "My salon is different. I had to work for years to get it recognized as the premier establishment that I wanted it to be. For women to have the space to talk and a platform to be *heard*. Now that it's a success, I thought to do it again here in the country. But maybe I would have been better focusing on London, and Jacquie and Nora could have set something up of their own."

Beatrice's eyes were shining. "You are so talented with people, Georgina. You may not have the same magnetism as the Duke of Hawthorne. He is a force unto himself. But you have this earnestness that makes it easy for people to be vulnerable with you. When we visited Mr. Powell at the vicarage, he opened up to you almost the moment we were through the door. Maybe it takes more time for it to happen here for the entire village, but those individual connections are how it starts. It's real and valuable and it's because of *you*. Nora and Jacquie asked you to help them for a reason."

"Thank you," she said, humbled. "It means a lot to me to hear you say it."

"You will have everyone so comfortable that they won't even realize that you're also passing them radical pamphlets, or whatever it is that you're secretly planning."

"I did think to have a table of leaflets," she admitted.

Beatrice grinned. "You see? There is plenty of space for fashion and foundation to collide here in the country. The ball has a purpose here. You have a purpose here. Do not doubt it."

"And I thought you said *fashion* and *country* were words that ought never to go together."

"Maybe I was wrong," she said, with a twinkle in her eye. "Just this once."

CHAPTER TWENTY

The ladies dispersed from the drawing room after supper the next evening, and Georgina thought to go to the village when Cecilia bounced into the room. "Oh!" she announced. "I thought the room quite deserted. I was about to practice my pianoforte."

He smiled at her. "You are in luck, Miss Sinclair, as I am off to the tavern. The room is yours."

"It is ever so late already, Mr. Smith. Maybe you would prefer to listen to my playing? You are from London, after all, and I could not have a better teacher of what is passable in town."

"You would do best to seek the opinion of Lady Honora," he said. "I've no ear for music. But I am sure you play beautifully. Young ladies so often do."

She giggled and leaned closer, placing a hand on his forearm.

Georgina plucked her hand away at once. "Miss Sinclair, do not forget yourself. Do not flirt with gentlemen at house parties until you are *well* past your first Season."

She blinked her eyelashes as if she had a stye, doubtlessly an attempt at a flutter. "Oh, but this doesn't count," she said. "Away from the city, a young woman such as myself can attend dinners and entertainments that she would never be allowed to do in the city. What is a house party without a little flirtation?"

"Have you been reading such things in a novel?" he asked. "A girl such as yourself should not be thinking of any flirtations with a gentleman. There are too many unscrupulous men out there. You would be wise to keep yourself chaperoned at all times."

"Mr. Smith, are you trying to tell me that you are one of them?" she breathed.

"Permit me to be blunt with you, Miss Sinclair. You are a girl who ought to still be in the schoolroom. I do not fancy a flirtation with you, and you should beware of *anyone* who would take you up on your offer to flirt at your age. It is not appropriate at all for you to be here with me, and I am leaving this room this very instant."

He strode out of the room, hearing her indignant gasp. He would need to talk this over with Beatrice later, he thought, shaking his head. She would know how to address the situation with Cecilia.

When he got to the Rose & Thorn, he stood outside, raking his hand through his hair. He had planned to talk about the ball tonight, but he suspected that this wouldn't be as easy as his previous sojourns to the tavern.

The Rose & Thorn was the village's alehouse, but it also doubled as the inn. The rooms on the second floor could be rented to visitors, and there was but one guest staying in Rosedale Village these days.

The Earl of Sinclair.

Georgina eyed the door again. It would be best to just go in as if nothing were out of the ordinary, he decided. Sinclair didn't know that he and Beatrice were having an affair. Any awkwardness would be on his side alone. Maybe he would be lucky. Maybe Sinclair wasn't the type to sit all night in an alehouse with the locals.

A dull roar of appreciation sounded from inside, and Georgina sighed. It seemed that Sinclair's popularity in the military and as Society's darling had followed him all the way to Rosedale.

With a deep breath, he pushed open the door and strode inside.

The heroic, handsome earl was in the thick of things. His tankard was raised high in one hand, the crowd was cheering around him, and a dartboard was lodged with a quivering dart in the dead center of the ring.

Georgina sighed again and went to the bar. Keith grinned at him. "You're not the only visitor from London these days, young George," he said as he pulled him an ale.

He slid onto a stool. "It appears not. And an earl is far more interesting than a mere mister."

"Do you know him then?"

"We've met," he said.

The owner of the general store was seated beside him, and the village baker was on his other side, and he started to talk to them both. Interest in the idea of a ball hosted at Rosedale Manor grew among the men gathered around the bar, and he felt more hopeful that people would be curious about the subsequent events that he had planned for Rosedale.

Sinclair went to the bar and took a stool beside Georgina. Up close, he could see that the earl looked tired and worn. He cast his eye over the group, and they dispersed. Georgina supposed that skill was due to his military training.

Sinclair raised his tankard to his lips. "I'm in a thorny situation," he said, his tone dour. "I don't know what to do, Smith."

"Call me George," he said.

"Right. George. Well, you're up at Rosedale Manor, aren't you? With my wife and my sister?"

He mulled over the words, wondering if there was a veiled warning in them, but Sinclair looked too dispirited to be threatening. "Yes, I'm a guest at the manor."

"Then you know all about my situation, don't you?" He gestured around the room. "These folks know it, too. You can't hide anything in a village, if you've given any thought to misdeeds here."

"I'll keep it in mind." But his misdeeds were done. He was sleeping with this man's wife.

"I've come to Rosedale to get Lady Sinclair back, George. Can you help me?" he asked. "You can talk to her. Make her see sense. Her place is with her husband, not with her friends."

"Lady Honora and Miss Lockhart are exemplary women," he replied, staring hard into Sinclair's eyes. "I will hear no slight against them."

Sinclair frowned and studied his tankard. "I remember you were there when my engagement was announced at Hawthorne Towers. You arrived at the house party with Miss Lockhart, didn't you? You know that she and Lady Honora—my fiancée until that moment—found themselves in a compromising situation."

The earl's voice was pitched low enough for secrecy, but Georgina pushed his stool closer, glancing around to make sure there was no chance of being overheard. "I would support them and their choices to the death. If you thought to come to Rosedale to interrupt their life—"

"No, no. I wasn't happy to think of my prospective bride in love with another woman, but I have no quarrel with them," he said, surprising Georgina. He laughed and clapped him on the back. "Did you think I had never seen such carryings on between my ensigns and lieutenants? But after they sold their commissions, most of them settled into marriage. I thought it would be the same for Lady Honora. Instead, I have been saddled into a less than blissful union with a woman to whom I never would have offered my hand in marriage."

"It doesn't sound as if you care much for the lady." Georgina glared at him. He wouldn't tolerate any threat to Beatrice.

"I want an heir, George." He frowned and drummed his fingers against his tankard. "The sooner, the better."

"I can't help you. Lady Sinclair is not inclined to take suggestions," Georgina said.

Sinclair scowled. "I don't know what else to do. I wanted to wed so I could have a family, which is more important to me than life itself."

"Marriage is not the only way to enjoy a family," he said softly.

"That's true enough, isn't it? I am not related to my brothers-at-arms, but I considered each of them to be brothers in truth. I would have died for them, and them for me. But you know how I got the title, don't you? While my fellow soldiers and I faced death in the field, my flesh and blood brother battled a wasting disease. He died eight months ago." His face spasmed.

"May he rest in peace. I am sorry for your loss."

Sinclair pulled out a monogramed handkerchief and wiped the tears from his cheeks. "Perhaps you think it isn't manly to cry."

He put his hand on Sinclair's shoulder. "There are endless ways to be a man."

"I promised myself that I would name my firstborn son in honor of my brother. If this is my only opportunity to do so, then I must have Lady Sinclair back." He paused. "Perhaps once we share a home again, things will be easier between us."

Georgina sighed. There truly were no secrets in villages. He might as well share the invitation to Sinclair as well as everyone else in the tavern. "Rosedale is hosting a ball in two weeks' time. You could try to talk to Lady Sinclair at the party if you come to Rosedale." Maybe this was Beatrice's chance to have a happy marriage after all.

Georgina nodded to Keith, who had drifted back to them. "Everyone is invited, Keith. Everyone in the village, from the farmers to the shopkeepers to the vicar."

Keith's eyes were on Sally, and there was a soft look in his eyes. "I'm glad to hear of entertainment from the manor. This is the sort of thing the Banfield family used to do now and then. It's good that the daughter has a mind to continue some of the old ways."

Nora would be happy to hear it. He tucked away the compliment to bring back to her.

"You're a good man, George," Sinclair said. "I appreciate it."

"Oh, I need to mention something to you," Georgina said, remembering Cecilia's advances before he left. He ought to tell Sinclair as well as Beatrice. "Your sister should have the influence of a governess for a time or so yet. She flirted with me tonight before I left the manor. I gave her a lecture, but I think she might need more guidance before her Season."

Sinclair looked outraged. "My sister! If she is engaging in any sort of improper behavior, it must be the influence of Lady Sinclair." He bit off the words. "I have been mistaken in thinking we could ever have a union in truth."

Georgina stood and leaned over Sinclair. "Lady Sinclair is a decent, kindhearted person," he snapped. "But you wouldn't know that, would you? She might as well be a stranger to you. For your information, Lady Sinclair would never do anything to hurt your sister. Cecilia looks at her as if she hung the stars. You should be ashamed of yourself for thinking so ill of your wife."

He pivoted and left the earl spluttering behind him. Beatrice was warm, loving, and generous. She would make a wonderful wife to any man lucky enough to have her, and instead she was shackled to this man who thought so little of her?

Georgina yanked his cravat away from his neck as he started the short walk to the manor. He passed the brick wall near the bakery and noticed with satisfaction that the bills he had posted were still up.

He kicked at a stone in his path. He hadn't wanted to think much this summer about Beatrice's marriage. The act of having an affair didn't bother him. He had known too many *haut ton* marriages that were no more than a facade, with no foundation and no roof. They were made for nothing more than to enshrine the division of society into its neat patrimonial parcels.

Beatrice could make her own decisions. She had chosen to leave London. She had chosen to pursue pleasure with him. Together, they had chosen to engage in a summer liaison. But his feelings for her were changing, growing stronger by the day. He no longer liked to think of her returning to Sinclair as his wife, bearing his child.

Yet maybe over time, Sinclair and Beatrice's marriage would become a happy one. Georgina couldn't imagine spending time with Beatrice and trying for a child and *not* falling in love with her wit and charm in the process. Sinclair wanted a family. Beatrice so clearly wanted connections in her life. Raising children with Sinclair, helping with his sisters, could be the connection that she was looking for.

Georgina's heart ached to think of it.

If only Beatrice were *his* wife. He entertained a lot in London, in order to maintain connections and to encourage people to support his causes. Beatrice would be a wonderful asset at those entertainments. She was a sparkling conversationalist. Society's elite might snub her, but Georgina suspected that his dinner guests and the salon attendees would love her. He thought of the politicians that he often invited, many of whom would be delighted to talk to her and be swayed into signing bills based on the strength of Beatrice's persuasion.

How had he never thought of this before? Beatrice could be his partner, in every way that counted. His partner in the salon, his partner in life. Together, they could conquer anything that stood in their way.

But Beatrice was already someone else's wife. She had always said that she would return to Sinclair. And Sinclair was determined to have her back.

He let himself into the manor. Exhausted, he gave one long look down the dark hallway to the library, then went up the staircase to bed. He was too out of sorts tonight to be good company. Beatrice would understand, he told himself as he slipped into his room.

CHAPTER TWENTY-ONE

It was the middle of the afternoon before Beatrice came upon Georgina. She hadn't seen him all day, and now she found him ensconced in the library, an untouched cup of coffee and a sweet bun on his desk, yawning as he made notes in his ledger.

Georgina was spending his days talking to all and sundry in the village and going out after dinner to the tavern. He hadn't come to see her last night in the library, so she knew he must be exhausted.

"Georgina, working yourself into a decline is no way to help others," she said, tugging the pen out of his hand. "Do you need to push yourself so hard every day?"

He sighed. "Hawthorne has written to me again. I worry about the situation in London. It's for the best that I'll soon be back there to help out."

He had told her all about the threat of the raids. "Hawthorne will protect his own," she said. "You know he and Phin are doing their best."

"Their best can only stretch so far."

"You can't worry about everything."

Georgina gave her a look. "I don't. But there are some things more under my control than others. Where we can help, we should."

Beatrice studied the desk, scattered with paper. She picked up a foolscap and skimmed a sentence or two about manufacturing conditions. The next paper was about coal mining. Another for wage equity, yet another about hosting a music benefit to raise funds for the poor.

"You do so much," Beatrice murmured, feeling embarrassed.

What had she done since she had arrived here? Exactly as she had wanted. Nothing more or less. She pressed a hand low against her belly. That would come to an end soon enough.

"It's never enough," he said, looking up at her. "I know you might not want to talk about it, but as the Countess of Sinclair, you are in a position to help so many. It needn't even take much of your time. You could arrange donations through the earldom's staff. You could sponsor charities. If you're going back to London soon, then it might be time to start thinking about it."

Beatrice shrank away. Her father's gambling had forced the Eversons to rely on the charity of family and friends too many times. She loathed feeling indebted. All her life, she had avoided either giving or owing.

But she had wealth now, and it wasn't as if she had planned to spend it all on diamond parures. After all, she had been helping Nora with the household expenses all summer. Beatrice flushed. Her circumstances when she was growing up, and Nora's position now, might have been strained, but neither of them had known true neediness. She had helped Nora first out of a sense of shame, and then through friendship. She had always supposed charity to be personal. But Georgina was right. Donating money could help dozens of people, and they didn't have to be people she knew.

"Maybe you could help me look at foundations to support," Beatrice said. "Maybe I could visit the salon and help with your events there." The idea of work instead of leisure didn't fill her with dread as it once did.

"You don't have to do that," Georgina said, lowering his eyes to the letter in front of him. His voice was cool. "We can work with donations."

Beatrice blinked. "I would be happy to help. I have liked working with you to arrange all the details for the ball."

"You will be busy, won't you? Aren't you planning to have a child with Sinclair after you return to London?"

She froze. Had Georgina somehow guessed her secret? No, it was impossible. "I don't want to talk about Sinclair."

She stood behind Georgina and trailed her hand across the shoulders of his wool coat. Tendrils tickled her nose as she kissed his nape, where his hair brushed against his collar. The paste that he used to style his pompadour smelled like almonds and vanilla. His hair was already messy, so she pushed both hands into his copper red curls and gently massaged his scalp, moving her fingertips in circles.

"God, that feels good," he said, relaxing into her touch.

"I could make you feel even better."

"We're in broad daylight in the middle of the public rooms of the manor," Georgina said. "This is altogether riskier than I might like."

She kissed the tip of his ear, and then his cheekbone. "What is life without a little risk?"

"Beatrice!" he complained.

"My bluestocking has a different place that wants kissing?" she asked.

"Many places. Just not at this very desk."

"Meet me in my bedchamber in five minutes," she said with a grin. "You must be tired. Let me help you."

Georgina looked down at the papers in front of him, and he blew out a deep breath. "Give me thirty minutes to finish up," he said, and looked up at her with a smile. "Then I will be all yours."

Beatrice made quick work of disrobing after she reached her bedchamber. She browsed through her wardrobe and selected a pair of drawers to slip on and a silk dressing gown to wrap around her body. Georgina may have said half an hour, but she knew how he could get lost in his letters. Sometimes they absorbed entire afternoons.

Georgina wasn't the only one who could write a letter, she thought as inspiration struck. Her hand wasn't neat, and she lacked flowery phrases. But what was the value of a long letter anyway? The point of her missive was short, and she was done with plenty of time to spare. She scrawled the addresses on the back of each letter and set them on the desk, ready to be franked.

Georgina slipped into the room almost an hour later, easing the door shut. "I don't think anyone is around," he said. "But, Beatrice, we should be careful during the day."

"Why should we care? Jacquie and Nora have figured out by now that we are having an affair. Given the eyes I've been making at you since I arrived, I don't think the servants would be surprised."

"What about Cecilia?" he asked.

That gave Beatrice pause. She wasn't sure what to think about Cecilia. She wouldn't want her to know that her new sister-in-law was cavorting with another man mere months into her marriage. "I hadn't given it any thought," she admitted.

Georgina nodded. "We should wait until tonight."

Beatrice raised a brow. "I think not, my darling scrivener. We shall simply be quiet. We can manage that, can we not?"

"Well, we can try," he said, his hands busy on the front ties of Bea's dressing gown.

"No. This time is for you," Beatrice said, slipping out of his reach. "You have been working so hard. You deserve loving care."

There was so little time left. She wanted to show Georgina how much she treasured every moment of it.

She untied the silk dressing gown and slowly shrugged it off, exposing her body clad only in her lace drawers. She loved the intensity in his eyes as he watched her every move. She ran her hands over her own full breasts, cupping them and brushing her thumbs over her nipples. "Today is about *your* pleasure," she told him.

"It pleases me to watch," he said.

"It pleases me to touch," she replied, and she stroked her hands down her waist. She untied her drawers and eased them down her hips. "But what I really want to touch is *you*."

She untied the knot in his cravat and tossed it aside, followed by his coat. The double-breasted waistcoat came next, and she pulled his shirt from his pantaloons, tugging it over his head. Beatrice paid lavish attention to his bared breasts, stroking and sucking his nipples until he threaded his hands through her hair and moaned with pleasure. Beatrice knelt at his feet to pull off his tight leather boots, then pushed his pantaloons and smalls down his legs, giving his hips a fond squeeze.

Beatrice drew Georgina to the bed, rolling him onto his front and straddled his muscular thighs. She swept her hands down his freckled back, pressing her thumbs into the muscles beside his spine and feeling his body loosen and relax beneath her touch. She pressed her palms below his shoulder blades, and across his shoulders, before running her hands up and down his biceps. "You are so strong," she said. "Not at all what I would expect of a bookish bluestocking."

"It's the horseback riding," Georgina said into the pillows. "I ride all the time while I'm in London."

Beatrice continued her exploration of Georgina's body, intent on relaxing every inch of him. She ran her hands through his hair and over the delicate curve of his neck, where she was pleased to note the pulse that quickened due to her ministrations. Georgina's quiet sounds of pleasure delighted her as she pushed her fingers into those strong muscles. She kneaded her hands into his firm buttocks and upper thighs.

"You certainly must sit a horse better than I do," she said. "Though I suppose that isn't saying much. I've no eye for horseflesh."

"As long as you've an eye for *me*, I won't complain."

Bea shifted and lay down beside him, drawing herself close at his side and moving one leg firmly on top of one of his to spread them apart. She dipped her fingers between his legs and found his center, damp and ready for her, and she slid deep inside. Georgina cried out into the pillow, his back arching as Beatrice stroked him, listening for the ragged pants that would tell her that he was close to his release. She withdrew and cupped his sex with her palm, her fingers swirling around his nub and bringing him ever closer.

"Beatrice," he moaned, and Bea quickened the tempo of her fingers until he cried out into the pillow, his hips jerking.

Bea curled up beside him and stroked his back as his breathing evened into slumber. This was the first time that she had ever had a sexual encounter designed purely for her lover's benefit, she thought, surprised at herself. She kept watch over Georgina until her own eyelids felt heavy.

It was dark when her eyes opened again. Disoriented, she lay there and listened to Georgina's steady breathing. For all of their stolen moments flirting in the library and walking in the gardens and wading in the lake, this was a first. They had never slept together in the same bed.

They had avoided the luxury of dreaming of forever.

Georgina stirred. "Have we slept the evening away?" he asked, yawning.

"I believe so, my chevalier."

He sat up, the sheet falling away from his body and pooling around his waist as he stretched. "I say, we've missed dinner, haven't we?"

"We must have."

"How far does your offer of taking care of me go?" he asked with a sidelong glance at her.

"I could ring for Reina," Beatrice said, blinking.

"I think it's too late for Reina," Georgina mused.

"I could forage for something. It's been a few years since I've been in a kitchen, but I could make do."

"Perfect." He fell back against the bed, bunching the pillows beneath his head.

"In fact, I have the perfect idea for a nightcap."

"Dare I hope that it's smuggled from France?"

She smiled, thinking of the first time she had seen Georgina at Rosedale when she had pilfered her brandy, so many weeks ago. "Warm milk should do nicely."

Beatrice took a taper with her downstairs. To her surprise, she saw a dim light coming from the kitchen. When she turned the corner, Cecilia was leaning against the wooden worktable, nibbling a piece of bread.

"What are you doing here, Cecilia?"

She dropped the bread. "Beatrice! I didn't think to see anyone here. I didn't see you at dinner."

"I am sorry to have missed it, but I fell asleep."

Cecilia wrinkled her nose. "You took a *nap*?" The scorn that she loaded into the word was clear.

She shrugged. "Don't take your energy for granted, Cecilia. People of all ages get tired. There's nothing wrong with sleeping."

Beatrice poked around the kitchen. She had hesitated to set foot in the kitchen, but she had to admit it was satisfying to be doing something for Georgina with her own two hands. She found the bottle of milk easily enough and started a small fire to warm it up.

Cecilia kept picking at the bread. "I couldn't sleep tonight."

Beatrice glanced at her, hunched over the table with a crease across her brow. Best to make a second cup, she thought, and splashed more in the pot. "Is there something on your mind?"

She scowled. "No."

Beatrice browsed the shelves and located a jar of honey. "Do you want to talk about it?"

"*No.*"

She didn't know anything about young people, but Beatrice suspected that this meant *yes*, so she kept talking. "I don't suppose you know where the cinnamon might be kept?"

"Why on earth should I be troubled to know where the cook keeps her spices?"

Beatrice recognized that tone. It was her own. She knew that Cecilia looked up to her, though she had tried time and again to create more distance between them. She didn't want to hurt the girl in the end. Georgina had told her that her influence on Cecilia was positive, but Beatrice wasn't so sure. She might be following Beatrice's recent change of manners, and she didn't like that idea at all.

"When I was your age," she said, "my family didn't have a cook. Of course, we also couldn't afford cinnamon, so I suppose I also wouldn't have known where it would be kept."

After a minute of searching, she discovered the spices on the shelf. She slid a pat of butter and a pinch of cinnamon into the pot.

"How ever did you meet my brother if you were so poor?" Cecilia asked.

"My father is a gambler, and he had his ups and downs. We led a precarious life," she said. "Thank goodness your brother was captivated by my beauty." Then she bit her lip. She shouldn't be flippant if she didn't wish to see it mirrored back at her at dinner the next night. "You are very fortunate to have a brother who will always look out for you," she said, and hoped Cecilia could hear the sincerity in her voice.

"I had another brother," Cecilia said. Her lips were pressed flat, and the bread in her hands was nothing more than crumbs. "He died this year. I never saw Adam much because he traveled so often with the army, but Richard was always there. He teased me dreadfully." A tear slid down her cheek. "I miss him," she whispered. "Every single day."

Beatrice went over to her and drew her into a hug. "I am so sorry about your brother."

"Adam returned as soon as we sent him word of the funeral.

But then he went straight to London to get married. He's been gone for so long, and I don't feel like I ever got to know him. I didn't know if he was coming back to Yorkshire or if he would just stay in London forever, and I couldn't bear to wait and find out. I came here as soon as I could manage it. At least now I have my brother again, and a new sister," she said. "I couldn't wait to meet you. Adam always says that family is the most important thing."

Her chest ached. She didn't know what to say. Sinclair wanted Beatrice out of his life after the birth of their son, and she couldn't imagine him allowing Cecilia to visit his spurned wife. She poured the spiced milk into sturdy glazed mugs, spooning in honey and stirring as if all her attention depended on the task.

"I wish your only worry was which handsome boy to dance with at your very first ball," she said, remembering how excited Cecilia had been to write out the invitations. She passed her one of the mugs.

"Oh. No one will want to dance with me." Cecilia took a sip.

"There will be dances aplenty for you. I promise." Georgina and her ever efficient ways would see to it, Beatrice knew.

Her lip trembled. "I have no best features," she said with bleak conviction. "No one will take notice of me."

"Who told you such nonsense?" Bea said sharply.

"All the girls at school said so," she said with a sniff. "And I was the only one in my class who had never been kissed!"

"You probably were not missing much from the local boys," Beatrice said, but she reflected on her own days at school. She hadn't been popular. But she had known love in the arms of her dearest friend Jacqueline, and she remembered burning with fires that seemed greater than the world had ever known. She had felt like the first person alive to feel such passion for another woman.

Cecilia picked up a copper pot and looked at her reflection in its bottom. "Look at me. My eyes are too large and too far apart. My lips are too thin. I do not fill out a ball gown in the least." Her voice was cold and fierce, but her face crumpled as Bea looked over her shoulder at the pot. "And look at *you*! You could be on an advertisement for—oh, something wonderful. Like face cream. Or perfume. I would die for eyelashes as long as yours. Or a Cupid's bow in my lips. Or hair that curled instead of just…being there."

Beatrice hadn't thought it was in her nature to be maternal. Although she knew she was pregnant, the life within her womb didn't feel quite real yet to her. But this poor girl in front of her tugged at heartstrings that Beatrice had thought withered long ago.

"You might not be classically beautiful in the way of a drawing on a tin of soap," she said, ignoring Cecilia's fresh wail of grief. "Few people are."

"I hate that all of my cosmetics have beautiful women on them," she cried. "It's all I see. I am not beautiful, not in the least. Must they remind me?"

"But you are memorable. Look at your face again. What you have is worth more than skin-deep beauty. Your eyes are large and full of curiosity and warmth. Your lips might be thin, but they are a very pretty shade of pink. And look, there—you have a quirk of your lips that is most amusing when you hear something that you agree with. Your face is expressive, and it has its own prettiness."

"But your beauty won you an earl," Cecilia said, scowling. "You just said so."

Beatrice smiled. "My beauty may have first caught his notice. Beauty often does. But there are so many ways to attract notice. You can do it with what you say, or how you laugh, or dance. Anyway, it's what you do *after* someone notices you that makes for real attraction."

"What if one is naturally dull after they are noticed?" She stared down into her mug.

"You aren't. But if you were, it wouldn't matter. Men who can't wield a sword still find a way to fight duels. They simply use pistols. You need to identify your strengths and use them in the best way you can. Don't try to use tools that other people *think* you should have. Ignore those women on the soap. The trick is to be yourself. No one can be like you, Cecilia. Own your own power."

Cecilia caught her eye. "Maybe."

She remembered Georgina's words to her. "Don't live your life running away from things that don't make you happy. You should discover what you want and pursue it. Find what you want to run toward." Beatrice sighed, wishing that the advice was as easy to take as it was to give. Her own life was a mess. What business did she have in trying to give Cecilia any type of guidance? "Now go to bed."

Cecilia grumbled but got to her feet.

"And one more thing," she said. "Ceci...please call me Bea."

She beamed. "Good night, Bea."

CHAPTER TWENTY-TWO

Georgina smoothed her hand over the long red wig on its carved wooden holder. She was ready for the day in her white embroidered muslin and her pearls, but she didn't want to wear the wig. It was hot. Heavy. Sweaty in the summer sun.

Legrand fussed with his coat. "Do you ever think about adding padding to the shoulders when you wear a suit?" he asked, frowning as he smoothed the wool over his front. He had made the coat himself, and it was tailored perfectly for his short thick frame.

"No," she said and glanced at him in the mirror. She tousled her hair a little for the pleasure of seeing Legrand roll his eyes at her affectation, and she wished she didn't have to hide her hair under the wig. "Are you considering it?"

"I was thinking I might. But I'm not sure."

"We've known each other for over half a decade, and I don't think you've ever padded anything in all that time, have you? I've stuck a wool sock down my smalls sometimes if I'm wearing my tightest pantaloons, but I thought you didn't much like doing that?" She rose to her feet and grasped him by the shoulder, looking him in the eyes. "Has anyone at Rosedale said anything? I'll browbeat the butler for you if I must. I would knock the sense into anyone who isn't treating you right."

Legrand wagged a finger. "Although I appreciate you rushing to my defense, Gina, you know I like to fight my own battles. This has more to do with aesthetics. I wish to look my very best today."

Legrand had narrow shoulders and a wide hip, and he dressed

better than Georgina did, with a flair for patterns and brightly colored waistcoats that looked magnificent on him.

"You're a handsome enough chap," she said with a wink. "Do you fancy making a new type of coat?"

"Lady Sinclair's maid has caught my eye," he announced. "Reina is a most elegant woman. I plan to let her know my intentions today."

Georgina pinned the wig to her short curls and smoothed it into place. "I wish you luck. But then I would advise against the padding. If you think she is ready to take your hand in marriage, then she should accept your shoulders the way they are."

He sighed. "She has seen my shoulders, along with the rest of me, and says she loves me. But it almost feels too good to be true." His voice held a thread of longing. "How many people have we known like us who have unhappy endings?"

"You deserve love as much as any of us, Legrand." Georgina clapped him on the shoulder. "We all deserve happiness, and it should be celebrated wherever we happen to find it."

"If I am successful, you know that I will have to give up my post. A valet cannot be married, after all."

Georgina paused. A life without Legrand? She would miss talking to him every day. And yet..."Does this mean you would open your tailoring business?"

He grinned. "Someday to be the finest in London, I hope. Someone needs to bring bright color into fashion again. I tire of seeing drab hues on every gentleman I see."

She hugged him. "This has been your dream forever. I would be delighted to see it come true, Legrand. That is, as long as you would have time for your favorite customer?"

He laughed. "You would always be welcome."

Georgina went to look for Beatrice to talk about next week's ball and to tell her that she might soon need to hire a new lady's maid. She found her in her room, worrying her lip as she arranged roses in the vase on her bedside table.

"You look upset," she said.

Beatrice jumped and gave her a drawn smile. She was pale, with dark shadows under her eyes. Perhaps she was unwell.

Georgina came closer and kissed her forehead. "What is troubling you, damsel?"

"Oh, it's about Cecilia," she said, twisting away.

"Your midnight discussion last night?"

"Comparing herself to advertisements for face cream and the like! It's awful," she said with a glare. "She is a lovely girl, and she is so tied up in her looks. I remember she talked of it when we were shopping a few weeks ago as well."

How had Georgina ever thought of Beatrice as selfish, when it was so far from the truth? "We can do something about that, if nothing else." She thought for a moment. "Wait here. I am going to my room to ring for Legrand. I need his help."

She was back in a few moments with a slim parcel wrapped in cloth. "I have asked Legrand to collude with the maid who is taking care of Cecilia, and to bring us the offending articles."

Beatrice smiled. "I should have guessed you would have a solution."

Legrand returned soon with a basket, its contents wrapped in white cloth. He whipped off the cloth with a flourish. "I present to you the creams, ladies."

Georgina picked up a shallow tin of lip salve and untwisted the lid. The silver itself was engraved with curlicues, but on the underside of the lid, there was a watercolor of a lady with bright eyes and a bright mouth and improbable proportions.

"The image is pretty," she remarked and looked up at Beatrice. "Are you sure that she doesn't like it?"

She nodded. "She was distraught last night. She said she hated them."

Georgina pulled at the twine around the package and revealed a thin blade, a pot of glue, and a brush. "This is what I use to paste up the bills in town."

She ran the edge of the blade around the perimeter of the lid and pried the little illustration out. "Do you have a hatbox?" She grinned. "I ask, and yet I know the answer. You must have a half dozen, don't you?"

Beatrice went to the closet. "Does it matter what size?" She emerged with two boxes, each covered in floral printed paper.

"Not at all. If you would care to sacrifice them, I thought to take a little patch and re-paper Cecilia's cosmetics with something beautiful. Just for her. It might make her smile."

"What a wonderful idea." Beatrice beamed.

They made quick work of the project together. Georgina showed Beatrice had to apply just enough adhesive so the paper wasn't lumpy and spotted through with glue. "You should come with me some night to practice with posters," she said.

Beatrice held up the last jar of face cream and lifted the label from its front. "You know, I would have expected you to suggest we use handbills instead of hatboxes."

Georgina laughed. "Perhaps we could replace Cecilia's curling papers with seditious pamphlets next. It is wise to educate the youth, after all."

She went to call for Legrand again to give the creams and salves back to the maid, where they could be returned to Cecilia's room.

Legrand tucked the goods into the basket. "Please allow me to put these away," he said to Beatrice, gesturing to the hatboxes.

"Thank you, Legrand," she said. "I would appreciate it. They were on a rather high shelf."

He lifted the boxes onto the top shelf of the closet with ease, and then he paused. "Do forgive me, my lady, but these are very fine fabrics you have stored in here."

"I bought a great deal of yardage from the general store this summer," she said. "I don't know what to do with half of it."

He came out with a length of crimson wool twill. "The texture is so smooth, and the fabric has a wonderful heft. This was made locally?"

"Yes," Georgina said. "Nora tells me there was a thriving industry here very recently, until they were no longer able to compete on price. The demand wasn't there to support the trade."

"I can understand why. The work is far too fine to be cheap, and it's too labor intensive. They would never have been able to keep up with the market of inexpensive cloth being woven farther north. Their costs would have been too high, with not enough profit at market."

The words sank in, and it felt like a cloud lifted from her mind. Madhavi had been right when they had last spoken at the beginning of the summer. Georgina had been too exhausted and too overworked to think straight all this time. She had missed all the signs in front of her. She flushed at her arrogance, thinking that her own work was more important than anything else.

"The people here aren't indifferent to the idea of the salon, are they?" Georgina asked, thinking aloud. "They simply have more pressing concerns. Like employment."

"What do you mean?"

"Why didn't I think about the boarded-up shops? The closed up cottages? Even the reaction of the villagers when you spent so much coin on your visit to the shops, Bea. They told me that they were no longer worried about their quarterly bills, but I never put all of it together."

"Put what together?" Beatrice asked.

"Half the village is struggling to survive now that the weaving industry has left it. Mr. Powell told us that many of them are relying on charity from the church. They don't know what to do next. You were right, Bea. You told me that people didn't want a lecture. They want to go to events that would interest them."

What had been the term Beatrice had used to describe herself on their walk to the village, so many weeks ago? *Specifically interested*. The problem was that she hadn't paid any attention to where their interests lay. Her mind raced. In a way, it was a relief. She had been so worried about her failure to build an extension of her salon, but in retrospect, that had been selfish. Her feelings paled in comparison to the needs of the village.

"We can help them get the industry up and running again," she said, taking the fabric from Legrand and studying it.

"How would we manage that?" Beatrice asked.

"If they were intent on setting their prices low, then they might not have thought of the alternative. They can market their fabrics as suitable only for high-end fashions, couldn't they?"

Legrand nodded. "I would be thrilled to work with fine fabrics like these."

"We could help them market it to show that Rosedale is a destination for these weaving techniques. They don't have to compete on price, as long as they are known for being specialists and for providing good quality. We shall need advertisements."

"More handbills and labels?" Beatrice said, her eyes twinkling.

"Exactly. And this time, it's all about the aesthetics. Like you said about the ball when I was too foolish to listen to you. The *presentation* is important." She grabbed a sheet of paper and a pencil and started scribbling notes. "Oh, I have so many letters to write."

"They could use the rose theme to their advantage," Beatrice mused. "The bolts of cloth themselves could be sold in bags with roses on them when they ship them out, which would put people from other parts of the country in mind of Rosedale when they think of fine fabrics. Didn't you tell me that you know embroiderers and lace makers looking for work? Maybe they could relocate here?"

Georgina stared. She had told Beatrice all about Mrs. Lewis and the Luddites in Nottingham when she first arrived at Rosedale. She was surprised that Bea had remembered. "That is a brilliant idea." Beatrice blushed, and Georgina pressed a kiss to her lips.

"I can just imagine the coats I could make when I open my shop in London," Legrand said. "If I may count on the custom of such gentlemen as our friend the Duke of Hawthorne, then I think the consequence of this town could be considerably raised."

A rush of pleasure raced through Georgina. This is what she missed most about her Tuesdays. Working through problems and coming up with practical solutions. There was no greater pleasure in her mind.

The pleasure was all the sweeter to be sharing it with Beatrice. If only they had more than one week left of their holiday.

CHAPTER TWENTY-THREE

Beatrice was taking tea with Jacquie, Nora, and Ceci when the butler announced a visitor for Nora. She smiled into her teacup. It must be the visitor that she had arranged, without Nora knowing.

Lady Mildred entered the drawing room, and the look on Nora's face was all the reward that Beatrice could have asked for.

"Aunt Mildred!" she gasped, throwing herself into her arms.

"Honora, my dear girl." She patted her on the back. "Miss Lockhart." Her gaze sharpened on Jacqueline, who hovered near the sofa after her curtsy. "I should give you both a scold after you ruined the opportunity for me to have an earl as a nephew and for Nora to have him as a husband."

Beatrice's stomach lurched and she regretted the cake that she had with her tea. This was not the reaction that she had expected. Her nerves soared as she realized that she had yet again brought trouble to Nora, where she had least intended it. The letter she had written had been more of a gamble than she realized.

Nora's face fell, but she lifted her chin high. "We are very happy here together, Aunt Mildred. If you cannot support us, then I would remind you that there is an inn in the village."

She gasped. "You would send your only aunt to a *public inn?*"

"Yes. I would," Nora said. She went to Jacqueline's side and took her hand. "I might not have had the backbone to do it before, but I've changed, Aunt. I will not accept less than what I deserve."

To Beatrice's surprise, Lady Mildred drew out a handkerchief and wiped away a tear. "That's your mother's character showing through," she said, her voice gruff. "My sister was a spirited woman. You are so much like her, Honora."

Nora looked at the painting of her parents on the wall near the fireplace. "I miss them every day."

"As do I." She paused. "I miss you every day too, my dear girl."

Nora's face was resolute. "I have missed you as well, Aunt Mildred. But I will not cut out my own heart to appease your sense of propriety, which I cannot share."

"I wouldn't ask you to, Honora. I was hoping we could talk, not of propriety, but of property."

"What do you mean?"

"I have no children of my own, as you know. I had always planned to leave you my inheritance. But the older I get, the more I wish to share it with you now, and enjoy it together." She looked at Jacqueline. "All of us."

The three of them hugged, and Lady Mildred wiped away another stray tear or two. "Enough of this sentimentalism," she announced. "Tea is in order." She noticed Beatrice. "Ah, Lady Sinclair! Thank you for the letter. I was pleased to receive an invitation to your ball."

Nora shot a startled look at Beatrice. "You arranged this?"

She nodded, then gasped as Nora hugged her tight. "Thank you," she whispered in her ear. "Thank you so much. You have no idea what it means to me to have my only family here again."

Beatrice felt the need of her own handkerchief as tears welled in her eyes. "I wanted to thank you for your generosity to me this summer. You have been a good friend, Nora. I appreciate what you've done for me."

"I should be thanking you, Beatrice, for all the candles and cloths and sugar and tea."

"Your forgiveness is much more valuable than any of that," Beatrice said quietly. It had helped to heal wounds inside her that she would never have known about if she hadn't come to Rosedale to expose them. The friendships she had made here were precious beyond price.

Lady Mildred interrupted them. "This young person here says

that she is Sinclair's sister, and that he is staying at the inn? Why, he must come tonight to dinner! Let us celebrate the good fortunes of Rosedale together."

Cecilia beamed at them. "I would love to have my brother here among such happiness."

Everyone looked at Beatrice, who sighed. For Cecilia, she suspected she would do anything. "Of course, Sinclair should be invited to dinner."

❖

Sinclair was an imposing presence in the drawing room. Beatrice gave him a wide berth at first, talking with Jacquie and Georgina. She didn't want to speak to her husband more than necessary. But then she thought she should at least greet him, as it would please Cecilia, so although her feet felt like lead, she walked to his corner of the room and found it in herself to smile.

"This is our first entertainment that we are attending together as a married couple," she told him.

"Almost three months after the fact," Sinclair said. "There must be some couples with worse records than us."

Cecilia bounded up to them. "Thank you for coming to our party," she said to her brother. "Lady Mildred has allowed me half a glass of watered wine." She sounded awed by Lady Mildred's largesse.

"You must have been on your best behavior to have won such a prize," Beatrice said.

She smiled. "I want to show Adam my tins." She thrust her glass at Beatrice and rummaged in her reticule.

"Tins?" Sinclair asked.

Cecilia withdrew one of her face creams that Beatrice and Georgina had re-papered. "See, if you unscrew the lid, there's the prettiest blue flower paper!" Her voice was dreamy. "Bea, thank you ever so much. I love all of them."

Beatrice blushed under Sinclair's scrutiny. "I replaced the original illustrations in her creams with papers from my hatboxes, as the drawings were upsetting her."

"It's the nicest thing anyone has ever done for me," Cecilia said.

"I'm going to show Lady Mildred." She flounced off, forgetting her wine.

"She seems so much happier than she was before," Sinclair said as he watched her chatter to Lady Mildred.

"She was grieving," Beatrice said. "Time and a change of scenery has helped her."

"Or it has been you who helped her," he mused. "But I can't deny that the country air has done us both good. I have been thinking a great deal, Lady Sinclair."

She gritted her teeth. "Oh?"

"I was angry when we wed." Sinclair took a deep breath. "I apologize for my harsh words. I regret that we have started our married life separately and with such rancor. Could we start again?"

"What do you mean?" Beatrice asked, pressing a hand against her belly, her muscles tense.

"Let us return to London as friends, instead of enemies. Isn't that what you had offered me on the night of our engagement? Friendship?"

"It is hard for me to envision you now as a friend, my lord. After I bear your child, are you still planning to forbid me from seeing you or your family again?" Her voice cracked as she thought of Cecilia.

Sinclair looked away. "As I said, I was angry. I should not have treated my wife and the future mother of my child with such disrespect. I hope you know that I would never hold you to that bargain. It was beneath me to have ever proposed it, and I have thought about it with shame every day."

Beatrice thought of all her wasted emotion this summer, worrying about her future, dreading the growing strength of her relationships, knowing that they would need to be severed. Anger simmered inside. She didn't need to make any decisions about forgiveness now. They had a long marriage in front of them for her to figure out how she felt about any of it. "Thank you for saying the words."

"I also have had a letter from your father."

Beatrice grimaced. "What is his news?"

"Mr. Everson has burned through all the money I gave to him and has asked for more." He frowned. "I could not believe it at first.

That money, carefully managed, should have kept himself and your mother in comfort for all their lives."

"My father is incapable of managing anything carefully," Beatrice said. Embarrassment had her cheeks feeling hot. "I apologize on his behalf."

"You were right to warn me of him at the beginning of our marriage. You have nothing to apologize for. I told him we will not finance his journey to ruin."

"It's the right choice," she said, her heart heavy. "Maybe someday he will learn from his mistakes."

He nodded. "I should have trusted your word from the beginning. So, do we have an agreement? Shall we return to London and give this a proper try?"

She didn't want to agree, but there was no hope for it. He was her husband, and they had a life to start together. "Yes. We will."

❖

Midafternoon on the next day, the butler announced that additional guests had arrived. Beatrice was excited and pulled Georgina downstairs as soon as they heard the news.

Hawthorne's tall frame blocked the light for a moment, and Georgina's heart leapt. Too surprised to say anything, she swung around to see a mischievous smile on Beatrice's face.

"Lady Sinclair issued an invitation to me," he announced as he entered the hallway with Sir Phineas. "I am sure it is mere politesse. Nothing more than a thank you for my wife's engagement party. I am gratified by the attention, nevertheless. I must admit that I am nonplussed that the invitation didn't come from my beloved cousin, Lady Honora. Nor from one of my dearest friends, Gina."

Georgina slapped his shoulder. "If you show up wherever I am, Your Grace, you may always be assured of the warmest of welcomes."

"Excellent. The very warmest is what suits a duke, after all."

Phin rolled his eyes. "He is unbearable, Gina. I do not know how you ever put up with him in Paris." He gathered Beatrice in his arms and gave her a kiss on the cheek. "You have left me too long alone in London, Bea dear. It is not the same without your charms."

"My charms must be sadly lacking," Hawthorne said to Georgina with a sigh.

She snorted. "That isn't what I recall hearing about you."

Hawthorne bowed to the company at large, who had wandered into the foyer to see who now had joined the party, and seized Nora's hand, bringing it to his lips. "My lady, I am delighted to see you again."

"The last time we met, your duchess was not best pleased with me," she said, blushing.

"Worry not, it was not the first time that we failed to see eye to eye." He grinned at Beatrice. "Lady Sinclair. I was overjoyed to receive your letter."

"I was overjoyed to write it, so I am glad we both got pleasure from it."

Hawthorne chuckled. "The pursuit of pleasure is all one needs for a good life, is it not?"

Beatrice looked at Georgina. "Once upon a time, that is all I believed in," she said. "Your protégé has shown me there is much more to be had, however."

The duke was soon whisked away by Lady Mildred, who insisted on setting him up personally in the last of the suites. The Banfields were distant cousins to the Hawthornes, and Lady Mildred was proud of the connection.

The addition of two more houseguests meant that another leaf needed to be added to the dining room table, and the appearance of a duke was occasion enough to set it with their finest silver. Nora and the butler debated the merits of their best bottles of port and cognac from the cellar that had been curated by Nora's late father.

"Hawthorne prefers a Bordeaux to anything, if you should happen to have it," Georgina mentioned as she passed by them.

She strode up the stairs and found Hawthorne in his rooms.

A surge of pleasure rose over again, but it wasn't romantic. It was simple happiness to see the man who had been the best of friends to her for some of the most important years of her life. Gratitude welled up in her heart. It had been thoughtful of Beatrice to include the duke in the ball that had come to mean so much to them both.

"Where's Sir Phineas?" she asked. For the first time, thoughts of the man that she had once been wildly jealous of didn't affect her in the least.

"He's in the bedchamber, resting. Between you and me, his seat on a horse needs work. Some gentlemen don't ride nearly as much as they ought to."

Georgina gave him a look. "Do not mince words with me, Hawthorne. You aren't talking about horse riding."

"No," he sighed, extending his booted legs in front of him. "It was perhaps unkind of me to indulge in such nocturnal activity when our daytime journey also relied so much upon his seat."

Georgina leaned against the windowsill. "I envy your happiness," she said. "I have done something foolish in the extreme, Hawthorne, and I fear I will never win what you have."

He raised a brow. "Do tell, my dear."

"I have lost my head over Beatrice." It was an understatement. She was drowning in need for her.

"Ah, the charming Lady Sinclair. So this is why she invited me to your ball. She wanted to impress you. Phin and I were wondering if there was some reason beyond wishing a ducal endorsement of your salon."

"I haven't felt like this about anyone before." Except for the duke himself, but Georgina declined to remind him. "She is wonderful."

"And very married."

She sighed. "Therein lies the rub. It's damnably complicated."

Hawthorne laughed. "If you're having trouble with the rub, then I have overestimated your ability all these years." He paused, steepling his fingers together. "Do forgive me, but I have spent some time with Lady Sinclair at Hawthorne Towers while my wife hosted her during her engagement. I confess that I found her wit amusing, but shallow. I am not sure that I would trust her to love you the way that you deserve to be loved."

"She isn't shallow. Beatrice is intelligent, compassionate, and thoughtful, but she hides her true self behind a wall of arrogance. She has dropped the pretense this summer and I have had the pleasure to get to know her. And love her."

"Maybe her behavior this summer was the act, and the arrogance is her natural mien. Did you consider that angle? Lady

Sinclair seems the sort to go after what she pleases, and to do anything within her power to get it."

"Am I such a prize that she would go to such lengths?" Georgina shook her head. "Beatrice can behave any bloody way she pleases, though you are free to think what you want of her. I know my own mind, and my heart. How very rarified you are these days, Your Grace."

His lips thinned. "I am trying to protect you."

"I don't need it, Hawthorne." She shoved away from the windowsill. "The lady is going back to her husband. She won't have me anyway."

"Phin and I weren't planning on a long stay, as I'm concerned about our friends in London. You are welcome to come back with us in the carriage, if your affair is over." He considered. "Unless Phin has trouble with the horse again, of course. Then you could ride his stallion back to town."

Georgina sighed, but she knew she would go with him. After the ball, and after Beatrice left, there would be nothing more to tie her to Rosedale.

Dinner that night was marvelous. The meal was simple enough, though the cook had been in a dither due to Hawthorne's appearance. They had never had anyone so grand before at Rosedale. Cecilia was indulged by Hawthorne, who endured her prattle with the single-minded focus that made people love him, and censured by Lady Mildred, who scolded her at every table manner that she forgot in her excitement to be talking to a duke.

It was a noisy crowd around the table, and Georgina grinned at Nora. She was a shy woman, but she had wanted to fill Rosedale Manor with people and laughter and vibrancy. Beatrice had done this, Georgina thought as she looked at friends and family sitting together. No matter what happened with the ball, or with the salon, Beatrice had arranged this special moment for them all. Georgina raised her glass to Bea at the other side of the table and winked. For this alone, it had been a successful summer indeed.

CHAPTER TWENTY-FOUR

The party had been late to break up, with so much news and gossip from London. After dinner, they had taken tea in the drawing room, Cecilia showing off her indifferent skills at the pianoforte for the company.

After everyone had gone to bed, Beatrice still felt the buzz of excitement thrumming in her veins. It had been wonderful to see Nora reunited with her aunt, and Georgina with Hawthorne. If nothing else, then she had brought some happiness to people she cared for this summer. She started to head toward the library, but before she was two steps outside of her bedchamber, she found herself walking to the ballroom instead.

Beatrice stood in the entry, her hands pressed to her cheeks. The ballroom exceeded her expectations for tomorrow's event. It was pure, unadulterated romance. Roses bloomed riotously over a white wooden trellis in one corner. More roses were twined around poles that were propped up at intervals against the wall. Pots of hydrangeas had been donated by dear Mr. Powell and placed beneath the windows. Mrs. Talbot's prized lilies were nodding near a brace of chairs.

The terrace doors would be open tomorrow to combat the heat of the night and from all the new beeswax candles that she had purchased for the chandeliers. Beatrice unlatched one set of doors and let the magic of a summer evening drift in and flutter the curtains.

She could see now what she had refused to admit before. She

had planned this entire room, had placed every vase and every rose and every curtain, entirely for Georgina.

Because she was in love.

What danger the country hid under its innocent charms. What temptation had lain in wait for her here in the gardens. What a calamity to befall a married woman. A friendship was one thing. An affair was quite another. But love?

She was in deep trouble. Deeper than the lake where she taught Georgina to swim. More complicated than the knotted mess of her hat ribbons after a walk through the roses.

The feeling scared her. Wasn't love meant to be like a lightning bolt upon first sight? She hadn't felt that way when she first saw Georgina. She had been looking for an affair. Something temporary.

Somehow her feelings had changed into a maelstrom of emotions that she couldn't remember feeling before this summer. Compassion. Concern. She wanted to do whatever she could to make Georgina smile, to help her with her work. She wanted every opportunity to nestle up beside her and kiss her cheek and straighten her cravat and smooth out her petticoats.

This wouldn't do at all.

The pregnancy had changed everything. She was duty-bound to Sinclair, and she would return to London with him as his wife as soon as the ball was over.

"Beatrice?" Georgina called out from the hallway.

He stood in the doorway and Bea's heart stopped for a moment, caught by the earnestness on his face. He wore trousers and a loose shirt open at the neck, sleeves gathered and billowing.

"Georgina," she sighed. It felt natural to stretch out her arms, to beckon to her lover. Let the romance of the moment overwhelm her.

Georgina walked into her arms, and she clung to him, inhaling his woodsy bergamot scent.

"Look at what you accomplished," he said, pride in his voice. "So much of this was you, Beatrice."

I did it for you. But instead she summoned a cocky smile and twirled around. "Yes, and of course it all turned out splendidly. Perfection. Did you have any doubts?"

"None at all, damsel."

The sincerity in his eyes felled her, and Beatrice dropped the facade. She took a deep breath and looked around the room again. "We did this," she said. "Together. People will have an evening of joy and happiness. They will want to come back to Rosedale, again and again."

"I hope so. Shall we dance?" Georgina asked with a laugh. He was so handsome standing there. Her hero. How could Beatrice say no to one more night?

That laugh clutched at Bea's heart. Such a cheerful sound that she had grown attached to over the past few months. It would be hard to live in the stoicism of the Sinclair household after this. Sinclair was a serious man. Except for her stay at Rosedale, Beatrice defaulted to a bored air of fashion that never included bursts of laughter unless at the expense of others. Those sarcastic quips that once fell so easily from her lips seemed so foreign to her now.

How different she had felt during these few months. A little naked and vulnerable. In the darkness of the ballroom, she felt like a new person. More like the self she had always yearned to be, but who she had wrestled down under the weight of her own pretensions and fears. One couldn't hurt if one always left first.

The day after tomorrow, Beatrice would once more be the first to leave.

She curtsied and took Georgina's hand and was startled when he swept her close and pressed his palm against the small of her back. "This is no Almack's," he murmured. "We needn't watch out for any sticklers here."

They danced together, legs brushing against each other, arms gripping at one another. There was no music except for the steady beat of their hearts, their mingled breaths and the occasional sigh, and the sound of their shoes on the wood floors.

Georgina's arm was tight around her waist, grounding her in the moment. It was almost too much for Beatrice. Overwhelming with its emotion and poignancy. She leaned in and pressed her lips against his, wild to forget this moment and to lose herself in the bliss of lovemaking.

But even that was different tonight. They tumbled onto Beatrice's quilted bed in her yellow bedchamber, and she thought with confused affection of the billowing curtains and the chipped crockery and the spots on the vanity mirror, all mixed together with the sweet press of Georgina's fingers against her sex. She felt equal parts anguish and elation when she found her release. It had all become so dear to her, and it was slipping through her fingers faster than she could hold on to it. She lay in the dark underneath Georgina, panting and sweaty and sad that she couldn't even enjoy this last night together, with the shadow of their separation looming overhead.

❖

Beatrice didn't think she had ever felt nerves as tightly drawn as she did on the evening of the ball. She had pushed aside her dinner, managing a spoon or two of soup while fretting about everything that could go wrong. The Duke of Hawthorne sent her an amused look that sent a shudder into the pit of her stomach, but it didn't quell her urge to check on the ballroom and make sure the front drive was swept.

It wasn't her house, she reminded herself. None of this was her responsibility. If the evening was a fright, then it would have a kind audience to overlook its flaws. Even if the evening was a success, it would do her no credit. For all that she had nurtured the details of this event with Georgina, the real prize at stake was Jacquie's and Lady Honora's wishes to bring the community together. Georgina had done so much to make sure that there were enough subsequent events to host through the rest of the summer and the autumn.

This ball therefore was only the beginning, and the least important part of the whole.

The real reason for her nerves, she knew, was because this was her last night at Rosedale.

Beatrice pushed a spear of asparagus on her plate and smiled at Cecilia, who sat beside her chattering away. At least she would have Cecilia by her side when Sinclair moved them to Yorkshire.

In Yorkshire, she wouldn't have Jacqueline to visit, or Phin to walk with. She wouldn't have Georgina to love.

Georgina was sitting next to Hawthorne, laughing at something as he bent his head and murmured in his ear. There was something in the way that he looked up at Hawthorne that bothered Beatrice.

Like he was marvelous. A god among men. Georgina didn't look at *her* that way, she thought with a nasty start. And why should he? Hawthorne was the champion of people such as themselves, a friend to any who professed to love their own, a protector of the community.

In fact, Hawthorne sounded an awful lot like Georgina.

And nothing at all like Beatrice.

Georgina deserved someone like Hawthorne. She knew that he had experienced a youthful and unrequited love for the duke which had ended long ago. From Phin's account, and from her own witness of the sizzling looks that passed between them, the duke was deeply in love with Phin. But even if Georgina and Hawthorne were not meant to be together, surely Georgina deserved someone good and noble and charitable like himself.

It was one more reason that she should leave with Sinclair tomorrow.

❖

When the crowd finished trickling in through their informal receiving line, and the musicians tuned their instruments, Georgina felt a thrill pass through her. Almost everyone in the village had showed up.

Beatrice had been right. Everyone wanted to peer at the trellis, and more than a few couples had sneaked a kiss beneath its arch. It was beautiful, romantic, and memorable.

Nora clapped her hands in the middle of the ballroom. She hated attention, but Georgina and Jacqueline had practiced this moment with her, with Beatrice and Cecilia acting as the audience. As many times as she had rehearsed it, she had said today that she was still nervous. Georgina held her breath as the murmuring died down to silence.

"I would like to thank everyone for coming to Rosedale Manor to attend our ball tonight," Nora announced. The enthusiastic applause left her blushing. "As many of you know, my dear friend Miss Lockhart has come to live with me. We would like to welcome the ladies of Rosedale Village to gather here once every few weeks to attend a salon. Our plan is to offer afternoons of discussion, debate, and education, about anything that interests the people in this community." Nora cleared her throat. "But the first event we will hold is open to everyone. I understand that the village has suffered with employment issues since the weavers left town for other opportunities. Lady Gina and her cousin, Mr. Smith, have been working hard to find a way to ease this problem. I would like to invite Mr. Smith to say a few words about his endeavors."

There was a sudden increase in volume as people turned to each other and started to talk.

Georgina pushed through the throng and joined Nora in the middle of the room. "Wonderful job, Nora," she murmured, shaking her hand.

Nora smiled. "I owe it to you. Thank you for being here this summer and for helping us so much."

Georgina bowed to the room and raised a hand for silence. "I am very pleased to announce that my cousin and I have been able to contact many of the Rosedale weavers. We have proposed a new plan to them to revitalize the industry and attract other tradespeople who work with fine fabrics and trims. Lady Honora and Miss Lockhart will open the manor next week to host discussions about how to support the local industry. Lady Mildred has pledged to help wherever possible, including investing in machinery, as the weavers have told me that the starting costs were one of the major barriers to economic progress in Rosedale."

Georgina pointed to a table near the trellis. "And if anyone is interested in reviewing some of the ideas that will be addressed at the salon, we have a selection of leaflets for you to take and read at your leisure."

Nora smiled. "We hope you all enjoy tonight's ball, and we look forward to talking more over the coming weeks and months."

The cheers were boisterous, and Georgina felt relieved. They had done it, she thought. Through everyone's efforts, it was going to be a success. Now she could relax and enjoy the evening.

Georgina kept an eye on Beatrice as the evening got underway. In one breath, she was introducing Hawthorne to Mrs. Talbot, and in another she was consulting with the butler on some detail of the supper that they had planned. She fixed Cecilia's hairpiece in the corner, then turned to laugh with the baker and his wife. She was popular and in demand.

It was clear that everyone in Rosedale had come to love Lady Sinclair. Georgina was delighted for her sake.

Beatrice danced the opening set with Phin, but Georgina was waiting for her before the last strain of music finished. "Everything looks beautiful tonight, does it not?" She kissed her hand and murmured, "Including and especially yourself."

"You are ever so dashing tonight, George. Am I to hope that you will ask me if I am free for the next set?"

"You have guessed correctly, damsel." She lowered her voice. "By the way—it's Gina tonight."

Beatrice blinked. "Oh!"

Georgina grinned and adjusted her cravat. "I wanted to dance with you. I want this to be a night to remember."

Beatrice glanced at something beyond her shoulder and beamed. "Sally and Keith from the Rose & Thorn are here."

Georgina turned around to see Sally and Keith deep in conversation. Sally's hand was on her hip and Keith was staring down at her like a man half-starved. "I think maybe they'll make a match of it," she said. "They always seemed sweet on each other when I spent my evenings there."

The pair drifted past them on their way to the refreshment table in time for them to hear Sally complain to Keith, "I do wish this was altogether a different sort of entertainment. I am so looking forward to the lecture series on the local architecture that George promised to us. Do you think our tavern will be featured? We had a king pass through here a century ago, after all."

Georgina raised a brow. "You see, Beatrice? I was right. I should have pushed harder for a lecture series as the first event."

Beatrice gave her a playful shove. "There is nothing so universally pleasing as a dance, Gina. You were always quite in the wrong about this and you know it."

"I admit to nothing. But may I have the next dance?" she asked.

Having Beatrice in her arms tonight in public was a thrill that she thought would last her a lifetime. This was pure joy, each movement bright and energetic and delightful, swinging her lover on her arm and darting among others in the formations of a country reel. It was every bit as wonderful to be with Beatrice in public as it was in private.

She only wished they could have this all the time.

Looking at Bea's shining face, laughing in exertion as she twirled, Georgina knew without a shadow of a doubt that she was in love.

They walked to the edge of the dance floor, Georgina's heart still full, when a deep voice boomed in her ear. "I believe that is my wife."

Sinclair had arrived.

CHAPTER TWENTY-FIVE

C ecilia was most insistent that I put in an appearance," he said. "I could not find it in me to disappoint her."

"Of course not," Beatrice replied, her face softening. "She was on her best behavior in anticipation of the dancing. Lady Honora and I thought it unexceptional for her to attend a country dance."

"If anyone has anything to say about it, the Hawthornes will quash any disagreeable rumors," Georgina said.

"Lady Sinclair, might I steal a dance from you this evening?"

She hesitated but nodded. "I am free for the next set."

Beatrice and Sinclair walked off toward the dancing, leaving Georgina restless with pent-up adrenaline and wretched for having witnessed their reunion. Not that it was romantic, or even friendly. But it gnawed at her that Sinclair had the right to stride into the ballroom in search of his wife. He had the right to speak to Beatrice and to expect her to bow to his wishes and be available when he demanded it.

She seethed. Women deserved so much more than what they had under the law. They didn't deserve to be in such subservience to their husbands, to swear to honor and obey. Any number of the women who attended her salon had escaped unhappy marriages and refused to submit to another. She considered it a mission in her life to help provide other options to women besides matrimony and the patriarchy.

But none of the work that she had done would stop the woman she loved from going back to her husband tomorrow.

Hawthorne appeared at her shoulder like an apparition. "Your lover has been claimed by her husband again?" he asked.

"I suppose she has."

"We could shock them all by dancing together, you know," he said. "If you wanted to make a stir."

"I do not. And your duchess would have both of our heads if we made such a scene. I know I needn't remind *you* of her habit of policing of public affections." Georgina rolled her shoulders, edgy and uncertain.

"You know she will return to him," Hawthorne told her, watching the Sinclairs dance. "You shouldn't let it upset you."

She tore her eyes away from them. The married couple. The pair who belonged together because of faithless words spoken in a chapel. She had been at their wedding. She had thrown rice with the rest of them.

It didn't matter how she felt, she reminded herself. The fact of the matter was that Beatrice was leaving, and she was going back to London as well. The affair was over.

Mr. Powell joined them, and she introduced the vicar to the duke.

"If you ever find yourself in London, Powell, do look up my address or drop word for me at White's. I host many dinners and entertainments that I believe would be to your liking," Hawthorne said with a wink.

He stammered his thanks, his round cheeks flushing.

"I have a matter of some delicacy to discuss with you," Georgina said to him. She glanced at Hawthorne. "Perhaps we could remove ourselves to a quieter corner."

She couldn't look for one more instant at Beatrice dancing with the earl. She led them out of the ballroom and into the rose garden outside, sighing with relief to leave the heated room, the music and laughter still ringing in her ears.

"Mr. Powell," Georgina said, "You may have heard the news from London about increased persecution of men like us in some of the places we tend to congregate."

Hawthorne nodded. "It's difficult these days in the city."

"Do feel free to say no, as this may put you in some danger, but I wished to speak with you about the possibility of offering protection now and then to men that we may know in London. Some have nowhere that they can safely flee the law if they are under any suspicion. I was thinking that Rosedale might be far enough away for them to escape for a time, until they are no longer under investigation."

Mr. Powell looked thoughtful. He pushed his blond hair away from his face. "That's a right generous thought you had, George. As it happens, I do have extra room in the vicarage. I would be delighted to host a friend now and again."

"It is very kind of you to accept," she said. "A vicar's protection would offer respectability and safe haven until they are on their feet again."

"Indeed, anyone might benefit from the fresh country air," he said, nodding. "And my currant biscuits might be just the thing to help perk them up."

Hawthorne grinned. "If your biscuits don't do the trick, I shall send you a case of my best brandy with any visitor who might come this way to you." His deep voice turned serious. "Along with my deepest thanks."

Mr. Powell bowed. "I am most gratified to be able to offer any assistance that I can."

Georgina felt the tension ease from her body. Finally, this was a way that they could try to help at least the individuals, if they could not always help the masses. She slapped Hawthorne on the back and shook Mr. Powell's hand. "Now let us return to the dancing, gentlemen."

❖

After the last guests had drifted out, and Jacquie and Nora had hugged her tight in elation over the ball's success, and Cecilia had yawned her way up the stairs to bed, Beatrice went to the library. Her head was full of music, and her eyes were full of stars. This was a night of possibility, of hope.

Maybe everything could change.

Beatrice had one last secret to reveal to Georgina. She hadn't planned to tell her about her pregnancy, but while she was dancing with Sinclair, she realized that she couldn't leave Rosedale without taking a risk and gambling her heart. Maybe she was her father's daughter after all, unable to be prudent, willing to risk it all.

Maybe her heart would break in the process. But she had to try. She couldn't believe that she hadn't thought of the solution sooner. Georgina, with her love of problem solving, would surely be delighted with her.

Georgina was already in the library, her back to the door, gazing out the window into the inky darkness.

"Lost in contemplation?" she asked, her voice light.

Georgina tossed a smile at her. Beatrice pressed herself tight against her back and laid her cheek against her shoulder blade, her arms clasped around her.

"Waiting for you," Georgina said, her hands coming up to cover the ones that Beatrice had wrapped around her ribcage.

Somehow it was easier to talk tonight without looking at her face. "Everything feels different now," Beatrice said. "*You* feel different. You seemed distant tonight after we danced."

She was quiet, and Bea found herself holding her breath.

"I am sorry," Georgina said after a long pause. "You're right, it does feel different now. Sinclair wants you back, Beatrice. I saw how he looked at you when you were dancing in his arms."

Beatrice pressed her face against Georgina's coat, burying her nose in the wool. "Yes," she whispered. "He wants to leave tomorrow. But we can change all of this."

Georgina carefully unlocked her arms and stepped away, turning to face her. Her short curls seemed even messier than usual. Her face was pale, the freckles standing out in stark contrast. "I don't think we can, damsel," she said. "All good things must come to an end. This was our good thing." She smiled without humor. "Maybe it was the best thing. But you are married. And you are leaving."

"It doesn't have to end, Georgina."

She sighed. "I cannot follow you to Yorkshire. My life is in London and I am not interested in uprooting it. I have obligations. Responsibilities. This has been a wonderful summer, but I need to return to my salon after having been away for so long. You know that this is my life's work."

"I don't mean for you to follow me to Sinclair's estate. What if we could have it all? Together?"

Georgina's eyebrows knit together.

"I am pregnant, Georgina. I am carrying Sinclair's child. But he doesn't know it yet."

"I shall wish him happy when he finds out," she snapped and turned away from her.

Beatrice grasped her hand and turned her around. "He doesn't know," she repeated. "He doesn't trust me, so I have yet to trust him with the information. I thought at the end of the summer, I could leave Rosedale and say my good-byes with my head held high and my heart intact. But I can't, Georgina. I just can't." She took a deep breath. "Because I love you."

Georgina's face didn't register any emotion. She simply stared.

Beatrice faltered. This wasn't how she imagined her reaction. But for all their midnight conversations, they had never spoken of love. What if she was wrong about how Georgina felt about her?

"Don't you see?" Beatrice asked. "The answer was there in front of me all along, and I didn't realize it. Sinclair already suspects me of being loose in my affections. He didn't trust that I wasn't already pregnant on our wedding night. I was outraged, and hurt, and I fled here. But maybe it all happened for a reason."

"A reason?" Georgina repeated, her tone skeptical.

"Don't you *see?*" she repeated. "We could claim that this baby is *yours*. Parliament will grant a divorce if I had proof that I was adulterous. Your confirmation and my growing belly would be all the proof anyone could ask for. I know Sinclair will not accept this baby as his. He won't want to raise another man's child. If Sinclair and I divorce, I could marry you. We could be together. Wouldn't it be wonderful?"

Georgina backed up until she bumped against the desk. "Divorce?" she sputtered.

"I know it would be a scandal," Beatrice continued. "But if we start the proceedings now, maybe it would all be done during the winter, and old news by next Season. My marriage has been so brief that it will be hardly remarked upon. Everyone will be delighted that Sinclair is available again on the Marriage Mart."

She deserved to be loved. Who better to love her than Georgina?

A muscle worked in Georgina's jaw. "You might think you could weather the scandal, but it would be awful. It would ruin us both." She turned away, crossing her arms across her chest, as if she couldn't even bear to look at her anymore.

Beatrice felt it like a blow. "Isn't love worth it?" she said, but she felt less certain now. Her heart thudded beneath her breastbone.

"Love could be worth it—if you weren't already *married*. I can't handle a scandal like this. Not a divorce scandal."

"Why ever not?" she cried. "This could be our opportunity."

"Because the scrutiny is unbearable, Beatrice!" Georgina spun around to face her, her eyes wild and angry. "Because the court investigators are relentless. The journalists and the cartoonists love to lampoon anyone involved in these kinds of affairs. Our likenesses would be pasted up in every shop from here to the other end of England, for everyone to snigger over. And there are not enough handbills in the world for me to cover them all."

Beatrice scowled. "What do I care for scandal? Why should *you* care? Your friends at the salon would never judge us. Neither would Jacquie, or Nora. The Duke of Hawthorne would stand beside you. We would have friends, allies."

"You are so quick to dismiss all I have created and all I have achieved," she snapped. "I won't do it. I can't. If they look too closely, if they discover that Lady Gina of the ladies salon and Mr. Smith of the Sinclair affair are one and the same, it will be a scandal to far eclipse the divorce. And it would be all about *me*. My identity splashed across the papers, gossiped about in the coffee shops. My likeness pasted up in the newsprint shop windows, saying God knows what about me. About others who are *like* me. Lives would be at risk. Do you know how careful I have been through the years to keep my name out of anything like this? I have *never* in my life been hauled before the courts, and never will I consent to it. Not for you. Not for anyone."

Beatrice felt as if she were hollow, a mere shell that could blow away in a wisp of a breeze. "Georgina, I swear I would never have proposed it to you if I thought that you would be at risk," she said. "I would never put you in that position. I didn't think—"

"You still aren't thinking." Georgina inhaled sharply. "You are selfish in the extreme if you think to embroil me in your schemes without one thought to what it would mean to me. You haven't changed at all since you met me here, have you? I thought you saw a greater purpose, how all of our actions intertwine."

"I just think—"

"Stop thinking and *listen*. This will not happen. You will not cry for a divorce. Neither Sinclair nor I would ever want to be involved in this utter nonsense." She whirled around and strode out of the library.

Beatrice felt her legs tremble, and she sank onto the sofa. She had been so sure that Georgina would see the rightness of the situation. She could give her this child. They could live like a family. Yet Georgina didn't want it. She didn't want *her*.

Maybe she hadn't thought it through. She would never have suggested divorce if she had thought that it would put lives in danger. But if Georgina had stayed and talked to her, maybe they could find another solution.

The truth must be that Georgina hadn't wanted to stay. It seemed clear what Georgina truly thought of her. Nothing more than the upstart countess that everyone else seemed to think of her too.

Swallowing hard, Beatrice left the library for the last time.

Tomorrow she was leaving.

CHAPTER TWENTY-SIX

It was folly to miss someone who one had only known for a summer, Beatrice thought, leaning her head against the glass window of the carriage on the journey back to London. But she missed Georgina. She missed her eager conversation about the issues of the day. She missed the almond scent of his pomade, the bergamot that perfumed his cravats, the wool of his suits. She missed the sparkle in Georgina's eyes when she came across a challenge, her determination to save any damsels that came across her path, her constant support and loving touch that reminded her that she could be relied upon.

But when this damsel truly needed saving, Georgina had turned her back.

Beatrice frowned as she stared out the window. Ceci was prattling on about the excitement of going to London, interspersed with Sinclair's amused replies. She would have liked to have joined in so she could tell Cecilia about the lions at the London Zoo, with the promise of a visit to Gunter's for flavored ice afterward, but her heart wasn't in it.

Sinclair had been a perfect gentleman at the ball last night, and now he looked at her with warmth in his eyes. He had asked her to come back with him so they could start their family, and she had agreed.

Everything had changed between them. She felt a little sick at the thought of telling him that she was already carrying his child. How would he react? How could she explain that she had hidden it from him, and now she was three months into the pregnancy?

The journey to London was interminable. When it was over, she was glad to be in her own bedchamber at last, pleading fatigue and asking for a tray to be sent to her rooms instead of taking the meal downstairs in the cavernous dining room.

Although Beatrice was grateful for the privacy, in truth the bedchamber didn't feel like hers at all. She had slept once in this bed, after her disastrous wedding night. It felt like a lifetime ago now. The colors in this room were too dark, the furniture too heavy and ornate. She stared at the ceiling in the pitch-black and tried to remember the scent of the roses from Rosedale, and the pattern of the little white flowers on the yellow wallpaper.

The next day was no better, nor the next. She hadn't realized how the days would blend together when they weren't filled with anything. Before her marriage, there had always been entertainments to attend, or she would pass the time with Jacqueline shopping and gossiping and flirting. It was September now and the cream of high society had left London weeks ago for their country seats. The dregs still seemed inclined to titter over her supposed premarital eagerness in the bedchamber. The result was that she was invited nowhere and had nothing to look forward to.

There was little enough pleasure from anything that happened during the days to remember them by. Living in a grand house with servants to attend to her every whim, and having a fortune to spend on anything that pleased her, had been her most devout dream for a long time. She had prayed for it. She had schemed for it. She felt like she had earned it. Yet it all dwindled to insignificance when she didn't have anyone to share it with.

There were dinners every night with Sinclair and Cecilia. But they were formal and stilted and Beatrice would have begged off except for the message it would send to Cecilia. Though she realized with dismay that even her relationship with Ceci had changed. She was trying her hardest to impress the older brother she barely knew by behaving with perfect decorum, but with arch manners that Beatrice hated. Was this how Beatrice had appeared to others? With paste personality instead of authentic jewel?

Shopping on Bond Street failed to cheer her. She poked around a fragrance shop with Reina, but it reminded her of laughing with Georgina as they relabeled Cecilia's creams and powders. She came home dejected and spent another restless night staring at the ceiling. How she yearned to turn over and be in Georgina's arms again, to open her eyes and find the familiar cozy bedroom at Rosedale around her, like the return to London was simply a bad dream.

Why had she ever brought up the idea of divorce to Georgina? She had thought herself so clever, finding a solution that she thought would please all of them. But because she hadn't thought it through, she had hurt the person she cared about the most. It was a bitter pill to swallow, but she knew that it was hers to take. She had been thoughtless, and selfish, and all the things she had thought she had outgrown during her country sojourn.

Finally, she had to face the first Tuesday since her return to London. Beatrice had never guessed that a day of the week could hurt so much.

Cecilia found her in her bedroom and plopped on her bed. "Let's go to Gina's salon today!" she announced, her face shining.

Beatrice hadn't seen much of her this week except at dinner. Sinclair had hired a new governess who kept her charge on a tight schedule with deportment lessons and museum visits.

"Where is Miss Jansen?"

"Probably looking for me. I thought if I had a prior engagement with you, then she wouldn't drag me to another lending library."

Beatrice had never gone to Georgina's salon in Mayfair, though she had heard so much about it over the summer that she could imagine Georgina gliding into her drawing room, calm and cheerful, ready to moderate any sort of discussion that might occur. Everyone who gathered there loved her, Beatrice was sure. The keeper of their secrets, the solver of their problems. Always ready to shoulder a burden or rescue someone from harm. Steady, reliable, trustworthy Georgina.

No one there loved her as much as Beatrice did. No one there could have spilled so many secrets and revealed so much to Georgina as she had, and been entrusted with her own secrets in return. But she knew she wouldn't be welcomed today among the bluestockings and intellectuals. She might have a smart mouth, but that was all she had to offer them except for money.

Besides, Georgina didn't want to see her again. She had made that clear.

"I will not be going, Ceci, but Miss Jansen can accompany you."

Her face turned mutinous. "After all the time we spent with Gina in Rosedale, how can we not visit her? She will think it rude in the extreme."

"Gina will think no such thing. She has many visitors. I shall not be missed. You may go ahead, and if Miss Jansen thinks it uncommon, then tell her to speak with me." She might not go to the salon, but she would sack any governess who refused to consider it educational.

"I want to go with *you*, Bea," she said.

"Your choice is between going with Miss Jansen and not going at all, so you had best decide now," she said.

Cecilia scowled. "This is not fair," she muttered, then pushed her way out the door. "I won't go without you."

It didn't feel fair to Beatrice either.

Deciding she was in sore need of a distraction, she called on Phin for a walk. His droll humor never failed to lift her spirits, but she wasn't able to summon more than a smile or two.

"Why are you so severe today, Bea?"

"This is my usual comportment," Beatrice drawled, but she knew it wasn't quite working.

"You have seemed different ever since you returned from the country. Is it Gina?"

She gasped. "How would you know?"

He shrugged. "Gina tells Hawthorne most everything, and he of course tells me. I apologize, my dear, but you know how it goes. When one of us has heartache, we all must share the burden." Phin patted her hand, tucked into the crook of his elbow.

"I love her," she said. It was the simple, unvarnished truth. There was no secret to it, and no shame. "I love her, but she would not have me."

"She was always going to choose the salon. You know how devoted to her work she is."

"She certainly is not so devoted to me," she said with an artificial laugh.

"It isn't personal. Gina has always had big dreams, and a very specific platform that she wants those dreams to take place on."

"I understand that her work is important," she said. "She thinks she has no time for love. But when we were together, it was magic. She understands me, like no one has ever understood me. And I understand her."

Beatrice was silent for the remainder of their turn around the park.

If this were true, she thought, then she needed to fight for it. It was the most important thing that she had ever experienced. It had changed her life.

The summer affair was meant only to be a holiday. But now that she was back among the bustle of London life, she realized that it had been a new beginning. When she hadn't been paying attention, everything had changed inside her.

Regardless of Georgina and their affair, she did not want to go through with her marriage. If she stayed with Sinclair, it would be choosing the safe route. It would be running away from happiness. Georgina had been right from the beginning. Why should women be forced to stay with their husbands under such narrow restrictions? Wasn't she her own person? Shouldn't she have her own rights?

She knew now that she shouldn't have asked Georgina to stand up with her to petition the courts for a divorce. But even without Georgina waiting by her side, she would have to find a way out.

She would have to rescue herself.

CHAPTER TWENTY-SEVEN

Mother Mary's was a shabby tavern tucked between a pawnshop and a brothel, surrounded by a maze of alleyways. It was a far cry from the Rose & Thorn's thatched roof and whitewashed walls, Georgina thought as he stepped out of Hawthorne's carriage and into the night.

There were eyes everywhere in this part of the city. Not only the tired eyes of those who huddled in doorways and begged for their suppers, but also the relentless and unforgiving eyes of the law.

"Come on, Hawthorne. The evening is wasting, and we've never once let it slip through our fingers."

He craved comradery tonight, the society of friendship and easy love if he could find it. His heart was shattered, and this was the best way he knew to soothe it. Mother Mary's was unlike anything he could think of compared to Rosedale, and it was a guarantee that no one who passed through these doors would remind him of Beatrice.

"Are you sure you want to do this?" Hawthorne asked.

Georgina jabbed at him with a sharp elbow. "Afraid?"

"Simply trying to watch out for you," he sighed. "As usual."

He paused with his hand on the old iron doorknob. "What's that supposed to mean?"

"All those nights in Paris, Georgina," he said, his hooded eyes intense. "Who protected you?"

"I stood up for myself," he said in a low voice, furious, pushing up against the duke. He might only come up to his shoulder, but he didn't care. He shoved him in the chest. "Where were *you* when I walked from my father's house to yours during all those nights? I held my own against the men who tried to take more from me than I wanted to give." He hated to remember the ugliness of the Paris, the scuffles and assaults and jeers that he had endured. He preferred to relive it in his memories as glamorous and romantic.

Hawthorne caught his fist as Georgina flung it at him. "Where was I? I was waiting for you," he said, his voice like a velvet rope ensnaring him, still with the power to heat his blood after all these years. "I was watching for you from the windows. I was paying my servants to give me news of you, to follow you when they could. I was worrying myself sick about you, more nights than I could count. That's where I was, George."

Georgina felt his world tip on its axis. Confusion and anger and the old tendrils of love warred within him, and he shoved at the duke again. "Why didn't you ever say anything?" All that wasted time. Why was the duke mentioning it now?

"You were a stripling. A mere boy of twenty, as green and gentle as anyone that ever passed through my doors. Where I felt like an old roué already at thirty." The ghost of a smile teased his lips.

"I didn't care about that," he said, fresh pain lancing his bruised heart. "I was old enough to make my own choices. I had loved you, Hawthorne. When I told you I was leaving Paris for London, all you said was that you would give my name to your British bootmaker to make sure I had the right tassels." He spat out the words.

"Because who had ever heard of Mr. George Smith?" Hawthorne asked. "No one had been to school with you at Eton. Or Oxford. No one at White's knew your name. Who was this mysterious man who appeared from thin air? You needed a duke's introduction. My protection."

Deep down, Georgina recognized the truth of it, and he hated it.

He shouldn't care, and he yanked open the door to the shouts and hollers of the men inside, people he was familiar with, a place for good cider and warm hands and forgetting. He had protected enough people himself to know that they were all connected in this community. Everyone watched out for each other when they could. Together, they were stronger.

But he had been so in love. Georgina could have had his heart's desire, but the duke had chosen to withhold it. He felt the truth of it twist deep as he tried to shelve it away with the hurt and betrayal that he felt over Beatrice.

Hawthorne could follow him or not, he thought sourly as he pushed his way into the throng and found an empty chair. He hooked it with his ankle and pulled it toward him, throwing himself into it with a deep sigh.

Hawthorne found him soon enough, and with a glance, cleared the chair beside Georgina for himself. He settled himself as neatly as if he were in sitting in a waiting room for the Prince Regent.

There were no princes here, Georgina thought. Or princesses. Only rogues and wastrels and ne'er–do–wells. A shunned society of big hearts and lost dreams.

"I don't need a nursemaid," he said to the duke.

Hawthorne ignored him. He raised a brow at a waiter, and a rum punch was brought around straightaway. Georgina was annoyed but then decided that he might as well take advantage of it. Mother Mary's punch had knocked him on his arse more than once, and he was willing for the oblivion of alcohol.

A warm body pressed close, perching on the arm of Georgina's chair. "It's been a long time, Georgie my lad," a voice cooed in his ear as a broad hand palmed its way through his hair.

Georgina sprang up from the chair. He would have known that voice anywhere, and there was but one man he allowed to call him Georgie. "Charles!" he exclaimed and clasped the man tight.

Charles Hollister was a second son of a minor peer whose allowance had been cut off long ago for exactly this sort of behavior. He was a sight to behold, Georgina thought with affection as he kissed his cheek. Tonight, Charles had painted his face chalk white and rouged his cheeks and darkened his thick lashes. His wig of big bouncy curls bobbed against his wide shoulders, and he looked for all the world like a courtesan in a bad play on Covent Garden. The costume that he wore was from the last century, sporting a saucy ribboned stomacher and battered hip cages that had seen better days.

Many of the men who frequented Mother Molly's liked to experiment with their dress in a casual way and put on female affectations in the privacy of the tavern, and the owner kept a retiring room full of old theater costumes and cosmetics for his patrons' pleasures.

"*Charles*? You know I wouldn't have come to Mother's to dress like this, just to be called a name like that," he said in mock reproof.

A lazy grin spread over Hawthorne's face. "Madam, you are gorgeous no matter who you are tonight." He caught his hand and brought it to his lips.

One of the damnably likable things about the man was his acceptance of everyone without question, Georgina thought. His anger thinned as he studied the duke, majestic and arrogant and beloved. He had agreed in an instant to come with Georgina tonight, and had always supported him. He always would. Georgina's heart filled. He could ask for no better friend than this. He gave the duke's thigh an affectionate pat, then turned his attention back to Charles.

"Do tell me who we have the pleasure of addressing?" Georgina asked.

Charles curtsied and rustled his full skirts up to his hips like a French cabaret dancer as he came back up. "Why, I'm Petty Mischief." He winked.

Georgina laughed. "Of course you are." He had been up to mischief many a time with Charles over the years, drinking and placing wagers and stealing kisses when the mood struck them both.

"Will tonight be your lucky night, sir? Will you peek beneath old Petty's skirts?" He sat down again on the arm of Georgina's chair and rolled his shoulders forward so that his bodice gaped at the front, a rouged nipple peeking out.

Who had he been fooling? He had wanted to escape thoughts of Beatrice tonight. But how she would have loved to be here. Flirting with Petty, laughing with Hawthorne. Longing overtook him, and he could almost smell her jasmine perfume instead of the cheap scent that Petty Mischief had spritzed on himself.

The duke poured more punch for the three of them, and Petty leaned across Georgina to take his glass. Georgina wrapped an arm around his waist to steady him, as it didn't seem to be the first glass that he had enjoyed tonight.

"Alas, I am in no mood for pleasure tonight."

He wanted to, in theory. It was the reason he had dragged Hawthorne to Mother Mary's in the first place. But Beatrice still plagued his heart. He picked up his glass and drained it.

"You, not in the mood? Have you taken a monk's oath? I've

rarely known you to turn down the opportunity to polish a knob on a night like this."

"I met with heartbreak over the summer," Georgina said, accepting another glass of punch from Hawthorne.

"Who's the poor sod who hurt my Georgie?" He scanned the tavern. "I'll break his face for you."

"It was a woman. Another man's wife." Georgina grimaced as the potent combination of rum and wine staggered him, but the fuzziness that started to blur his memory of Beatrice's eyes tempted him to stare down the bottom of another glass.

"Will you need a second?"

He frowned. "I think I'm on my fourth, Miss Mischief. But you can make me the happiest of men by pouring me another."

Hawthorne took his drink away. "He means for a duel, dear George. Though if there is to be such a thing, consider me aghast if I am not your first option."

"I would be a lovely second," Petty argued. "I'd cut a most dashing figure standing in the fog at dawn."

"There's no duel," Georgina said. "She has chosen to stay with her husband. It is the lady's prerogative."

"What would you have chosen?"

Georgina stole his glass back from the duke and took another drink. "I didn't get a choice."

"There's always a choice!" cried Petty Mischief. "I could have chosen to marry to please my parents, but instead I chose acting. Here I sit, broke but happy."

"I love her," Georgina said. "But I didn't tell her." Saying the words out loud was cathartic. "I could have been a father," he choked out. "She's carrying a child."

"If you love her, then go get her."

"The lady knows her own mind. If she wants to come and get it, then she knows where to find me." Tuesdays at two in the afternoon, to be precise. It was when she didn't show up today that he knew it was really and truly over, and he had decided to get really and truly drunk.

"What about what you want?" The duke's big hand was on his shoulder, and Petty's smaller hand was on his knee, and for a moment he considered wanting what might be available to him right this very moment. But there was Phin to consider, and Georgina thought it might not be fair to him if he tried to take a taste of what he had once wanted so long ago from the duke.

"I'm too busy to have what I want. I work all the time, Hawthorne. You know that."

"Is this the life you dreamed about when you left Paris?"

Of course it wasn't. He had expected to return to England, work hard, find someone to love, and then carry on the work by their side. When it didn't happen, he had doubled and tripled his efforts until the salon had taken over almost all his time.

Maybe that had been the wrong approach. Maybe spending all his time working had prevented him from getting the opportunity to ever find love. Maybe it had taken resting for a moment and catching his breath in the country to find what he had spent a lifetime looking for and had become convinced he could never have.

Georgina had found the love of his life this summer. Beatrice might be flawed, but she was still a jewel. And so was he. They could glitter together if he just gave it a chance. If she would still have him.

He realized that things would need to change, and he thought he might know how to do it.

"How have you been these days, Petty?" Hawthorne asked.

"Life is bleak, my loves. So I shall be glad that you are providing the punch tonight, as I haven't a farthing left to my name." He said it with a laugh and a roll of his eyes, but Georgina could see the shadows in his eyes. He tossed back his glass with a grimace.

"What happened?" Georgina asked.

"I was put in the pillory every day last week, and the acting troupe I was working with sacked me for not showing up." He made a moue with his lips. "I had a good role coming up too. A nice bit of Shakespeare. Now I've about a week's worth of money tucked in my boot for my room and board, and after that Petty Mischief might need to turn to Petty Larceny or worse." He laughed.

Georgina patted his knee. "If you're hard up, I have just come from the country where I think you could find a friend," he said, thinking of Mr. Powell. "If you would like, I could write a letter on your behalf and you could be there before your board runs out."

"He's a country vicar but a good man," the duke added.

"I daresay a vicar is just the sort to like a spot of mischief for Michaelmas." He pressed a noisy kiss on Georgina's cheek. "Much obliged, gentlemen. Are you both quite sure you don't want any mischief for yourselves tonight? I'm in the mood to celebrate, and two gorgeous men as yourselves would be just the ticket."

The door to the tavern snapped open and the mood changed as Phin rushed in. "There's not much time!" he shouted. "Everyone, out! The police are coming."

CHAPTER TWENTY-EIGHT

This was the risk they took by socializing with each other like this. Consequently, they were accustomed to moving fast. Chairs were pushed over and the men scattered. Mother Mary's had several exits, and it wasn't long before everyone was out of the tavern and disappearing into the streets.

Phin pushed Georgina and Hawthorne in front of him, herding them roughly to his waiting carriage. Georgina made a wild grab at Petty Mischief, taking him by the hand and hauling him inside. The easiest mark to spot running away from a molly house was a man dressed in women's clothing. Petty had already lost his afternoons to the pillory, but this time it could mean losing his life.

The door was hardly closed behind them when Phin rapped on the roof to tell his driver to speed away. "Make haste!" he shouted.

Hawthorne clasped his hand and brought it to his lips. "Sir Phineas, my knight errant," he murmured. "My endless thanks."

He shook his hand away. "What were you thinking?" Phin asked, his voice filled with anguish. "You could have been killed."

"No one would dare to touch a duke."

"They would if they didn't *know* you were a duke."

"It was my idea to go to Mother Mary's," Georgina broke in. "If you're going to lecture anyone, it should be me."

"You have more sense than this, George," Phin snapped. "Drinking and cavorting with God knows who for God knows why."

"Can a man not have a little fun?" Georgina asked.

Petty Mischief glared at Phin. "We all deserve to have fun."

"Is this so different from the parties you host at your own house these days?" Georgina shot at him.

"Of course it's different. There are safe places—"

"Not for all of us," Petty Mischief snapped. "Maybe for you lot. Look at you three and your fine coats. If I could hawk your jeweled buttons, I'd have room and board paid for a year. If you hadn't been born into the wealth and the titles, this is where you would be every night, too."

His face went ashy under the white makeup. Georgina looked at him in alarm. "Are you going to be sick?"

He shook his head and slumped against the carriage seat. "My clothes. They are at the tavern. All I've got is this costume."

"Don't worry about that," Georgina said. "You can borrow from one of us."

"You don't understand," he said, bringing his hand to his forehead. "All of my money was in my boots. And my boots are in the tavern. It's lost to some policeman's pocket by now."

They looked at the delicate silk dancing slippers laced onto his feet.

"You may not have boots," Hawthorne said, "but we will get you back on your feet again. That is a solemn vow."

Georgina looked at him. "You'll be coming home with me tonight," he said. "I'll take care of you." He could well afford to replace the money that Petty had lost.

"How did you hear about the raid?" Hawthorne asked Phin.

"A friend knocked on my door to tell me, and I ran out to warn you. He went to another tavern that was rumored to be targeted tonight as well."

"It's getting intolerable," Georgina said.

Hawthorne cracked his knuckles. "There's no choice anymore," he said grimly. "We're going to have to fight back with everything we've got."

"We've tried to think of ways to help," Georgina said. "You and Phin are doing all you can to invite people to your homes to protect them from the risk of being in public. I shouldn't have disparaged your parties," he told Phin. "You know I respect the work you've done to protect the community, and I am grateful that you came out tonight to warn us at Mother Mary's."

"We can't fight," Phin said, eyeing the thunderous look on Hawthorne's face. "The law won't listen to us if there's a scuffle."

Hawthorne smiled gently. "We won't shed blood. I have a different sort of fight in mind."

Georgina sat up straight on the leather seat. They had talked about this before, but the duke had been reluctant. Now it appeared that he was all in.

Hawthorne nodded. "My dear gentlemen, it is time for me to finally take my seat in the House of Lords. We will see then how easy they will find it to persecute us after they discover how much power a duke of the realm can wield."

❖

After a week's worth of fitful sleep, Beatrice decided that she was ready to speak with her husband. She found him in the library. It was a different sort of room compared to the one at Rosedale Manor. Sinclair's library was sleek and elegant. The books had all been bound in matching leather and were organized by size with military precision. The oak furniture gleamed, and the chairs all matched.

She told herself not to think of the cheerful jumble of armchairs at Rosedale, and what she and Georgina had done on those chairs, lest she blush.

"Lady Sinclair," he greeted her.

"Sinclair, we must speak," she said. "I know we agreed to return to London to start up our life together as a married couple, but I must confess something." She took a deep breath. "I do not wish to be in this marriage any longer."

He stared at her.

"I can leave whenever you wish, and you need never see me again. I promise," she continued. "No one would follow me. Society would be on your side in the whole affair. You could claim abandonment. You could even claim that I have died, if you wish to be truly free of me." She swallowed. Now she would have to tell him about the baby, and he would demand she leave this very instant.

Staring down a future without the prospect of a comfortable income was stark. But living without integrity was now unbearable.

Nora and Jacquie would help her, she knew. She could live in one of their country cottages and learn to weave. She smiled. The image of poverty of a country cottage no longer made her shudder. The people at Rosedale would welcome her. She imagined Sally taking care of her bouncing baby girl, and Mr. Powell popping in to ply her with biscuits.

"Whatever are you talking about?" Sinclair asked.

Beatrice looked him in the eye. "The marriage was a mistake," she said.

He blinked. "Three months ago, you announced to the world that you were engaged to me. Do not forget that I paid your father's debts, my lady. We have a bargain."

"I didn't think I had a choice to marry, but I thought if I could just choose the right person, then everything would work out." She touched his hand, her eyes imploring. "I am sorry for the harm that my family has done to you and your sister. I didn't consider the consequences of my actions, and it was reprehensible of me to have taken away your choice in the matter when I forced your hand in marriage."

He stared at her, his mouth twisting. "All this is to mean that it isn't mine, then."

She blinked. "I—what?"

"Cecilia told me. She said she heard you being sick a few times at Rosedale. I thought for sure this meant you were pregnant, and I was prepared for it to be my child. Our child. But now you are speaking of leaving? Whose child is it?

Unmoored, she tried to find steady ground. "Cecilia told you?"

"Yes. You must know Ceci thinks the world of you, and she is excited about the prospect of a niece or nephew. But she doesn't matter to you any more than I matter to you, does she? You would throw away her chance at sisterhood, at being a loving aunt? For what? For *who*?"

"I do believe I am with child," Beatrice said. "And you were right. It is yours, conceived on our wedding night."

He turned from her. "How am I to believe this now? Why would you hide my own begotten child from me?"

"I am not trying to hide," she said. "I was going to tell you. I just thought you would prefer to be well rid of me, and of any trace of our life together. You could be happier with someone else."

"I don't have someone else, do I?" His eyes flashed with anger. "I have you. Or I thought I did. God, Beatrice! I thought we could move beyond these past months. Make the best of things. But you are only interested in your own selfish gains."

"I'm trying to think of you!" Beatrice cried. "And of Cecilia! You would both be better off if you had never met me!"

"We did meet you. You became part of our family when you vowed before God and man to be my bride. But whose babe is in your belly, threatening our happiness?" His face twisted and he looked grim. "The only man in that house party was Mr. Smith."

"It's yours," she said firmly. "But I don't care if you never believe me. The words on our marriage contract are legal and binding. I am aware of that. But I am also aware that this house is no prison. I can leave at any time. I don't need your permission or anyone else's. I don't care if we separate, divorce, or if I never see you again. But I am not living here in a house where my husband disdains me." She looked him dead in the eye. "I'm worth more than that." She picked up her skirts and walked to the door, then turned. "I will leave by the end of the week."

There was a lot to be done to pack, assuming Sinclair allowed her to take what she had bought with his money since their marriage.

But that could wait.

After all, today was Tuesday.

CHAPTER TWENTY-NINE

L egrand trimmed one last curl and set his scissors down. "Finally,"
he said. "Now your hair won't be brushing against your collars."
He rubbed pomade between his palms and styled Georgina's hair.

"Thank you, Legrand. I love it." She angled her neck and looked
at the shorter cut in the mirror. It was still long enough on top to
muss into a pompadour when she felt like it, but it was shorn almost
to the skull at the back and at the sides. It wasn't at all fashionable.
But it felt good. She had needed a change.

"What would you wish to do with this, Gina?" Legrand lifted
her long red wig.

"It served me well," she said, giving it a fond look. "I needed
its security for a long time. But now I think I will give it to Mother
Mary's for their costume room. Maybe Charles would like it the
next time he decides to engage in Petty Mischief."

Charles had left for Rosedale that morning in Georgina's
carriage. As he had promised, Hawthorne had sent over a case of his
best brandy to present to Mr. Powell with his compliments.

As Legrand dressed her in her new frock, her mind wandered.
Her heart felt lighter this morning. When Hawthorne had announced
last week that he was going to take his rightful place in government,
she had felt a huge sense of relief. She had been so concerned
about the raids, but she had hope now that threat might come to an
end if Hawthorne was successful in petitioning against such harsh
persecution in the House of Lords.

The raid had also reminded her of what was important. Love,

and happiness, and living. She deserved to have a life of her own, not just her work. With any luck, she could have it all.

"When is the wedding?" she asked Legrand.

At least one of them had a happy ending to their summer love affair.

He smiled. "My lovely Reina has agreed to a Yuletide wedding. I should have my tailoring shop open by then, with a snug living quarters above stairs. I have been looking at renting space, but it has been difficult to find a premium location."

"If you need an investor, I would be happy to buy a building for you," she offered. "It would be the least I could do to thank you for all your years with me."

His smile was all the answer she needed.

She had also made some decisions about the salon.

Madhavi was waiting for her in the drawing room when she came downstairs. This was the second Tuesday since she had returned from Rosedale.

"Have you given any more thought to my idea?" she asked as she entered the room.

Madhavi stared at her. "Gina, your hair!" she gasped. "Your *dress!*"

She touched her hair. "I cut it," she said. "I feel like a different person these days, Madhavi. The country air did me good."

She touched the skirt of her peach silk chiffon dress. She would never stop wearing the embroidered white muslins that she so loved, but she had decided that maybe she didn't need to wear them every day. She didn't need to be so black-and-white with her approach in life. There were many ways to support industry without literally wearing examples of it all the time on her body.

"Now, our agreement?" she asked again with a smile.

Madhavi withdrew a few folded pages from her reticule and smoothed them open. "I have some concerns," she admitted. "I love the idea of running the salon with you, Gina. Thank you for offering me a full partnership in what you have built here. Running the events all summer has been a joy and I loved every minute. But it's exhausting, and I saw how exhausted you have become over the years."

"If we share it together, then we won't have to worry about that."

"What happens if you go away again? You thought you would be away for a few weeks, but it was three months."

"I don't have any plans to go away again."

"What if I want to go away? Would you handle everything again by yourself?" She shook her head. "I am not willing to be put in the same position that you were in for so many years."

Georgina thought for a moment. "What if we made the salon into a cooperative?" she asked slowly. "What if we all entered into an agreement, with the women who attend most often and who are the most interested? Anyone could host events here, or plan them. You and I could perhaps head a committee to oversee it, but we would all participate in the work."

Madhavi smiled. "I think the idea is perfect. If anyone wanted to create any sort of offshoot, like the one you just created, it would be easier to do. Neither of us would be responsible for putting our lives on hold to do it."

"I didn't put my life on hold this summer," she said. "I put my *work* on hold, and in doing so, I discovered that there is more to life than just the work."

It was past two o'clock, and women began to enter the salon. Georgina and Madhavi explained their plan, and it was met with a great deal of interest.

As the conversation dwindled and they were getting ready to wrap up for the week, the butler announced two more visitors.

Lady Beatrice Sinclair and Miss Cecilia Sinclair.

Beatrice paused in the doorway, and Georgina knew without a doubt that she wanted to make a statement. She was dressed to the nines. It must have taken Reina over an hour to perfect her curls and to paint her face. Her eyes were rimmed with black kohl and her lips shone with cherry color. Her muslin was impeccably white with rows of wide black lace banding the fabric. Her gloves were fashioned from the sheerest black silk up to the elbow.

It was bold and dramatic and unexpected.

Georgina loved every elegant inch of it.

Beatrice snapped open her fan, and with delight Georgina saw that every stick of it had been recovered with newsprint. Black-and-white print danced across the ivory sheets as she fluttered her fan in front of her face.

Beatrice's brows rose when she saw Georgina, her eyes taking in her peach dress and short hair.

"I do hope I am not too late," she drawled.

Cecilia was bouncing on her heels. "I wanted to leave ever so much earlier, but my sister insisted on a grand entrance." She rolled her eyes but beamed.

"Too late for what?" Georgina asked. Her heart was hammering. What did this mean?

She swished in with the air of a duchess. "Cecilia has declared herself to be quite the bluestocking. She wished to be presented so she could bow at the feet of their queen."

Cecilia giggled and made a little curtsy. "If you take members that are not yet out in Society, I would be very happy to attend when I am in London," she said shyly.

"Of course you are welcome," Madhavi said, grinning at her.

"I, on the other hand, am here to present a proposal to Gina. Simply a trifle." She pressed a single piece of paper on the desk where Georgina took the minutes and pushed it over to her with one manicured finger.

Georgina picked it up. All it had written on it was *A Treatise in Which Beatrice Everson Declares Everlasting Love for Georgina Smith.*

Beatrice locked eyes and leaned in close. "As you can see, it's a proposal for something much bigger. If it's popular with its intended audience, it could be a long running series," she said, then dropped her voice. "It took me all summer, but I have figured out what I want to be running toward, Georgina. You. I've been waiting for you my whole life."

How Georgina wanted to kiss her, right then and there. But a roomful of women was watching them and buzzing, and she wouldn't give them a show. At least they were far enough away not to be overheard, though Georgina knew that the love between her and Bea would be clear to anyone looking.

"I love that you have discovered what you're passionate about," she murmured with a wink. "I especially love that it's me. I love you too, Bea." This was why she had wanted to reduce her hours at the salon. She wanted to offer a full life to the person she loved, not a life squeezed around letter-writing and meetings and lectures. She wanted to build a life with Beatrice together instead of fitting her into the life she had carved out for herself alone.

"I'm leaving Sinclair, and may have nothing," Beatrice said. "But I am here to offer my all, and to work with you if you wish to have me here."

"Always," she said.

With pride bursting inside her, she introduced Beatrice and Cecilia around the room. Georgina saw without any surprise that she had been right. These were no Hyde Park snobs, refusing to shake hands or curtsy. Beatrice was going to fit right into her Tuesday afternoons.

In exactly the same way that she fit into Georgina's heart.

CHAPTER THIRTY

Beatrice told Georgina that she was escorting Cecilia back home, and then she would return sometime later so they could talk. Her heart was full. The expression on Georgina's face when she had read her "treatise" had told her everything she needed to know, but she longed to hear the words from her lips as she held her close.

Cecilia was vibrating with excitement during the carriage ride. "I thought a house party was enough of a thrill before my first Season, Bea!" she exclaimed. "But now I have the privilege of saying that I have been to a bluestocking salon as well. I will be the envy of every debutante I meet next year."

Beatrice peered at her. "And what did we discuss you would say to those debutantes, Ceci?"

She grinned. "That they are welcome to join too, any time they wish."

After they arrived at the townhouse, Beatrice went in search of Sinclair. She found him in the gallery, his arms clasped behind his back as he stared down the long hallway of Sinclair ancestors.

When she came close enough, she saw that he was looking at a specific painting. The man that smiled back at them had the same cleft chin, blond hair, and dazzling good looks as her husband, and he brimmed with youthful energy. He was painted with a possessive hand on the shoulder of a dark-haired woman with sparkling eyes and a sweet smile.

Sinclair cleared his throat. "Richard," he said. "My brother. And his wife."

Sympathy tugged at her heart. "This has been a hard year for you and your family. You must miss him terribly."

"He was taken too damn young. I never thought for a minute that I would inherit the earldom, but he never had the chance to fill his nursery."

She folded her hands over her abdomen. Life was so frail. So precious. So unpredictable.

"I had sworn never to return to England," he said, his eyes still on the painting.

Beatrice knew he had been passionate about the army, but the words were charged with an intensity that she suspected meant something much more. Whatever it was, it was none of her business. She was no family to him anymore, as curious as she was.

She swallowed. "I apologize for having interrupted your contemplation, my lord."

"You are not interrupting at all."

"I will start preparing my belongings today to leave," she said. "I wish to be fair. Would you prefer if I took only what I brought from my father's house? Or would you be willing to gift me with whatever I have purchased in the past few months? I must warn you—I was overexcited at the jeweler's in our first week of marriage."

She may have just declared her love to Georgina, but she wanted to be sure that she had her own money if she needed to set up her own establishment. They hadn't talked about the future, after all.

"I recall the bill," he said dryly. "If you are determined to leave, then I shall not stop you. You are welcome to anything that you have bought as Lady Sinclair, with my blessing."

She made a move to leave and stopped when he raised a hand.

"But I wonder if we are overlooking a solution, my lady."

"What solution would that be?" she asked.

He hesitated. "I am in love," he announced.

Confusion hit her. "But you know I don't reciprocate your feelings, my lord."

"Not with you! Good God, no. I have a mistress."

"A mistress? You are in love with your *mistress*?" She blinked. "You *have* a mistress?"

Sinclair looked again at the painting. "Mistress is perhaps not the word, though I support her financially. I always will. I love my brother's widow. Eliza."

Beatrice didn't know how to react. This was shocking. She would never have guessed such a thing of the straitlaced Earl of Sinclair.

"I had courted Eliza and intended to wed her. But my brother was a better prospect compared to a second son. Her father spoke to my father, and they convinced Richard that it would be for the best for both families if they were to marry. When Richard proposed to her, I knew I could not bear to live in England. I purchased a commission and never looked back."

"You must have hated him," she said. How could his father have interfered like that?

"Not at all," he said, surprising her. "He did his best by our family, and hers. He didn't love her, but he did his duty. Because of my own stubbornness, I fled the country and wasn't there at his deathbed. I wasn't here for my sisters when they mourned him. And I wasn't here for Eliza, who handled everything on her own while I made the long journey back to England."

"Why did you come to London looking for a bride if you love her?"

"Eliza refused to have me."

"She doesn't love you?"

"She and Richard were wed for over five years without issue, and she would not marry me as she didn't think she could give me a son. I love her too well to lose my heart to another, so I decided to come to London and make quick work of choosing a bride for the sole purpose of begetting an heir. I have no more brothers, and no one to leave the title to. I thought I could find a woman to wed who wouldn't care about me. Someone passionless but devoted enough to family to help me with my sisters."

"Lady Honora," she said softly. "She would have been perfect."

"My cousin, the Duchess of Hawthorne, had known about her inclinations for other women. She urged me to choose Lady Honora as my bride."

"But then I came along." She was starting to understand.

He sighed. "You, Lady Sinclair, are full of passion. You flirted with me at every opportunity. You were so single-minded in your determination to marry me that I was convinced you would want a devoted husband, which I could not promise to be. I was worried that if I didn't return your passion, you would find out the reason why. If you ever discovered my affair with Eliza, I didn't think I could trust you to keep it a secret. For her sake, I could not bear the scandal."

"You could trust me."

"I know I can trust you now," he said. "But could I have trusted you then?"

Beatrice thought of herself before the summer, angry and snide and wounded. It felt like a lifetime ago. "Maybe not," she admitted.

"Now you are telling me that you would give up being a countess and you wish to leave."

"Which means neither of us wish to be married to each other," Beatrice said.

"Yet it's ideal for me if I *am* married. Perhaps it might be useful for you, too? If we simply…stay married? For convenience's sake?"

"What are you proposing?"

"My plan was always to return to Yorkshire and Eliza. If I am married to you, then I can be with Eliza until the end of my days, without casting aspersions on her character. You can keep the London townhouse if you wish. I don't expect to be here often. Or you could buy another one. I have funds enough. You could even move in with your lover."

This was perfect. She just had one more thing to reveal that would make sure that Sinclair would never come after Georgina for a duel. His identity would always be safe this way, even if it risked sacrificing all of the goodwill that he seemed to be willing to extend to her now.

If she told him her own truth, she could protect Georgina. But it might mean that Sinclair would cast her aside after all.

She was ready for it. Come what may, she was ready to take a stand and align herself with her community.

"It wasn't Mr. Smith who I fell in love with this summer," Beatrice said. "It was Lady Gina."

He was quiet for a minute. "Then the baby really is mine?" he asked.

She blinked. "You would have offered me this bargain if you thought the babe might *not* be?"

He nodded. "I know how much you mean to Ceci. When I watch her with you, I can see that you would make a wonderful mother. It doesn't matter who the baby's father is. We would raise it to be our own. If it's a son, he will inherit the earldom. If it's a daughter, she will be a grand heiress. Either way, our child will be welcomed into our family."

"It really is yours."

Sinclair caught her around her waist and swung her around, whooping. "I'm going to be a father," he shouted, and he was so exuberant that he kissed the top of her head.

They were going to be a family, Beatrice thought, laughing as her husband twirled her and shouted for Cecilia. It was going to be an *unusual* family—but it was going to be theirs.

❖

Georgina was finishing up a letter when she heard the noise. At first she thought it was an animal outside. A cat, perhaps. But the scratching and scraping sounds were rather loud to be caused by an animal. Then she heard a stream of swear words, and she grinned.

She crossed over to her marble terrace and peered over the edge of the balcony. "Is someone there?" she called out.

"Georgina, I don't understand how you used to do this every night in Paris," Beatrice grumbled from below.

"Do you have solid footing on the ivy?"

"No." There was a pause. "To be honest, I haven't even left the ground yet."

She laughed. "Come through the door, my damsel in disguise. Climbing up a wall of ivy might be ambitious for your first night of skulking around."

A few minutes later, Beatrice opened the door to her bedchamber. "I had wanted to make a grand entrance," she complained as she went into Georgina's outstretched arms.

"You already did that at the salon this afternoon. You were magnificent." Georgina kissed her forehead.

"I was so worried that you wouldn't want to see me," she said.

"I am so sorry for what I said after the ball. I would never have gone through with the divorce without your consent, and I would have dropped the idea as soon as I realized how dangerous it was. I should have thought harder about it."

Georgina hugged her closer. "I know you would never put me in harm's way."

They lay down on the bed, Bea snuggled against her with her head on Georgina's shoulder. Beatrice told Georgina all of what she had learned about Sinclair. "I would never have guessed that he was a man pining over love lost. I hope he finds peace with his Eliza in Yorkshire."

She stroked Beatrice's waist. "That's all I want these days. Peace." Georgina moved her hand to cover her belly. "And family."

Beatrice's hand covered hers. "We're going to have a baby," she said, kissing her shoulder. "I don't know anything about children, you know. It will be good for me to have extra parents involved. Assuming that Sinclair and you both *want* to be involved." There was a note of hesitation in her voice.

Georgina sat up so she could look into Beatrice's honeyed eyes. "I want to be involved in every minute. If you want Sinclair to help with the child, then I will make sure to get him here. I will find a way to work with him, if it would please you. Even if I have to convince him at sword point." She paused. "In fact, I might prefer if it's at sword point. I have not yet forgiven him for his poor treatment of you."

"My chevalier in truth," she said, eyes shining.

Georgina took her hands and held them tight. "I love you, Beatrice. I want to have a life with you. Maybe it will be messy and complicated. It's certainly going to be different. But I want it all. When I thought I only had a summer with you, I spent every second trying to memorize the shape and scent and feeling of our days together. Now we have the chance at an endless summer in front of us."

Beatrice laughed. "Even though autumn is upon us now?"

"In my heart it will be summer, and our love will always be in full bloom." She brought Bea's hand to her lips and kissed it. "I worried for so long that I would never be anyone's first choice. I was devastated in Paris when I thought Hawthorne didn't love me in return. I was so scared of being second best that when I returned to London, I worked as hard as I could to be considered the best with the salon. I never thought that I was running away from the chance of love, until I saw you before me."

Beatrice smiled. "I love you, Georgina. You will always be my first choice. I love your optimism and the way you just make everything *better*. The summer was extraordinary, and it changed my life forever. When I thought love was a gamble that only foolish people made, you showed me how to win every hand we're dealt, with honesty and strength."

"Do you want to know what I think?" Georgina asked. "I might need a kiss to convince me to tell you."

Beatrice cupped her cheeks in her hands and drew her lips against hers, kissing her deeply. Sweetly. With the promise of forever.

"I think you should live with me," Georgina said. "Stay with me."

Beatrice kissed her again. "Always. No matter where the journey takes us, or how hard the road might be, let us live every day like we're on holiday."

EPILOGUE

One Year Later

The carriage trip to Yorkshire took longer than planned, but Beatrice didn't think anyone would mind. It was difficult to transport a six-month-old baby any distance, after all, and of course they had to make an extended detour to Rosedale so he could meet his honorary aunts Nora and Jacquie.

Richard was content to be bounced on Georgina's lap for the time being instead of wailing and carrying on, and Beatrice decided to count it as a blessing. One of many, she thought happily as she looked at Georgina's profile and the baby on her lap.

"We are lucky," she said. "Our baby has lots of people to love him."

Georgina pressed a kiss to his fair head. "That will be true all of his life." She took her hand. "And it shall be true for us, as well."

Beatrice leaned over and kissed her. "You have given me more than I could have dreamed, my gallant knight in blue stockings."

It wasn't long before they rumbled up a long drive and stopped in front of an elaborate garden. It was the first time Beatrice had seen the Yorkshire estate, and it was magnificent. Sprawling and majestic, it soared three stories high with spires and towers protruding from its corners. Once upon a time she would have wanted it for her own, but she no longer felt those pangs of envy. Her life in London satisfied her more than she could have ever imagined.

Beatrice stepped down the carriage steps first, stretching with relief as her aching muscles celebrated their freedom from the confines of the conveyance. She was almost knocked off her feet when Cecilia ran out the front door and threw herself at her.

"Bea!" she cried. "It's been *forever*."

She laughed and kissed her cheek. "It's been less than three months. I was by your side at the end of the Season, Ceci."

"It feels like forever." She picked up Richard and cooed at him while Georgina exited the carriage. "He's grown ever so large!"

Her sister, Meredith, came over to greet them. She was two years younger than Cecilia and had come to London for the first month of Cecilia's Season. Her governess had whisked her back to the country before she could get into any mischief. She was a dark haired and brooding girl, and Beatrice thought fondly that they would have their hands full when it was her time for a Season.

Meredith took the baby. "I shall bring him inside," she announced.

Cecilia hugged Georgina. "Thank you ever so much for the pamphlets that you sent last month, Gina. I do hope you brought more in your luggage."

"I travel nowhere without copious amounts of newsprint," Georgina said. "You may have all the scientific treatises that you could wish for, tucked away in my valise."

Beatrice was delighted when a maid brought them to a suite of rooms with adjoining doors. They would have the freedom to visit each other at night with discretion. They had decided that it was going to be a lovely long stay in the country, until Yuletide.

She and Sinclair had continued to develop their friendship during her pregnancy. He had gone to Yorkshire to win back Eliza after they had parted ways last year, and Eliza had promptly made arrangements for them both to stay in London until the birth of their son. Georgina had bonded with them on their arrival in London, with all three taking such anxious care of Beatrice that she had resorted to sending notes to Phin and Hawthorne to rescue her from their hovering ministrations. They took her on secret rendezvous to Gunter's to offer respite and to soothe her pregnancy cravings. She smiled at the memory.

Georgina poked her head through the door that joined their

rooms. "This house is like a palace," she said. "I have an enormous writing desk in my sitting room and a bookshelf that the maid told me they cleared just for me."

Beatrice beamed. "I wrote to Eliza and told her you would need it for your letters and the books you brought with you. Do you like it, my love?"

"I love it. I will finally be able to start compiling my lacemaking book."

"It will be a success, just like everything you touch." She put her hand on her cheek and kissed her.

The salon had grown even more in popularity this year, which Georgina credited to the wider ownership of the society by its own members in a collective. It had inspired creative ideas and a vibrant environment for debate and scholarship. Georgina had been delighted to have more time to herself than she had ever had since leaving Paris, which she had spent thus far by Beatrice's side with Richard.

Now she planned to spend time working on a book that would display different hand-worked lace patterns and techniques to help encourage participation in the industry, based partly on the discussions she had with the weavers and workers who now populated Rosedale. Through her contacts at the salon, she had been able to gather lace swatches and personal accounts from women about their labor in textile art from all across England. Next year, Georgina and Beatrice were hoping to take time to travel so Georgina could showcase the book during a lecture series on female industry.

After they had refreshed themselves, they found Sinclair and Eliza having tea with Cecilia and Meredith. Sinclair was wearing the waistcoat they had gifted him from Legrand's tailoring shop, which had proved successful in its first year of operations.

"I do hope you have settled in," Eliza said, shaking their hands.

"Thank you, we have. This will be a wonderful holiday," Beatrice said.

"And we do enjoy our holidays," Georgina said with a sidelong look at Beatrice. "The most marvelous things can happen, after all."

Sinclair bowed to them. "Whether it is for a holiday or a season, you must always consider yourselves welcome here."

Beatrice and Georgina sat together on a sofa, immodestly close with clasped hands that went without any notice from the people they were gathered with. They were here together, among people who accepted them, and that made it wonderful beyond measure.

Beatrice looked around the room and counted her blessings again. She had family, friendship, and love. All of it might be considered unconventional, but she knew that the people in this room were delighted to be part of it. What more could she have ever bargained for?

About the Author

Jane Walsh is a queer historical romance novelist who loves everything Regency. She is delighted to have the opportunity to put her studies in history and costume design to good use by writing love stories. She owes a great debt of gratitude to the local coffee shop for fueling her novel writing endeavors. Jane's happily ever after is centered on her wife and their cat and their cozy home together in Canada.

Books Available From Bold Strokes Books

Calumet by Ali Vali. Jaxon Lavigne and Iris Long had a forbidden small-town romance that didn't last, and the consequences of that love will be uncovered fifteen years later at their high school reunion. (978-1-63555-900-2)

Her Countess to Cherish by Jane Walsh. London Society's material girl realizes there is more to life than diamonds when she falls in love with a non-binary bluestocking. (978-1-63555-902-6)

Hot Days, Heated Nights by Renee Roman. When Cole and Lee meet, instant attraction quickly flares into uncontrollable passion, but their connection might be short-lived as Lee's identity is tied to her life in the city. (978-1-63555-888-3)

Never Be the Same by MA Binfield. Casey meets Olivia, and sparks fly in this opposites-attract romance that proves love can be found in the unlikeliest places. (978-1-63555-938-5)

Quiet Village by Eden Darry. Something not quite human is stalking Collie and her niece, and she'll be forced to work with undercover reporter Emily Lassiter if they want to get out of Hyam alive. (978-1-63555-898-2)

Shaken or Stirred by Georgia Beers. Bar owner Julia Martini and home health aide Savannah McNally attempt to weather the storms brought on by a mysterious blogger trashing the bar, family feuds they knew nothing about, and way too much advice from way too many relatives. (978-1-63555-928-6)

The Fiend in the Fog by Jess Faraday. Can four people on different trajectories work together to save the vulnerable residents of East London from the terrifying fiend in the fog before it's too late? (978-1-63555-514-1)

The Marriage Masquerade by Toni Logan. A no-strings-attached marriage scheme to inherit a Maui B&B uncovers unexpected attractions and a dark family secret. (978-1-63555-914-9)

Flight SQA016 by Amanda Radley. Fastidious airline passenger Olivia Lewis is used to things being a certain way. When her routine is changed by a new, attractive member of the staff, sparks fly. (978-1-63679-045-9)

Home Is Where The Heart Is by Jenny Frame. Can Archie make the countryside her home and give Ash the fairytale romance she desires? Or will the countryside and small village life all be too much for her? (978-1-63555-922-4)

Moving Forward by PJ Trebelhorn. The last person Shelby Ryan expects to be attracted to is Iris Calhoun, the sister of the man who killed her wife four years and three thousand miles ago. (978-1-63555-953-8)

Poison Pen by Jean Copeland. Debut author Kendra Blake is finally living her best life until a nasty book review and exposed secrets threaten her promising new romance with aspiring journalist Alison Chatterley. (978-1-63555-849-4)

Seasons for Change by KC Richardson. Love, laughter, and trust develop for Shawn and Morgan throughout the changing seasons of Lake Tahoe. (978-1-63555-882-1)

Summer Lovin' by Julie Cannon. Three different women, three exotic locations, one unforgettable summer. What do you think will happen? (978-1-63555-920-0)

Unbridled by D. Jackson Leigh. A visit to a local stable turns into more than riding lessons between a novel writer and an equestrian with a taste for power play. (978-1-63555-847-0)

VIP by Jackie D. In a town where relationships are forged and shattered by perception, sometimes even love can't change who you really are. (978-1-63555-908-8)

Yearning by Gun Brooke. The sleepy town of Dennamore has an irresistible pull on those who've moved away. The mystery Darian Benson and Samantha Pike uncover will change them forever, but the love they find along the way just might be the key to saving themselves. (978-1-63555-757-2)